Tapioca Pudding Next Door

Queendom Dreams Publishing
PO Box 93832,
Las Vegas, NV 89193

Printed in the United States of America

First Edition

ISBN-13: 978-0-9827-2232-9
ISBN-10: 0-9827-2232-X

Cover Design: Candace Cottrell
Editing & Typesetting: Carla Dean of U Can Mark My Word

For information regarding special ordering for bulk purchases, contact: Queendom Dreams Publishing, PO Box 93832, Las Vegas, NV 89193

Website: www.queendomdreams.com

Acknowledgements

As always, I give all honor and thanks unto Jehovah God. For without His grace, no talent that I have been blessed with would come to fruition. I thank Him for the past, present, and the blessings to come.

Extra special thanks for my entire U Can Mark My Word family on Facebook. Your support during this process has been invaluable.

Thank you to all along my path who have supported me in this journey. For those looking for a list of names this time, no can do. I'd have a whole other book filled with acknowledgements, and I know that's not the book you'd want to read from me. Anyone that's anyone knows who they are and don't need acknowledgment in a book to know how priceless they are in my life because I continually let you know personally. If you don't know, then maybe, just maybe, we might have to work on some things to change that.

My readers and fans of The Queen, words will never express the level of gratitude I have for you. Without you, I am just another person writing books. Prayerfully, you will stick with me along my journey and inspire me to want to give you more. It's because of you that I continue to press along this difficult road. It's because of your words, "Never give up," that I keep picking up the pen. I'd love to hear from you. So, do stop by The Queendom (www.queendomdreams.com) to keep in touch with me personally. Never too big to chat with you and can never have too many friends. Continue to spread the word.

For those wondering where the name "The Queen" originated from, the name came from my childhood fantasy of pretending I was a Queen (because I grew up in Queensbridge looking at the bridge all of my life). For many years, I have battled low self-esteem, and one day, I came to realize that I was in fact the Queen (in my own rite), and deserved to be treated as such. Never took on the name to indicate I was better than any (especially because I wish all women would recognize that they, too, are queens). I took on the name several years ago when listening to Mary J. tell me through her song that I was a queen. (Okay, so maybe she wasn't talking to me personally...lol, but I heard her loud and clear.) So, that's my story.

Gotta shout out my Queensbridge family...Family for life.

The Queen

Tapioca Pudding Next Door

The Queen

Queendom Dreams Publishing
www.queendomdreams.com

1

"Oh my goodness, Charles, this is it! This is the one!"

Charles Webb wiped his brow and shrugged his shoulders, although he didn't like the house. It was the eighteenth house they had looked at, and his opinions didn't seem to matter with the nine he had been perfectly content with. His wife Charlotte didn't seem to care about his feelings.

"You know which ones I'd prefer, but I don't want to look at any more houses."

The real estate agent stood by nervously frustrated because she too was sick of spending so much time trying to find the "perfect" house for Charles and *the impossible* Charlotte Webb. She too agreed that the previous homes looked much better. However, since the house they were standing in was selling for 8.6 million, which was slightly higher than the previous homes viewed, she was leaning with Mrs. Webb. The commission check from the sale was greatly needed, so she needed to find a way to get Charles on board.

"Mr. Webb, did you get a chance to see the spectacular view from your potential office? Since you'd be spending a great deal of time working from your home, I'm thinking a nice view would be important to you."

"Why would I care about a nice view outside when I'm trying to get work done? I'm thinking with an eight-million-dollar price tag, a view is the last thing I need to be concerned about. Not only that, why would I be impressed looking at someone else's swimming pool?"

"Charles! Stop being so grumpy! The child is just trying to make sure we'll be happy," Charlotte said, further irking the agent's nerves by referring to her as a child when there wasn't much of an age difference.

Charlotte habitually spoke in a condescending manner as if she was born of wealth rather than simply having married into Charles' hard work.

"Besides, you wouldn't have to look at their swimming pool if you're seated at your desk. You'd have that perfect view of L.A. during the day and the city lights at night. Since the house is sitting up on a hill, you don't have to worry about any window treatments obstructing your view. Maybe you'll finally find some inspiration to produce something worthwhile."

Charles groaned at Charlotte's attempt to sell him while insulting him like she always did.

"I know you loved the master bathroom and the balcony off of the bedroom. And do you know all of the wonderful treats I could whip up for you in this beautiful kitchen?"

Charles almost choked. "Charlotte, please! You travel almost half of every month. I can't remember the last time I had a good home cooked meal. If I'd known your promotion meant no more home cooked meals, I would have never given my blessing."

"How about we hire a cook to prepare you meals when I'm away?"

Charles looked at his wife as if she were crazy. Then he walked away, ignoring her comment to prevent saying anything that would cause another fight. He returned to the master bathroom, hoping the four-jet shower and Roman tub would help him accept the decision his wife of seven years was about to make. He was also frustrated with the house because it was not *kid-friendly* and offered no hope of his wife ever settling down to give him the children he desperately wanted and talked about prior to his engagement to Charlotte.

During the three years they dated, they would often talk about the large family they wanted. Charles was an only child to a single, struggling mother. While growing up, he fantasized about having a large family complete with a mother and father in the home. Now, his architectural career afforded him the luxury of being able to work from home to help care for his anticipated children. He intentionally chose a wife that would not be in danger of a ticking biological clock. He was forty when he began dating a twenty-seven-year-old Charlotte.

Charlotte was ambitious, appreciated the finer things in life, and wasn't afraid to work hard to have what she wanted. He just never counted on her becoming obsessed with her career as a Global Implementation Manager, which kept her in Japan more than it kept her home. When she was in the states, she spent countless hours at late-night meetings trying to secure new accounts for the company she worked for. When she was home long enough to find all of Charles' porno tapes he used to keep himself occupied, she threw tantrums as if the tapes were real women.

As Charles walked around the new house, he noted several spots he could make his hiding places for his tapes. His desire to design and build his own house was not an option with Charlotte. She wanted what she wanted, when she wanted it. Waiting close to a year was absolutely unacceptable. In reality, she didn't hold much faith in Charles as an architect. When they first met, he was the greatest, but over the years, she had constantly berated his work and compared his work to other successful architectures. She'd tell him instead of sitting in as an adjunct professor at the university twice a week, he needed to become a student and get more with the times and create more futuristic designs. The fact that he owned a firm that employed twenty-three other architects didn't gain him the respect he so desperately craved from his wife. His sixty-seven-year-old mother's opinion of how great of an architect he was didn't matter to Charlotte, because according to her, his mother was considered "old and still living in the past."

Charles' closest friends—Edward, Arty, and Larry—wished Charles would get rid of his wife and find someone who would truly appreciate him, his work, and show respect towards his friends and family. His wife also threw tantrums when she came home to find his friends in "her" home, although they were living in the home Charles had purchased prior to their meeting. It became her house when they married.

Of the eighteen homes the real estate agent showed them, he noted Charlotte's objections to any home that offered a place where he could entertain his buddies. The home they were standing in offered a large hall where she could entertain up to two hundred guests, and it was more on the elegant side rather than the recreational. A museum immediately came to mind, which was why Charles hated it.

When he walked into his would-be office again, he had to admit the view was stunning. Still, it wasn't as important as having a recreational area. He liked the idea of having an indoor and outdoor pool with sauna, but with his wife gone more than half the time, it wasn't that exciting. The fitness room was larger than the others, but he would have much preferred the third house they looked at which had a basketball court. Since tennis wasn't his thing, he wasn't impressed with having a tennis court, but he'd be willing to go along with having the house if it would be a reason for his wife to stay home more. Of course, she wouldn't go along with the twelfth house they looked at that not only had a tennis court, but a go-kart racing track, as well. The kitchen had been just as fabulous as the one they were standing in, but since the other house had something that Charles would use to entertain friends, it was a no-go. Charles also noted Charlotte's skillful way at avoiding conversations of finding children-friendly homes, despite her still promising to give him a large family. Now with him being fifty and Charlotte at thirty-seven, soon to be thirty-eight, Charles was starting to doubt his mother would ever see a grandchild. He felt they were financially comfortable enough for Charlotte to take time and give him children.

"Charles, we need to get to the real estate office so we can make a contract for this house," she said when she found him in the study.

"Don't I have a say in this, Charlotte? You can't just make this type of decision without us discussing it first."

"I don't see what's to discuss. My birthday will be here in three months, and I want to have thee most fabulous birthday party right here in my new home."

"Charlotte…"

He was about to debate with her, but decided to save his breath since he knew it was a losing battle. He was half tempted to tell her to buy the house by herself and move in it by herself. He knew not to argue any further because he had yet to receive his ration of sex since his wife returned over a week ago on her menstrual cycle.

Charles threw his hands up in the air. "Fine! Fine, you win! If this is the house you want, then this is the house you'll get. Anything to please Charlotte," he said with a note of sarcasm.

"So are you trying to imply that I shouldn't have what I want to make me happy? I earn almost three hundred thousand dollars, so don't act like you're giving me anything, Charles."

"Three hundred thousand dollars is your shoe money! You spend at least that on your shoes alone."

Charlotte gave Charles an evil eye. "What did you say to me, Charles Anthony Webb?"

Her calling out his entire name indicated the brink of a sex strike that could only be negotiated with the purchase of some new diamonds or other rare stone.

"If you'd like, we can continue this conversation when we get home about how you think I don't contribute anything to your pathetic existence."

The real estate agent was about to enter the study, when she heard

Charlotte's last comment. She quickly turned around, but Charles left out and brushed passed her without saying a word.

"I'm sorry. I didn't mean to interrupt," she said.

Charles continued to walk away as Charlotte answered, "Oh, don't worry. He acts silly sometimes, but we'll meet you at your office to get the contract going. I plan on having my 38th birthday here in three months."

"Wow! I wouldn't have thought you to be a day past thirty," the agent lied, whereas truthfully, with all of the makeup Charlotte was wearing, it made her appear to be in her late forties instead. And although her attire appeared to be expensive, it was not flattering for her 5'6", size-12 frame. From the moment she met Charles and Charlotte, she wondered what a handsome, athletic man like Charles could have possibly saw in Charlotte to make him marry her.

"Oh, you're too kind. I hang around my husband and feel like I'm getting as old as he. I travel so much, I know I hardly eat or sleep right. Hopefully, when we get this house, I'll get an instructor and take tennis lessons. I might even use the gym in this house. I have to definitely look fabulous by the time I hit forty. I plan on being every woman's envy by then."

The agent had to bite the side of her tongue to keep herself from laughing as she thought to herself, *Not in this lifetime, sister!*

"Well, I'm going to head on to the office so we can get you this house as soon as possible."

"I can't thank you enough for so patiently helping me find my perfect home, even though it is your job. Eventually, Charles will come around and see all of the beauty this house has to offer. I'm sure he'll thank us for picking a house with an office that has a view to die for. Maybe one day, he'll even look out of the window and become inspired to create some worthwhile designs. Then I'd be able to fill up my closet and not have my three sisters see a large closet not filled to capacity."

"Well, that closet is ten by twelve, so you'll have plenty of space to fill."

The pair walked out and the agent locked up the home, while Charles waited in the car.

"Are you sure he's going to be okay with buying this house? He seems really upset."

"He'll be fine. He'll get over this like he has to get over everything else. We'll meet you at your office."

The agent felt sorry for Charles. She even thought about getting to the office and lying to Charlotte about the house's availability, but since the needed commission check far outweighed her empathy for Charles, she'd say or do anything to make the sale.

"Mrs. Webb, I just want you to know this is a very good choice. This one was my favorite, also."

Charlotte smiled at her validation before going to get in the car with Charles.

"Sweetheart, I know you're not all that happy with this house, but it makes me happy, and you know when I'm happy, you're happy," she said, massaging the inside of his thigh.

Charles looked into Charlotte's eyes to see if they were saying what her hand was suggesting. He was so horny at that moment, he would buy her a twenty-million-dollar home of her choosing if she'd just let him have some loving.

"Tonight, Charles, tonight. We won't have any more stress of trying to find the right home hanging over our heads, so we can have a completely romantic night with lingerie and all." She raised her eyebrows and flashed a big smile.

Although he was happy with the promise, he hated when she said "completely romantic," because to him, complete should include oral sex. In all of his years with Charlotte, he lost hope of ever getting or giving oral sex. She would get very disgusted by the mere thought of it. During their courtship, she told him that oral sex was something to be shared only in marriage. However, seven years of marriage hadn't made her willing yet. Her idea of foreplay was blindfolds, feathers, and rubbing oils or lotions. Additionally, she felt a night of passion should be sufficient in a marriage once every four to six weeks because it kept the spice and helped to build the anticipation. He hated the feeling of rejection when he tried to get some more before she was willing to give it to him.

The only reason he was okay with his wife taking a job that kept her overseas more than at home was because when she was around, he couldn't watch his porno tapes to help relieve himself. Also, he didn't have to worry about her building him up just to let him down by falling asleep early before anything could happen. And he didn't dare disturb her rest to get sex. He made that mistake one time only, and she called him the equivalent of a rapist. He had never taken sex without her offering it since then.

They went to sign the contract for the house, but then she was too stressed to have sex until the deal went through without any hiccups. Since they offered the full asking price, the deal went through with ease, and they were closing shortly after the inspection. Still, Charlotte was too stressed to have sex because there was so much to be done in preparation for the big move.

2

Not even a week into the new house, Charlotte was off to Japan for three weeks. Charles kicked himself for ejaculating two minutes after entering his wife. She finally let him touch her the day before her departure, but he became so excited, he didn't get a chance to make his own self happy, which caused Charlotte to go on a rampage vowing to never let his "selfish-self" touch her again. She blamed his porno tapes for making him selfish and inconsiderate of her needs.

As quick as Charles saw Charlotte through the airport gate, he rushed home to find a porno tape in his secret hiding place to help relieve his back up. He searched and searched but could find none. Charlotte had obviously gotten hold of his collection. He had to drive almost forty miles to the store where he always purchased them. He had purchased fifteen DVD's to keep him occupied for a while. He was even planning to dedicate the entire next day to doing nothing but watching one movie after the other and masturbating until he had nothing left to release. The store was near his old home, and he realized he'd have to find a new store closer to where he now lived.

That next day, he didn't bother to put on any clothes. He walked around his home with nothing on, which Charlotte hated, and only put on his robe when he went outside to get his newspaper. An urgent phone call from his office briefly interrupted his masturbating festival. As he sat at his desk, he had to admit the view was spectacular and inspiring. He stood up to go to his window for a better look as the sun was setting. He stood hypnotized by its beauty until the sun was no longer visible. He laughed out loud as he thought how he'd never in a million years admit to Charlotte that she was actually right about something for a change.

Just as he was about to turn away and leave the window, he caught a glimpse of a woman with rare strawberry-blonde colored hair. She was wearing short shorts with a bulging behind and going into the house situated down the hill from their house. That was the first time he'd ever seen any form of life in that house. When he looked down and saw his nudity, he became embarrassed and quickly retreated from the window while wondering if the woman had seen him.

Over the next three days, Charles spent a great amount of time at the window hoping to catch another glimpse of the woman. He stood by the window while he took his phone calls. He stood there while he ate his food. He also moved his drafting table near the window. He hated that no other window in the house offered a view of that house. On the fourth day when he had to go teach his class, he drove by the house in hopes of some sign of the woman with the distinctive strawberry-blonde hair. Still no sign.

A month later while in the grocery store with Charlotte, out of nowhere, she asked, "Why is that hussy looking at you as if she's star struck?"

Charles wasn't trying to hear the nonsense. Leave it to Charlotte, everyone wanted her husband.

"We came here to shop and get home. Stop worrying about other people."

"But she's staring at you as if I'm invisible. She just don't know. I'll snatch that fake pink mop off her head."

Charles laughed. "Pink, Charlotte? Now you're getting yourself all worked up over some punk rock kid with pink hair? Give me a break," he laughed, as he continued to stroll down the aisle with the cart.

"It's not a punk rock pink. It's like…it's like…I can't remember the name for that colored hair. It's some kind of pink blonde hair."

Charles stopped dead in his tracks. "Strawberry blonde?"

"Yeah, that's it. Why, do you know her?"

"No!" he answered more excited than needed. "I just was trying to help you figure out what you were saying."

"Then who are you looking around for? If you keep stretching your neck like you're doing, your head's liable to fall off."

"Are we about done in here? I don't feel like being publicly humiliated today. We came for a few groceries so you could take off and leave me again. Let's just get what we came for and go."

That incited Charlotte and made her cause a scene in the store, as she often did. So much so, that the manager had to come ask if Charles was okay.

"Oh, so now you boys all stick together? How are you going to ask him if he's alright? You should be asking if I'm alright. He's the one who has these female dogs in here disrespecting me and trying to get with my husband." Her voice got louder as she made an announcement to all the women in the store. "Yes, you heard me right, ladies. He's my husband, and we are happily married. So, don't even think about trying to have my husband lest you have hell to pay."

Charles was beyond embarrassed. "I'll wait for you in the car. Maybe it's safe there."

"Yeah, you do that. Look at almost every woman in here staring at you as if they really think I'm going to just let them have my husband."

Charles quickly went out to his car, thinking, *You can take the girl out of the ghetto, but you can't take the ghetto out of the girl.* He left the store partly because he was embarrassed and needed to get away from Charlotte. The other reason was because he was hoping to see the strawberry-blonde woman.

As he got out of the car to help Charlotte load the groceries in, he noticed a strawberry-blonde woman leaving the store and walking to a white Acura. The same pimped-out white Acura he was sure he'd seen one of those days he drove by the house. He didn't get a good look at her, but he could tell she was beautiful. Definitely sexy.

Another month had gone by, and he had yet to see the woman again. Charlotte was walking around like Bridezilla as the days drew near for her grand birthday party. Since she extended an invitation for several of the neighbors, Charles hoped the mystery woman would be amongst the guests. Although he didn't have any details of the woman's appearance, he would often visualize her when he watched his porno, and it would enhance his obsession to see the woman who he knew nothing about.

The big June birthday extravaganza brought out many who desired to see how a bragging Charlotte was living amongst the rich and famous. Unfortunately, the one guest Charles was hoping to see was a no-show.

With classes being out for the summer, Charles spent all of his free time waiting by the window or sneaking off to the same grocery store where he caught his second glimpse of her. When his wife informed him that she'd have to spend the next two months in Japan, he didn't put up one objection like he would have prior to his new hobby of stalking his neighbor.

When his friend Edward invited him over for a Fourth of July celebration, he almost declined because of his fear of missing an opportunity to see the woman. Eventually, he resigned himself that he was chasing a ghost who may have been just visiting that one day.

At one o'clock that morning when returning from Edward's cookout, his patience finally paid off. She was outside cleaning up from an apparent party. Even in the night, she looked better than Charles could have imagined. Her skin was quite fair, as if she may have been bi-racial. Her strawberry-blonde hair was pulled up in a bun. She wore a bikini top, which boasted her ample bosom, and her tight abs that didn't know the meaning of fat only accentuated her perfectly round hips.

He stood in a dark office as he watched her every move. She made her way around the well-lit swimming pool picking up trash and placing it in a large bag. She had music playing low in the background that she swayed to as she cleaned. He wanted to run out and offer a hand since she obviously didn't have any help, but he knew he couldn't without making it known he was spying on her.

So, he continued to watch her pick up the last of the trash and take the garbage bag in the house, but she left the back door open. After fifteen minutes, he gave up thinking she would come back out, figuring she had headed to bed. As quick as he climbed on his bed after the hot shower he took while thinking of her sexy body, he realized his cell phone was on his desk in his office. He started to leave it, but his obsession wouldn't let him. He decided to get it and take one last look out of his office window.

Lo and behold, he saw her swimming in her pool. He pressed his face closer to the glass when she swam on her back, because it appeared as if she no longer had on a top. With the distance and the lighting, he couldn't be certain. However, the minute she stepped out of the pool and laid on a lounge chair next to the fire pit lamp, there was no doubt that she wore only what she entered the world with at birth.

Charles suddenly remembered the binoculars he had snuck out to buy for an occasion such as the one he was enjoying. As his eyes looked upon her from head to toe through the binoculars, his penis became so erect that he could hardly stand it. He jumped back from the window when she brought her knees up and spread her legs in his direction. It was almost as if she did it for his viewing pleasure. He could see so well with the binoculars; it was like he could almost feel the heat between her legs. He thought he could see the juices squirting from her where he stood. When she began fondling her own breast, he knew she was doing it for him. He hadn't cheated on Charlotte since he'd known her, but he couldn't understand why he was so intrigued by this woman to the point where he could no longer offer any guarantees about his fidelity.

The woman turned on her knees, doggy-style, shining a beautiful round ass in Charles' direction. Then, without warning, she up and went in her house, closing her door and shutting off the lights. Charles stood in the window another hour before going to bed, hoping she'd come back out for him to see more so he could finish jerking off.

3

The sound of a doorbell pulled Charles from his sweet dreams. He grabbed his robe and cursed during the long walk to the front door.

"If you're going to spy on someone, you're not supposed to stand in plain view while the moon is full and shining in your window. Otherwise, the spyee will see that you're spying."

Charles could hardly believe his eyes. He rubbed them, wondering if it was an extension of his dream. She was more beautiful than he thought and her body was better than any porno movie he owned. He couldn't form any words other than, "Huh?" Her beauty was enchanting to him. A haunting familiarity existed that instantly drew him into her.

She laughed and extended her hand. "Tapioca Pudding."

"Huh?" he repeated, that time confused.

"I'm Tapioca Pudding. My friends call me Tappy. Others call me Strawberry. Until we figure out who you are, you can just call me Tapioca."

"Tapioca? Really?"

"Yes, really."

Charles took her soft manicured hand into his.

"Boy, you must really be excited to see me. That or I interrupted you before you made it to the bathroom for that first piss," she laughed.

"Huh?"

Tapioca pointed down to Charles' erection poking at the inside of his robe. Charles became embarrassed.

"Oh my! I'm sorry," he said, trying to hide it.

"Don't be. I've seen more several months ago."

Charles looked confused by her words.

"Right after you moved in, I saw you in the window for the longest. I don't think you saw me, because when I stood there wondering when you'd notice I was able to see you, I never saw you look in my direction. I think you were captivated by the sunset. But, at least I didn't see a reason for you to be ashamed from where I was standing," she smiled.

Charles tried to keep his eyes on her eyes and not let them fall to her firm breasts covered with a light-yellow halter top that failed to mask her areola or thick nipples.

"I'm sorry, but I really do have to go. Please, come on in for a minute."

She came in while he went to the bathroom, where he had a difficult time getting his urine out because of his overriding sexual urge. When he left the bathroom, he found a pair of gym shorts to throw on along with a tank top that showed off his well-chiseled body. When he went back downstairs, he didn't see Tapioca. He looked around and eventually found her in the kitchen pulling breakfast foods out along with pans to cook in.

"What are you doing?"

"I figured since I obviously woke you up, you haven't eaten yet. I was going to fix you some breakfast. After the orgasm I'm sure we both had last night from each other, the least you deserve is to be treated to a nice, healthy breakfast fit for a king," she replied while breaking eggs in a bowl in a smooth, fluid rhythm that made it clear she was a pro in the kitchen.

"Excuse me?!" he asked, surprised by her blunt admission, while embarrassed by the fact that she was telling the truth. He gently gripped her hands. "Look, Tapioca, Tappy, or whatever you said your name was…please, please stop. I need you to stop and leave now. I don't think this is such a good idea, your being here. My wife would die if she knew anyone was in her kitchen. You're going to have to leave."

"Okay," she said disappointed. "Would you be more comfortable if I cooked you breakfast at my house and bring it back to you?"

"I don't think that would be good either."

Tapioca shrugged her shoulders. "Okay, fine. I'll just go fix my breakfast before I sunbathe by my pool. You don't have to watch if you're going to be offended."

"Offended?! Why would I be offended?"

"I don't know. You seem offended right now with my presence despite the many times I've noticed your car slowly driving by my house. I don't think there has been a single time I have looked out of my window and didn't see you looking in the direction of my house. But, I won't bother you again. Please forgive me." She wiped her hands on a towel and started towards the door.

Charles was screaming inside his head about whether or not to let this beauty, who wanted to give him attention, walk out.

"Wait!" he called out.

She turned, surprised.

"How about you cook the breakfast at your house and just bring it back. It's just my wife is very particular about her kitchen. I'd hate for her to know you were in here," he said, changing his tone. "I'm sure you understand."

She looked into his eyes and smiled. "I guess she would have a heart attack. That scene she caused in the grocery store was ridiculous. I guess that's why I was the only one who didn't get an invitation to the big event a few weeks back." Tapioca went to the door, then turned around. "You're more than welcome to come to my home to eat your food while it's good and hot."

Charles had his confirmation that she was the same lady from the grocery store.

"Do you mind if I ask how old you are? I'm looking at your face, and you can't be more than twenty-five. I can't imagine you being the cooking type," he laughed, not really sure of why he asked or if it mattered.

Tapioca laughed, while answering with pride. "Oh yeah, I can cook quite well. Many of the people around here can vouch for me. But, to answer your question, I'm twenty-four. I've been cooking all of my life."

Charles looked confused. "All of your life?" He was also embarrassed for lusting over a twenty-four-year-old.

"Yep, all of it! Long story. Maybe I'll tell you over breakfast."

Charles was intrigued, but was becoming increasingly nervous by the twenty-four-year-old in his presence. Somehow, the mention of her age made him feel guilty despite the erection her presence caused. Just watching her lips speak made him want to feel them on his pole.

"You know, on second thought, I think I better skip breakfast, but it was nice to finally meet you."

She looked disappointed again. "Well, technically, we never met. I told you my name, but you never mentioned yours."

"Oh, I'm sorry. I'm Charles…Charles Webb."

"Well, nice to meet you, Mr. Webb," she said, making him feel older than he already felt.

"Charles, please," he corrected, shaking her warm, extended hand that sent a shooting sensation down to his family jewels.

She seductively looked into his eyes. "Well, Charles it will be."

She pulled her hand from his that he held longer than necessary and then turned away. He watched her narrow waistline walk out of the door on her healthy-sized bottom. Fifty feet away, she turned halfway to find him still standing with the door open, watching her. She waved, and he quickly waved as he hurried to close the door.

He was back in his office window before she could make it down the hill to her house. He tried to hide when he saw her stand near her back door. She looked hurt, and he felt bad for hurting her feelings.

Though it was too hot to take his daily run outdoors at that late time of the morning, he took part of his run on his treadmill before going outside to run the last mile in the heat. No matter how much he tried to shake her from his thoughts, she wouldn't leave. He ran in the direction of her house, looking around to see if anyone was watching before getting up the nerve to ring her doorbell.

She came to the door surprised, wearing a white silk kimono with no trace of anything underneath.

"Charles! What are you doing here?"

He nervously looked around. "I was wondering if that breakfast offer was still open. I've been out running and kind of worked up an appetite," he said, covered with beads of sweat and a dampened t-shirt.

"Uh, oh…I guess I could whip you up something real quick. I was just about to jump in the shower to wash off this sweat from working out."

Her arm that was supposed to be keeping her robe secured wasn't doing its job, and Charles caught a partial peep at one of her breasts.

"Oh, well then, I won't bother you," he said, trying to play coy. "I could head on back up to the house and put something together."

"No, you won't! I won't let you do such a thing."

Charles noted the aroma of something already cooking. "It smells good already. Either that or I must be hungry."

She laughed as she stepped back and allowed Charles into her home. "No, it's not your imagination. I had whipped up a breakfast pie for someone. It's still in the oven."

"Oh, I'm sorry. You're expecting company." He turned back towards the door. "I'll get out of your way."

"No, Charles, it's fine. I just need to drop it off when it's ready. It's for one of our neighbors. I told you that I cook for many of the people around here."

Charles felt a twinge of disappointment. He wanted to think he was special.

"If you don't mind, could you give me about fifteen minutes to take a quick shower? I'm feeling really messy right now."

"Well, maybe I need to just head back up the hill," he said again, turning for the door. "I'm a mess myself. I don't want to get in your way."

"Please, come in and make yourself comfortable. You play Wii? I have a few video game setups in my game room, or you can check out what's on television in the great room. It's near the kitchen. I'll be back to keep you company shortly."

Charles was jealous of the fact that she had a game room and he didn't. While his home was by far larger in square footage, Tapioca's house was more homely and exciting to be in. His home felt like a museum to him, causing an echo with each word spoken, while her house felt more like a home.

"I'll wait in the great room then."

"Cool! I'll be back in a jiffy." Then she ran upstairs for her shower.

Charles decided to take a tour of her downstairs and marveled at her good taste. He wondered how a twenty-four year-old could afford to live in a house with a five-million or more price tag. He remembered still struggling through school and holding onto a small studio apartment he shared with his girlfriend back then. He certainly didn't own more than his piece of car that would run when it felt like it. He was almost thirty by the time he finally landed a good paying job in his field, which inspired his decision to one day start his own company. The company served him quite well over the years, but not without first struggling.

When he made it to her great room and looked at her collection of DVD's, he was stunned when he noticed she had an entire collection of adult movies sitting in the open for anyone to see. As he thumbed through the collection to see if she had anything he had yet to view, he noticed a ten-set collection titled "The Pudding Pop Series" that he didn't own. He picked up a couple of the cases and almost dropped them when he saw Tapioca as the star on the covers. He knew there was something familiar about her, but he couldn't recall seeing her in any of his porno movies. Though Tapioca was clearly biracial, the production company straightened out her curly hair and marketed her as a white woman with a lot of behind.

"Oh, you've found my collection, I see."

Charles was startled when he saw Tapioca wearing a new kimono, and he fumbled with the DVD's while trying to put them back on the shelf.

She laughed. "Don't be embarrassed. I'm not. I did those like five years ago. Thought I was going to be a famous movie star one day, but it didn't quite work out that way."

"Five years ago? That would have made you like nineteen?"

"Kind of. That's when that set was done. There were some long before then. I was about sixteen or seventeen."

Tapioca went in her kitchen to pull the breakfast pie out of the oven. The smell was overwhelming to Charles. His stomach growled.

"Boy, I better get you something quick."

Embarrassed that his stomach noise was audible, he tried to over talk it. "You were making movies since you were sixteen? How did your parents feel about it?"

"My parents? Try my mother. My mother was a hooker. Was until the day she died. I have three sisters, and neither of us knew of a daddy. There were many who came along wanting to be our daddy, but our mother couldn't stop doing what she was doing. Eventually, it cost her, her life."

"I'm sorry to hear that."

"Don't be. It was the life she chose."

"So how'd you get the name Tapioca Pudding? Is that your stage name," Charles asked, sitting at her breakfast bar as she whipped up pancakes from scratch with eggs and bacon. He was getting a kick out of her bending and reaching in her kimono, which offered just enough peeps to intrigue him even more.

Tapioca laughed. "No, that was our mother's crazy obsession with the many flavors of pudding. Our real last name is Pudding. I was named Tapioca because I was born white, although my mother is biracial. I got a little tint as I got older. Just a little," she laughed. "It must have come from my daddy, whoever he is. My other sister, who came after me and who also was lacking melanin, is named Vanilla. My sister who is brown complexioned is named Chocolate, and my yellow sister is named Butterscotch. All with the last name Pudding. Chocolate is the oldest. She's thirty. I came next, then Butterscotch, then Vanilla.

Charles burst out into laughter. When he collected himself, he apologized. "I'm so sorry. This just sounds too incredible to be true. I can't imagine what life must have been like for you girls."

"It was rough. Believe me. Living in the projects didn't help. Being practically white in the projects didn't help either. Chocolate stayed in fights trying to protect us. Sadly, she's in prison now for life."

"Oh my! What happened?"

"She stalked and killed the man who killed our mother. The police didn't do anything to put him away." She looked sadly into the pancake batter. "I guess you're probably wondering how I ended up where I am, huh?"

Charles wanted to know more than anything, but said, "You don't have to tell if it's making you feel uncomfortable."

"Please. I've told the story a thousand times. I'm okay with it," she said, with a quick rebound of her emotions and wave of her hand.

"Well then, I'd love to hear. I take it the porn industry must have been kind to you."

"Porn?! Please! That didn't do shit for me. My sister Chocolate gave me this," she said, waving her hand in the air.

"But I thought you said she was locked away for life?"

"That's correct. Chocolate was hard working and wanted all of us on a healthy path, unlike our mother. She liked to have died when my mother bragged that I was a big-time porno star. Chocolate was so disappointed with me. Right at the time when my mother was killed, Chocolate gave me an envelope and told me not to open it unless something happened to her. Three weeks later, I see my sister's mug shot on the news. When I went to see her, she told me to open the envelope and follow the directions. It was a lottery ticket. Chocolate had played faithfully since her eighteenth birthday, hoping to make a better life for us all. The same week she found out she had the winning jackpot ticket, we found out our mother had been killed. Chocolate hadn't told anyone that she won the jackpot. It was the missing ticket for the $130,000,000 jackpot. For the longest, people wondered why no one came forward with the ticket. It was in the envelope all that time. I took the ticket and split the pot, minus all the shit-load of taxes, for me and my sisters. I haven't done porn since, and here I am.

"Most of the people in this area don't like me because I'm single and attractive. I never get invited to anything around here. I've been called a 'welfare tramp' by women who don't even know me, but I don't give a shit about them. I'm here to stay, and I have no problem staying to myself. With money, it's hard to find real friends, so I don't really have those either."

"Where are your other sisters? Are you guys close with one another?"

Tapioca laughed. "You see, that's the problem with money. It makes for ugly bitches. Vanilla and Butterscotch are angry at me for setting a quarter of the jackpot in an investment fund for Chocolate. I'm hopeful maybe one day she'll get out of prison. My sisters disagree. They wanted the pot split three ways instead of four, so they feel as if I'm taking money from them. Chocolate left me the ticket, and it was my decision. She only asked that I look out for my sisters. She didn't say split the ticket, so they can stay mad all they want. They barely go to visit Chocolate. Butterscotch is in New York living like a rock star, thinking that money is going to last forever. Vanilla is in Pennsylvania somewhere letting some stupid guy spend her broke. She had a baby with him, and she buys the guy everything just to keep him. He doesn't even want her. The only time she comes to Cali is when he wants her here with him. Most of the time, he'll come without her. His ass showed up for my cookout yesterday, without her or an invitation, talking about 'we're family.' Family my ass! Every time I turned around, he was brushing up against my ass. Then he thought I was going to let him crash at my place because he was too drunk to drive. He really was, but he wasn't going to be staying in my house then go back to tell my sister more lies of how I want him so bad."

"He did that?" Charles asked, fascinated with the story as Tapioca placed two plates in front of him. One had large pancakes on it and the other with eggs and bacon.

"My sister stopped speaking to me for like six months because he told her that I was trying to get with his drunk ass. We were at an industry party together. I was invited and only brought his ass along because my sister asked me to keep an eye on him since she couldn't make the trip because of her pregnancy. He was at the party throwing money around like it was endless. I drove his fool-behind back to his hotel and dropped him off at the front door. The whole ride there he kept putting his hands on me, but he kept calling me Nilla, which is my sister's nickname. I had to fight him off all the way while driving. A few days later, my sister called and cursed me out for trying to screw her man. So, I say fuck 'em all! I have to live my life and not worry about other people and their insecurities."

"You are absolutely right. You are a very intelligent young lady. Wise and can cook quite well," Charles said as he swallowed the forkful of pancakes he shoved in his mouth.

It had been probably seven years since he last had home-cooked pancakes from his wife, and even that was made with Aunt Jermima. He couldn't remember ever having pancakes made from flour.

Tapioca smiled at his compliment. "Well, you sit right here and eat. I'm going to run this pie up the street before it gets cold."

Before he could say anything, she ran upstairs to throw on a camisole top and shorts, and then was out the door with the pie. After finishing his food, Charles went back over to her adult movie collection to see Tapioca's revealing covers. They were begging for him to watch, but he didn't know how long she'd be gone and didn't want her to catch him watching. He could hardly believe he was standing in her house after just seeing her through his binoculars the night before. She was taking longer than he wanted to hang around, but he didn't feel comfortable just leaving with her door unlocked.

She returned a half an hour later. "Oh my goodness, it's hot and humid out there today. I'm going to have to take another shower," she said as she ran back up the stairs before Charles could object.

"Well, I'm going to get…"

He was going to let her know he had to leave before Charlotte started calling to keep tabs on him, but Tapioca disappeared before he could finish his sentence. So, he decided to watch television until she came back down. The entire time he contemplated stealing one of her movies to watch in private, but he didn't want to chance it. The thought of an eighteen-year-old Tapioca was more erotic than a twenty-four-year-old Tapioca.

"Charles?" she yelled out over the rail from upstairs.

Charles came from the great room to the bottom of the stairs and saw her wet, long, curly hair hanging on her bare shoulders and a large towel wrapped around her body. He got an immediate throbbing from the look, which was more sensual to him than seeing her nude at the pool or on the DVD covers.

"Yeah, I'm here," he answered, clearing the frog from his throat.

"Oh good, you're still here. My shower drain is clogged up. I'm sure it's my own hair. Do you know anything about unclogging a drain? I could just call a plumber if you don't."

Charles thought about a drain he'd like to unclog, and the shower wasn't it.

"Sure, I could take a look at it for you. It's the least I could do after that delicious breakfast you fixed me." He patted his belly as he hesitantly walked up the long staircase.

The thought of seeing her bedroom was exciting him with each step, but he reminded himself that he was a married man and Tapioca was more than half his age…just like all the girls in the porno movies he watched. Unlike the girls in the porno movies, though, she was live and in person.

He entered her bedroom and found an extra large king-sized canopy bed with a mirrored ceiling. There were many mirrors in the room. She had a large nude portrait of herself hanging over her bed. With each step into the room, he was becoming more aroused. When he entered her bathroom and saw two sex toys on her sink, his johnson was ready to pop out of his shorts. Her standing directly behind him covered in only a towel, smelling fresh and clean, wasn't helping matters. When he bent to look inside of the drain, he could feel her breath and body heat on his back.

"Do you need me to get you a flashlight or something? I'm sure it's my hair. That's what it always is. I'm surprised I have any left on my head."

When Charles turned to address Tapioca, his lips almost touched hers because she was so close. "A screwdriver will do. Actually a Phillips. I just need to lift the drain trap and pull the hair from the drain."

"You make that sound so easy. I've got a tool box downstairs. I'll be right back."

Charles looked at the details of her contemporarily decorated bathroom. He didn't appreciate the architecture of it because he thought it was poorly constructed with the toilet closed off separately with the large tub and the large double shower divided by a wall from the double sink. He was about to pick up one of the sex toys, when he heard her coming. He wanted to smell it and see if her juices were still on it. He quickly stood back near the shower when she made it back to the bathroom. It took less than two minutes for Charles to unclog the drain. Again, he was kicking himself for being a two-minute man. He didn't want to leave. He wanted to be in her bedroom, in her presence. He liked feeling her near him.

"I have to ask, is that your real hair color? I've only seen that shade of strawberry blonde once before in my life. Very rare."

She held up a lock of her hair. "Got it from my momma. The color, that is. Guess I got the kinky curl from my daddy, whoever he was. My mother's hair was straight unless she sat under the hair dryer with big rollers. She always wished she had my hair, and I wished my hair was like hers. She had lots of body and bounce." Tapioca laughed. "I guess if she knew how much money it costs to keep unclogging drains filled with this stuff, she wouldn't want it."

Charles nodded, thinking back to his own past. "So do you have anything else that needs fixing while I'm here? I'd hate for you to waste good money on things easily fixable," he asked after snapping back to the future.

"Well…not really. I had another picture I wanted hung, but it's no big deal."

Charles wondered if it was another nude portrait. He wouldn't be able to stand himself if he didn't get to see it.

"That's no problem. Just tell me where you want it."

"Over there on that wall," she pointed. "The portrait is in the other room. I figured it wasn't a good idea to have it in there just in case I ever have guests or family stay over."

"This one you have is very artistic. It's very classy."

"Well, the other one is probably not as classy. It was painted from a photo I took. That was another reason my sister's boyfriend could not stay here last night. He went in that room and saw the picture. I don't need to tell you some of the vulgar things he said after seeing it. It's very erotic. I thought about hiring a handyman to hang it, but I don't feel too comfortable with letting people into my bedroom and them looking at my nude portraits. They get the wrong idea."

Charles became flushed by her words.

"Oh, I hope I didn't offend you. I wasn't talking about you. I hate when I call the plumber for my shower drain, and they always think I want to go on a date with them once they see my portrait. I figured most handymen would be the same."

"I understand. I'll be glad to hang it for you. I know it can't be easy being a single, attractive, young lady living on your own."

"Tell me about it." Tapioca laughed as she left the room. She returned with the large portrait, while struggling to hold the towel that was trying to fall from her body. "Here, grab this. My towel is trying to come undone. I need to hop back in the shower and finish washing the dried soap from my body. The water started backing up, and I had to get out. Thank goodness you were still here." She pointed to the tool box. "There should be whatever you need in there. I promise I won't be long."

After she shut the door, Charles looked at the sensuous portrait of Tapioca with her legs spread open, fingers inside herself, her right hand holding her right breast, and her facial expression displaying the orgasm she was bringing herself to. He could barely concentrate to get the mounting brackets on the wall correctly for the distracting portrait begging for his attention. The stopped shower forced him to focus on his task, but all the focus in the world wasn't speeding the blood out of his erection. Worse than that, he could feel a cool wetness on the front of his gym shorts, which would be visible once he turned to face her.

While Charles had his back to Tapioca, she ran to her bed, dropped her towel, and wrapped herself in her white kimono lying at the foot of her bed. Charles tried to pretend he didn't see her ass the minute the towel dropped. When she came and stood near him, he noticed the robe clinging to her still wet breasts. It was taking all of his energies not to touch her.

"I'm sorry, Charles. I didn't realize how much work was involved with hanging a picture. I thought for sure you'd be done by now."

Charles cleared his throat, but still his voice trembled. "Well, typically, it only takes a minute. I just wanted to make sure the wall will support the frame. I'd hate for it to fall in the middle of the night and scare you half to death."

He placed the frame against the wall, straightening it out without looking at the picture itself.

"So what do you think? Is it too risqué to hang in here? Maybe I shouldn't hang it."

Again, he cleared his throat. "Oh no! Oh…it looks great. I like it," he answered an octave higher.

"What do you like most about it? Do you see it as art or porno?"

He couldn't believe she was putting him on the spot like that. He felt like it was more porno than art, but he lied.

"It's definitely art. It's expressive. It's great!"

He did not want to stand there and be forced to watch her masturbate on canvas when he himself could not touch it.

"Well, I better get going. I don't want to take up your day. I'm sure you have plenty to do."

As she disappointedly looked down and saw not only his erection, but his wet spot, she said, "Charles, please don't go. I don't get visitors too often. I have this big house filled with all of this fun stuff, but never anyone to do anything with. Maybe you'd like to play a game of pool or a video game with me? I'd appreciate the company."

Charles didn't know which was more exciting: standing in her erotic presence or the chance to shoot pool without interruptions. Even better was the opportunity to play pool with a beautiful young lady who wanted to be in his company.

"Well, since you put it like that, I'll shoot a game of pool with you. I miss not having a pool table in my house. Charlotte hates them."

"Thank you, Charles. This means a lot to me."

She smiled and pressed her warm body against his to hug him. She didn't leave an air pocket between their bodies. Charles was sure Tapioca could feel his erection, just as he felt her hardened nipples pressing beneath his chest. He could feel the throbbing sensation of his manhood pressed against her soft body. She held him long, as if she didn't want to ever let go. That or she wanted him to make the next move.

He looked down at her as she looked into his eyes. Her mouth looked hungry, and he wanted to feed it. He moved his lips closer to hers. There was no objection. When he let his hands fall down her back, she pressed her body even closer into his. Their tongues locked as he rubbed his erection against her. Her robe loosened and then opened, revealing her youthful beauty up close and personal. His hands savagely caressed her bare ass. They moaned as they kissed. Her hand squeezed in between their bodies as it maneuvered its way inside of his shorts to find his hardness. She gripped it tightly while rubbing it back and forth. Charles felt like he would explode at any second when his fingers touched the surface of her wetness.

He stepped backwards and led her to the bed while peeling the robe from her body. She managed to pull his shirt from him that was wet from her hair and got his shorts down to his thighs. As they stood at the side of the bed, he inserted his middle finger into her as he bent to take her pink nipple into his mouth. She opened her legs wider to allow him deeper access as she climbed onto the bed. She held onto his cock while caressing the back of his head and let out light screams as he touched the more sensitive spots inside of her.

Inside his mind, he wanted to taste the tapioca pudding between her legs, but was worried about not pleasing her properly. It had been well over ten years since he had any oral sex. He was sure Tapioca had the skills to satisfy him. He knew what he was expected to do next when she pulled his fingers out of her and put them into both of their mouths for them to taste the juices. The only way he'd ever get to taste Charlotte was to sneak and lick his fingers after touching her wetness. Once, she had a fit and stopped everything when he kissed her immediately after and she tasted her cum on his lips. Three years ago was when he last tried it. But, not only was Tapioca allowing him to taste her from his fingers, she also scooted further back onto the bed, allowing him to take his tongue directly to the source. Tapioca was also gracious enough to help him along by moving her hips to help bring her to an orgasm.

That first orgasm made Charles' tongue go in deeper and provide more suction. He became more confident once her body started trying to run from the power of his tongue. Her screams would wake Charlotte in Japan. The more he realized he was pleasing her, the more he wanted to please her. It was probably twenty-five minutes before he came up for air. She had no problem licking his mouth and nose to clean her juices from his face, and when she was done, she had him lie on his back so she could lie on top of him in a sixty-nine position. He was about to start licking her some more, when she stopped him.

"No, sweetie, I got this. You just relax and enjoy the view."

"I definitely like this view," he said, looking inside of her pink lips, which were still talking as it continued to spout out juices.

He felt a volt of electricity shoot through his entire body when her mouth took possession of his brick-hard dick. His worst nightmare was about to happen as quickly as she took him in her mouth. He was about to blow at any second. He tried to stop her, but she wouldn't let up. His mind transcended to the collection of porno tapes featuring the lovely Tapioca Pudding. He imagined they were making their own movie. As his volcano erupted, she didn't let one drop of lava escape her lips. Charles watched as she sat up and swallowed the mouthful of his cum.

He was in love with her at that moment.

She turned her face towards his and kissed him, allowing him to share the aftertaste of his eruption. Charles kissed her for dear life. He wanted to let her know that he was in love with her. Then she stopped kissing him to go back down on him again. While his fingers played with her clit, she took his free hand and guided his thumb to her rectum. He wasn't sure what to do because he had never touched any woman's rectum. Again, she moved her hips around to help Charles please her. When his finger was deep inside her pussy, she pressed his thumb into her awaiting asshole. As nervous as it was making Charles, her erratic body jerking turned him on more. He pressed into both of her orifices as deeply as his fingers would allow.

Tapioca was going wild. Still, she held his dick inside her mouth. Charles knew this had to be the best sexual experience he had in his fifty years of living. He had oral sex in his life, but he had never been with a real-live porn star. Just the thought of him being inside of her pussy made him want to explode again. Tapioca sucked Charles until he came a second time.

"Damn, baby, I wanted to feel the inside of you first. I didn't want to cum again. I was looking forward to the main course."

"Trust me, I've wanted to feel you inside of me from that first day I saw it dangling in your window. I want to savor it longer. That's why I had to get the quickies out of the way. This pussy is going to give that dick the royal treatment it deserves, and I'm going to take my time with it—as much time as you'll allow me."

"You can have as much time with it as you can stand," he said, trying to sound cocky, while knowing full well that his wife was probably calling every phone in the United States to track him down. He'd think of a lie at a later time, but for the time being, he wouldn't let the thought interfere. He was having sex with a real-live, twenty-four-year-old porn star and didn't care about what hell Charlotte could raise if she found out.

"I take it you've never had anal sex?" she asked out of nowhere.

"Uh…uhmm…"

"You can be honest with me. I'll help you with anything you don't know but want to learn," she said seductively.

The mere mention of the word "anything" made Charles start to come back to life.

"Well, to be quite honest, I have never. It's been over ten years since I've enjoyed oral sex."

"Are you kidding? Ten years? But you're married," she laughed. "I could tell at first you didn't seem too experienced, but I guess it was like riding a bicycle. It all came back to you. You did a great job. Now when I'm alone with my toys, I can think about how good you ate my pussy or we could play with my toys together if you'd like," she said, adding extra seduction to her last comment.

Charles could not take any more. He wanted her at that moment. He pulled her into him for a deep kiss, and then he flipped her on her back as his mouth devoured her breasts. He was planning to fuck Tapioca's pudding with staying power. There would be nothing less than an hour, and if she wanted to teach him how to have anal sex, then he'd be a good student for his teacher. He wouldn't have any egos getting in the way of having the greatest time of his life.

He went down on her once again and helped prepare the wetness he was anticipating on his dick. Just as he was about to come up to insert himself inside of her, she stopped him.

"Sweetie, you're going to need to put on a condom. I have some in my nightstand."

"For what? I haven't been with anyone other than my wife for the past ten years."

"You should want to protect yourself just the same. Besides, I'm sure you wouldn't want an illegitimate child living next door to you."

Charles laughed. "Well, I think if I had to worry about catching something, it's too late. I've sucked up all of your juices. As for a baby, ten years with the same woman and no child yet."

"You're going to have to do this, Charles." She looked into his eyes unmoved by his argument.

"Fine, but I sure would prefer feeling you naturally."

She said nothing as Charles got up to grab a condom from her nightstand drawer. He became jealous of the thought of Tapioca using all of those condoms with another man. Just from a quick glance, he estimated at least fifty condoms. He didn't like the thought of another man kissing her mouth or sucking her breasts. He certainly didn't want another man to fuck her or taste her. He wanted to believe she didn't want to be with anyone else.

He hated the thought of being so close yet unable to feel her on him. Still, he put the condom on, hating the constricting feeling, but once his train entered Tapioca's tunnel, he felt like he died and went to heaven. However, he wanted better. During one of the times his dick slipped out because of the wetness, Charles pulled the condom off without her knowledge. Now that was the feeling of dying and going to heaven. Even Tapioca seemed to be enjoying the sex more. He turned her in many ways and was determined to last at least one hour. When he thought she was worn out and couldn't go on any longer, she would suddenly become aggressive and fuck him mercilessly.

"Are you ready?" she asked in between breaths.

"Ready for what?" he said between strokes.

He had her doggy-style, enjoying pulling her naturally long hair and slapping her ass, leaving his red handprint.

"It's time for you to learn how to ride from the backseat."

He almost lost his erection from the fear of anal sex.

"I'm good here. This feels great. Perfect."

Tapioca moved her ass forward, causing Charles to slip out of her. She grabbed his slippery hard penis and aligned it with her rectum. Charles pushed forcefully, trying to get his dick back in a hot, wet place.

"Easy, baby. Take it easy," she coached him.

He couldn't believe what was happening. He was about to have his first anal sex ever. She positioned her ass to help ease him inside. Charles watched the head enter and felt the instant gripping. Seconds later, his entire cock was lost inside of her ass. He could hardly contain the sensation. His body had involuntary twitching as his eyes rolled in his head. He felt his body convulse as Tapioca swayed her behind to the rhythm of an unheard song. He pumped up the beat while watching juices form on his dick. He had never seen anything like it, but it felt better than anything he'd ever experienced in his life. When her ass was bumping him harder, it caused him to lose the nut he was fighting to hold onto, and as he continued to pump in and out, he noticed the white oozing on his dick. It excited him more, and he continued to pound her asshole until he collapsed on her back.

When they collected themselves and she was able to get up, she noticed the condom on the bed and not on Charles.

"Charles! What is this?" she said, holding the stretched condom between her fingers.

He had almost dozed off and was delirious. "Huh? What?"

"Why did you remove the condom after I told you that I needed you to wear one? Damn! Why'd you have to mess shit up like that?" She was pissed off.

"I'm sorry. I didn't think it was that important. I won't do it again," he said, sitting up.

"You're right, because I'm not going to let you touch me again. Just get your shit and leave. All you men just care about your damn-self. Go!"

Charles stood up from the bed, surprised by how angry she was about what he thought was no big deal since they had already exchanged bodily fluids during oral sex.

"I'm sorry, Tapioca. I didn't realize you'd be so upset. I didn't mean to upset you like this. I'll leave now, but please don't stay angry with me. I'll do whatever to make it up to you." He was whipped. Just the thought of never touching her again was killing him.

Tapioca walked to her bathroom as Charles put his clothes back on.

"Just be gone by the time I come out of the bathroom." Then she slammed the door closed.

Charles stood downstairs for a moment, genuinely hurt about upsetting the one person who just moments prior gave him the best sexual experience in his life. Then he thought it was best that he just leave. As he opened the door, he saw a black guy with an urban street appeal pulling up in front of Tapioca's house. The young guy, who looked about Tapioca's age, got out the car flicking a cigarette and looked at Charles.

"Hey, Pops! You doing my sister-in-law?"

Charles was put off by the question. "Uh…excuse me? No! I live up the hill. She needed something fixed."

The guy laughed. "Yeah, if you say so. I won't be mad at you. That's a nice fat ass she got there."

Charles just shrugged his shoulders, unsure of what to say. He wanted to deck the guy for making such a comment about his new love. Instead, he began to walk away, but then turned when he heard the door open.

"Trey, what are you doing here today? The cookout was yesterday. The one you crashed."

"Damn, that's how you gonna treat your family? I was coming to see if you want to hit this spot with me. It's a movie screening I got invited to."

"Get your ass in here before one of my neighbors see you. I don't know why you have to come around here acting all hood."

Charles watched as Tapioca stepped back and let him into her home rather than sending him away. He especially didn't like the fact that the guy was in there with her while she was only wearing a robe, and especially after he had tried to come on to her the night before.

Charles couldn't understand why Tapioca would hang around her sister's boyfriend, knowing the strife the guy caused for them. He immediately went to his office window to see what he could see. Tapioca stood in the back doorway as if she were waiting for Charles to show up. He stepped away from her plain view of him and continued to watch.

Trey walked up behind Tapioca, pressing himself against her ass while reaching to fondle her breast. Charles was relieved when he saw Tapioca push him away and then go back inside her home, leaving Trey out there to smoke his cigarette or maybe marijuana.

A few minutes later, Tapioca reappeared wearing provocative clothes. She stood as if she waited for Trey to approve. When Trey rose from his seat to grope Tapioca like an octopus, she again pushed him away and disappeared once more. Tapioca came back fully dressed in jeans, heels, and a red halter top. Her hair hung loose. Trey got up from the chair he was lounging on and again started touching all over Tapioca as she fought him off. Charles was infuriated.

4

Charles camped out by his window until one o'clock that morning. At four o'clock, his internal alarm clock made him return to watch out of his office window. He saw Tapioca drying off after getting out of her pool. Charles noticed she had on a bikini, and he was glad she was alone. He watched her until she walked into her house. However, just as he was turning to go back to bed, he saw a glimpse of another person as she was closing her shutters. Charles tossed and turned for the next three hours, bothered about someone being with "his" girl whom he was with less than twenty-four hours prior.

At seven-thirty, Charles was back to his window looking for some clue. At nine-thirty, he noticed the shutters were open. At ten o'clock, his heart dropped when he saw Trey out back smoking a cigarette in his boxers. Charles tried to convince himself that Trey slept in a guest bedroom. He watched Tapioca bring Trey a breakfast tray outside to the patio table where he was sitting. As Tapioca set the tray on the table, Charles watched Trey's hand clearly go underneath the back of her paisley kimono while he buried his face in her bosom. Although she pulled back, her reaction was too delayed to convince anyone they had not slept together.

Charles turned away to recompose himself, only to turn back and witness Trey sucking Tapioca's breast through her open robe as she clutched his head. She seemed to keep her back to Charles' window as if she didn't expect him to witness what was going on. Tapioca then went back into the house with Trey hot on her heels, leaving the breakfast on the table.

It was afternoon when the pair reemerged, both with clothes on. Tapioca picked up the tray to take it in the house, while Trey sat out smoking a cigarette with a drink. He called her back out to share the view with him. He tried to get her to sit on his lap, but she was reluctant as her eyes continually shifted in the direction of Charles' window. Charles sat on the floor feeling like a wounded soldier.

Two hours later, the doorbell was ringing. Charles was so wounded he didn't want to answer it. He figured since he no longer saw the pair, they were in the house having wild, crazy sex. As he was getting up from the floor to answer the door, he noticed Trey back outside smoking again. He started to ignore the door, but the person was persistent.

"Look, I know how things may look from where you are, but it's really not like that," Tapioca said as quickly as he opened the door. She stood there holding a pie up for him.

Charles was surprised to say the least with her at his door and trying to convince him not to believe his lying eyes. He wondered why his thoughts even mattered to her. Was she planning on giving him another chance?

"Anyhow, I made this meat pie for you. I figured you must be hungry," she said as he took it from her hands.

She was about to walk away, but he called out to her, "Wait!"

She turned back.

"Why are you doing this? Are you trying to pay me back? I mean, you win. You got me back, but that's your sister's husband."

She looked embarrassed. "It's not how it looks, and they're not really married."

"You have a passion mark on your neck that wasn't there yesterday when I left. If that's not how it looks, then what?"

Her eyes teared up as she bit her bottom lip.

"Come here, don't cry." He pulled her to him with his free hand and hugged her before kissing her on the forehead. "Just get him out, okay?"

She nodded her head as she pulled away and pecked his lips before walking back down the hill to her house. Charles felt a rush of blood to his head when he looked up at his neighbor, two hundred yards away, watching from her window. Charlotte made it a point to befriend the woman as soon as they moved to the house. Charles knew she'd be calling his wife in Japan, and he expected a call any moment from his wife raising hell. He forgot to make sure the coast was clear when he let Tapioca in and out of his home the day before.

His growling stomach made him tear into the pie. As he delighted in it, he suddenly remembered her taking a breakfast pie to a neighbor while he waited in her home. He wondered if maybe she was sleeping with the other neighbors she also cooked for. He clearly recalled her saying none of the women liked her, which told him she wouldn't have been cooking for any women. The thought was more disturbing than her sleeping with her sister's boyfriend.

He went back to his office to see if there were any new updates. Again, Trey was outside smoking in his boxers. Apparently, Tapioca wasn't doing a good job of getting rid of him. A robe-clad Tapioca carried a cell phone to him outside and sadly looked up at Charles before going back inside.

That night, Charles declared he was done watching Tapioca. However, his two a.m. internal alarm woke him and his curiosity took him back to his window. He realized he was a glutton for punishment, and particularly when he stood watching Tapioca and Trey making out in her swimming pool. Tapioca looked completely willing as she exited the pool and led Trey to a lounge chair to resume their activities. She was in her own world, oblivious to Charles' existence. He watched them go down on each other before taking their act indoors.

5

Charles was so disgusted with Tapioca that he didn't want to fantasize about their time together anymore nor did he want to watch any of his porno collection either. Three days later, she was back at his door.

"Hey you," she said, with a smile on her face and guilt in her eyes. "Thought you could use some breakfast. Got you a breakfast pie and some pancakes." She held up her basket.

"I'm fine. I need to cut back anyhow," he said coldly, refusing her basket.

She looked sad. "Can we talk?"

"Sure, I'm listening."

"Can we go inside? I'd hate to feel like spying eyes are boring a hole through my back. I won't be long. I just feel I owe you an explanation."

"You don't need to explain to me why you're still screwing that lowlife guy even after I asked you to get rid of him when you came by the other day," he said, slightly raising his voice, but then recomposed himself. "Tapioca, you're young, you're beautiful, and who you sleep with should be none of my business."

"Maybe if you'd just let me explain… Look, I don't want you angry with me, Charles. I felt something with you the other day that I have never felt before in my life. I acted stupid and overreacted because I didn't know how to handle my feelings. I can't explain it, but I couldn't stop thinking about you from the first time I saw you. Maybe it was just lust, but when we were together the other day, I wanted you to be mine forever. I hate your wife. I hate how ugly she treated you that day in the grocery store. I hate that she has you and doesn't appreciate you, while I can't have you other than when you could steal a random moment with me. I know it may sound crazy, but I think I'm in love with you."

Tears poured from Tapioca's eyes as she laid her heart out on the ground either for Charles to accept or step on.

Charles looked around before inviting her into his home. He took the basket of food from her and led her to the forbidden kitchen.

"Tapioca, Tapioca, Tapioca. What am I going to do with you?" he said with a chuckle and shaking his head. "You can't think you're in love with someone one moment and then sleep with a completely different person the next. Why would you sleep with that man? He's so beneath you. He has no class at all. Help me to understand that."

Ashamed, Tapioca looked down, but Charles lifted her chin up.

"I wasn't totally honest with you about the Fourth of July or about the whole deal with my brother-in-law. I mean, Trey. He's not even married to my sister. They just share a baby, and knowing my sister, it may not be his."

"Whether they're married or not, he's with your sister. You shouldn't do that to her."

Tapioca took a deep breath and paced a few steps around the large kitchen. "Okay, so you know I did the whole porn thing, right?"

"Yeah." He nodded while walking near her, forcing her to look at him as she spoke.

"Trey and I worked a movie together long ago. We didn't date or anything; we just 'worked' together. It was business. I wasn't interested in hooking up with Trey on a personal level. So, when he asked if I had any sisters, I hooked him up with Nilla because he preferred a white woman even though I told him we were mixed races. Like I told you, to see Nilla, you wouldn't take her to be mixed. Her hair is long and blonde, and her eyes are green. Although he was with Nilla, he still kept trying to get me instead. I never told Nilla how I really knew Trey. I just told her that I knew him from parties in L.A. I also didn't know Trey would continue to relentlessly pursue me even though I hooked him up with my sister.

"He smokes weed, and down the road in their relationship, when they hit a rough patch, he told my sister while he was high how we really knew each other. My sister got mad at me instead of his ass, and when she got her money, she bought a house way across country and tried to take Trey as far away from me as she could. Since she was willing to spend her money on him, he followed her. Trey still does some work from time to time, and he is in Cali a lot. Depending on what type of mood she's in, one day, she'll beg me to keep an eye on him so he doesn't hook up with another woman and leave her ass high and dry. Then, on another day, she'll be calling and cussing me to stay the hell away from him.

"She's the one who sent him to my house for my cookout the other day. She's not even speaking to me, but she tells him to come to my house for my cookout. One thing you need to understand is that Trey and I have had a friendship for over six years. I just had no interest in a personal romance with him. So, although I didn't invite him, I wasn't going to tell him that he wasn't welcome to my home. That night at my cookout, when he got too drunk to drive, I was going to just let him crash at my place and sleep it off. I took him up to my guest bedroom, and he passed out as quick as his head hit the pillow. A few hours later after everyone left, I cleaned up out back and then went to take my shower. I was tired. While I'm in the shower, he walks in naked trying to kiss all over me. He said my portrait got him extra horny, and he figured I put him in that room so he could remember what he was missing. That's not why I put him in there, but I'll admit, I almost went there with him. He was turning me on, and I also remembered being with him on set. I started to justify it was alright to be with him for old time's sake, but I got it together and stopped things before it went all the way."

"So when you say you stopped it before it went all the way, how far was that?" Charles asked, not sure why it made a difference after everything he saw.

"It went too far to be innocent or an accident. I made him leave and told him to go wherever, but he couldn't be in my house drunk and stupid. I was stressed about it. That's when you saw me out at the pool swimming. That next day when you saw him, I obviously wasn't expecting him. I was with you and was hoping to spend the day with you. When he came, he was sober and invited me to a screening for some mutual former colleagues."

"He was sober? He reeked of marijuana, and I saw him still trying to touch you."

"I don't know. I just wasn't thinking about the weed. He smokes all the time. He acts crazy, but I don't be taking him seriously."

"You don't think it should be taken seriously when someone touches you when you don't want to be touched?"

Tapioca was getting confused and annoyed by Charles' chastisement. Every time she walked away, he stayed hot on her trail.

"I mean, yeah, it should be taken seriously. I don't know. I just never thought too much about Trey."

"So I see you ultimately put aside all of your inhibitions. How'd that happen?

She turned and boldly faced him. "You."

"Me?" he asked, surprised.

"Yes. When we were out together, we had a good time, but when we got back to my house, I was so upset with you still. I went out back to cry, wondering if you were watching the tears roll down. When I walked back in, Trey saw I was upset and acted like my friend. I told him about you, but I didn't tell him you were the guy I was upset about.

I told him that you were married and somehow I became so infatuated with the thought of us being together. We sat sipping on a bottle of wine while he talked to me as a real friend. He told me that I need to look out for myself first and shouldn't let myself get caught up with a married man who would never give up his life for me. After awhile, one thing led to another, and I didn't fight him anymore. While I was with Trey, I figured it would push you out of my mind. Then I decided I didn't want to lose your friendship. Even if we never sleep together again, I'd still like to have your company sometimes. I'd still want to share the meals I prepare with you."

"About that, I remember you mentioned that none of the neighbors liked you because they were insecure. Yet, you take food to many neighbors. How is that? Are these all the husbands you take food to?"

"All but one is married. It's just they'd be nice to me but would tell me their wives weren't too comfortable with me. I've invited them to my home, but they would never show up. It's always the husbands that would do the explaining or apologizing. I started off sending my baked goods for the entire household, but I later learned the women were not receptive. Still, the men would put in requests for my cooking. Unfortunately, I'd often have to sneak it to them. No matter what happens between us, I want to be able to bring you something from time to time."

"I have to admit, that was the best meat pie I have ever tasted. I would have never thought about trying any had you not brought it to me that day. I was so upset with you that I didn't want to eat your pie, but one taste and I was hooked."

Tapioca smiled, happy that she was able to please Charles.

"If you think that's something, you should taste my tapioca pudding."

"I did, and I think it was the best I've ever had, as well."

Charles felt more at ease with her. Tapioca looked confused since she knew she hadn't fixed him any yet. Then he pointed down to her shorts. She looked down and understood what he was saying. She laughed.

"Funny! You had me going there for a minute. But, really, I make a mean tapioca pudding. Most people tell me they don't like tapioca pudding, but then, I fix mine and they're begging for more."

"I remember you told me that you would tell me how you became a great cook."

"I've been cooking since I was a kid. My mother was never home or available to cook, so I did all the cooking. I used to watch all of the cooking shows, and I'd read cookbooks for recreation. Then I'd add my own twist and experiment. And there you have it," she said, back in a happy place.

There was an awkward silence.

"Well, I guess I better eat this good food before it goes to waste."

"Charles, I don't know if this'll make it okay, but Trey is gone and won't be coming back," she said, looking into his eyes. "I really did enjoy our time together and hope it wasn't our last time, even though I foolishly said it was." She stood directly in front of him and held his face in her hands. "I don't want to lose you. I don't want you to have to keep watching me from a distance when you could have me in your arms. I don't want to see you treated like a third-rate citizen when you deserve to be treated like a king. And if you can promise to take care of all of my plumbing needs, I'll promise to never again let another man touch my body."

She reached up and sensually kissed his lips until he reciprocated. Then he stopped her.

"Tapioca, I don't know. You're young and have your whole life ahead of you. Me, I'm fifty years old, married, and trying to start a family. I don't want you putting your life on hold for me. I hate the thought of another man touching this lovely body, but I don't think it'd be fair," he said, rubbing his hands down to her waist.

"And I hate the thought of you making love to her instead of me. I hate the thought of you being saddled to that bitch for the rest of your life because of children, but even more, I hate the thought of you being sexually deprived to the point where you have gone ten years without oral sex and have only had one anal sexual experience."

Charles got a quick rise by the recent memory. "Wow! I didn't think about it like that."

She caressed his rising erection that pushed his robe up. He leaned against the kitchen's island when she bent forward to take his throbbing member into her mouth. His hands played in her hair when he didn't know what else to do with them. He closed his eyes as she took him to ecstasy. When he slightly opened his eyes, he thought he saw someone move past his window. He watched a few seconds longer and didn't see anything, so he ignored it.

Just as he stopped her to take her to a more comfortable place in the house, the doorbell rang. He was going to ignore the door and take Tapioca to a guest bedroom, but he would have had to go past the door to get to the stairs. Unfortunately, the windows near the door were uncovered because Charlotte insisted on allowing people to see the beauty of her elegant foyer. He waited for the doorbell to stop, but the person would not go away.

"Wait right here a minute. Let me see who this is and get rid of them."

He kissed her lips, fixed his robe, and went to the door. It was his wife's spy from across the way.

"Mrs. Vanderbilt, how can I help you?" he asked, annoyed when he opened the door for the seventy-one-year-old nosey neighbor that stayed in everyone's business.

"Charles, I know I'm bothering you, but that homewrecker needs to leave. Charlotte asked me to keep an eye out on the house while she's away, and I'm sure she wouldn't be happy knowing the neighborhood tramp is in her home," she said in her raspy voice that had more than enough cigarettes in its lifetime. "I saw her here the other day, but at least she didn't come in. I saw her come in here a while ago with her basket of poison that she takes to everyone's husbands when their wives are away."

"Well, if you don't mind, I'd like to eat my basket of poison in peace. Please go to your home and stop worrying about who brings me or anyone else food."

"I see she delivers lip service, too. I'm sure Charlotte wouldn't appreciate that kind of behavior in her house. I told her I'd keep an eye out, and that girl has to go. If you want your pecker lip service, just don't do it in Charlotte's house."

Charles couldn't believe his ears. Mrs. Vanderbilt obviously was the shadow he saw at the window. She was really spying on him. He also was getting pissed with her continual reference to the house he worked hard to pay for as "Charlotte's house."

She continued, "I'm not leaving until she's gone, Charles. Charlotte told me to keep an eye out, and that's what I'm going to do. The only reason I don't tell Charlotte what you're up to is because it would crush her, and she'd end up in a nasty, bitter divorce, and I don't know who would end up in this house. That's why the last couple who lived here left. That tramp wrecked their marriage and his wife tried to kill him. This neighborhood doesn't need another situation like that. It doesn't matter what color you are, as long as you got a pecker to pee with, she's bringing her basket of poison."

He wondered what she meant about the previous home owners having their marriage wrecked. He didn't dare ask Mrs. Vanderbilt and make her know she hooked him with her tales.

She persistently went on as Charles' patience grew thinner.

"I saw you coming from her house the other day and the next one going right on in. I don't care about any of that. I'm just looking out for Charlotte's house…"

"Mrs. Vanderbilt, Mrs. Vanderbilt," he cut her off, "this is my house, not Charlotte's house. And I don't need for you to keep an eye on my house or my movements. If I decide I want to have friends over in my house, that's my business. If I decide I want to go to a friend's home, again, that's my business. What goes on between me and my wife, still, that's my business and not Mrs. Vanderbilt's. Now I'd appreciate if you'd move your foot from my doorway before your foot accidentally gets smashed as I close my door. Have a good day, Mrs. Vanderbilt," he said, as she quickly snatched her foot away before the door closed.

He waited a moment before going back to his kitchen. He couldn't believe her gall. He tried to act like he wasn't moved, but the truth is he didn't know what he was going to do if Charlotte caught wind of his indiscretions.

"I think you'd better go now. I don't know what's about to happen, and I just need to see what's what. This woman is watching me here and at your house. She just saw us in the kitchen."

"Oh my goodness! She's crazy! Why is she spying into your kitchen window or my house?"

Frustrated, Charles shook his head. "I don't know, sweetheart. I just need a minute to figure this all out."

Tapioca put her hands around Charles' neck. "Okay, but don't keep me waiting too long. If you need for me to get a hotel or something away from here, just let me know. I really want to be with you and please you," she said, before kissing his lips.

He pecked her back. "Okay, I'll let you know."

He escorted Tapioca to the front door, and Mrs. Vanderbilt was standing in front of her house with her arms folded. "Tramp!" she yelled as soon as Tapioca stepped out of the door.

Tapioca flipped her hand at Mrs. Vanderbilt as she sashayed her way down the hill. Charles watched her walk away until she could no longer be seen. Then he turned in Mrs. Vanderbilt's direction.

"It was for your own good, Charles. She's evil. She means you no good. Karen James could tell you what I'm saying. Ask her!" she yelled out, referring to one of the other neighbors who happened to be the only other African American couple in the community. Oddly, Charlotte didn't like Karen because she felt Karen was a scorned Jezebel with her sights set on Charles.

Charles went back into his home, slamming the large door. "Bitch!" he mumbled to himself since his erection was left unfulfilled. He heated up some of the food Tapioca left him. The more he ate, the angrier he became with Mrs. Vanderbilt. He thought of all the wonderful things he was about to do with Tapioca before the intrusion.

While he sat figuring out what he would do if Charlotte found out, the phone rang. It was Charlotte calling. He debated whether or not to answer because he figured Mrs. Vanderbilt must have gotten hold of her, and he didn't care to hear his wife's ranting.

"Hello," he answered in a grumpy tone, guessing he'd better just get it over with.

"Hey honey. How's it going?" she asked happily as if they had a happy marriage.

"Just busy with work. How about yourself?" he asked, not really caring.

"Things are great here. I think you should come here sometime. I keep trying to tell you that you could probably learn a lot about your profession. I think it would make you way more competitive as an architecture."

Charles could feel his temples pounding in his head. "Did you call to insult me, Charlotte, or did you want something in particular?" he asked, ready to shut her down.

"Why so testy today? I'm just trying to help. Also, I just learned I'll be here a little longer than anticipated and thought maybe my husband wouldn't mind coming to visit me for a day or two. I'm sure you'll eventually need sex, and I'm just trying to figure out a way to balance my career with my wifely duties."

The phone almost dropped from his hands. He couldn't believe her nerve. He didn't want to believe she was really convinced that once every four to eight weeks for sex was fulfilling her wifely duties. Not only that, he remembered a few years back when he went with her to Prague for business because he thought it would be romantic. She spent the entire trip berating him for not wanting her architectural advice that she continually offered in front of her colleagues, who looked at Charles as if they felt sorry for him. In addition, she refused him sex because she was angry with him for his making her look foolish in front of those colleagues.

"No, Charlotte, I don't think so. I'll just see you when you get back."

"Are you serious?" She dramatically acted as if something were caught in her throat. "Karen! Karen James! I know that witch got her claws in you the moment I left. I saw how she watched you at my party. I should have never let her into my house. Just because her husband is screwing the white girl down the hill, she has to seek out my husband. I will take the next flight out to let her have it," she spewed through the phone.

"Karen? Are you serious? Charlotte, please! Now you're just being ridiculous. You stay gone half the time around the world, and you want to accuse me of foolishness? The last time I saw Karen was at your birthday party because you, not me, invited her to show off your house."

"If not Karen, then who?"

"Who, what?"

"Who is satisfying your needs, Charles?" She paused, and just before Charles could respond, she said, "Please tell me you don't have any more of those filthy movies in my house. Charles, I thought we've been through this already. I want those things gone. Now!"

Charles rubbed his brows. He couldn't win with Charlotte.

"I have to go now. I have work to do."

"Are you rushing me off of the phone?"

"No, I'm going to discard all of those movies out of your home," he sarcastically lied.

"Fine! Just don't bring any more in there."

"Yes, dear," he said, placating her. "Anything else, dear?"

Charlotte scoffed. "Don't you get snippy with me…"

Before she could finish her sentence, Charles ended the call.

Charles paced for almost an hour trying to sort his thoughts out along with their consequences. Instinctly, he went to his favorite window after unsuccessfully trying to get work done. He got to the window just in time to see a tall black man closing Tapioca's blinds. Immediately, he felt his blood boil. Just minutes prior, he contemplated inviting Tapioca back in his home, not caring about Charlotte's spy. Although he didn't get a good look, he knew it wasn't Trey, and just hours ago, he was about to make love to her right after she promised to rebuke all men for him.

He spent the next few hours with his face pressed to his window, trying to get some clue of the man touching all over "his woman." Even after he went to bed, he continually got up once in a while to see. Still nothing. Before the sun could get up in the sky good, he was back at the window. Charles was becoming desperate. It was almost noon, and Tapioca's blinds were still closed. His concentration was out the window. He thought about going to ring her doorbell, but not only did he have to worry about spying eyes, he'd have to worry about a confrontation with the "he" inside of Tapioca's house. Instead, he decided to take a jog despite the high sun, and he'd slip a note in her mailbox.

6

It was 7:45 p.m., and he sat on the edge of the bed flipping the channels on the 42-inch plasma television affixed to the wall. His stomach was in knots. He had been unable to eat all day. He was hoping to eat soon enough. Thirty minutes later, there was a knock on the door. His stomach tightened, and he held his breath with each step to the door, exhaling as he opened it. There she stood in a trench coat in the middle of July, carrying an overnight bag. His heart danced with delight. He almost gave up on seeing her.

"Bob Johnson? Really?" she laughed. "Are you going to let me in, or am I going to have to open my coat right here in the hallway?"

Charles quickly ushered Tapioca into the hotel room he rented under his alias Bob Johnson so he could spend some uninterrupted time with the young woman who had captured his heart. He didn't care about the man he saw in her home the night before. He only cared she was with him at that moment.

"I had to think of a name quickly while I was writing the note. That's what came to mind first. I've never done anything like this before. I certainly didn't want to have to use my real name. It worried me when they asked to see my driver's license, though I was paying in cash."

Tapioca set her bag down and looked around the nicely decorated room.

"This is pretty nice. I would have been good with a Super 8 or Motel 6, though." She sat on the large bed and bounced on the mattress. "Wow! This is a really good mattress." She then stood up and walked over to a nervous Charles, wrapping her arms around his neck. "But, by the time we get through, they'll need a new one." She kissed him passionately.

Charles' stomach grumbled from his hunger.

"Have you eaten today?" she asked.

Charles was embarrassed. His loins were hungry for his personal porno queen, but his stomach was desperately in need of food. He wasn't about to tell her that he hadn't eaten since the day before, as he sat around like a love-sick puppy.

"I was going to order something once you got here."

"I know I'm like an hour late, but I didn't check my mailbox until four o'clock. Be glad I checked it today. Sometimes I don't bother to get my mail. When I thought about that nosey Mrs. Vanderbilt, I wondered if she snoops through my mail when I'm not around. That's when I decided to go get my mail, and to my surprise, I found your invitation to meet you here."

She took his hand and moved it inside of the coat she had yet to open, placing it between her bare legs.

"My pussy was so excited the whole ride over here. Can you feel the heat?"

Charles couldn't believe she was completely naked underneath her coat. Sure, he'd seen it in movies before, but he never thought anyone really did such a thing. Suddenly, his urge for food completely dissipated. His hungry loins became the priority. His fingers desperately went digging in search of the heat source, while Tapioca opened her coat and let it fall to the floor to expose her beautiful, erect pink nipples that Charles wasted no time sucking. Charles stopped long enough to get Tapioca on the bed as she helped remove his clothing.

"I need to have that big, black dick right now. Let me taste it."

Tapioca laid on her back as Charles brought his hardened tool to her mouth. He liked being on top of her and in control. As she licked, tasted, and teased, Charles' thoughts were to put his dick in her mouth and let it go as far down her throat as she could take it. He watched that a million times on his porno movies, and it made him want it more and more. Tapioca gagged a time or two, but she took him deep enough to cause him to ejaculate in record time. Charles was embarrassed yet again. That time for his inability to contain his release.

"I am so sorry," Charles said, as he sat on the bed beside Tapioca.

She laughed. "Yeah, that was kind of quick, but as long as you have some more ways to make this pussy speak your name..." she said, massaging between her legs.

"Uhm-hmm, I sure do," he replied, positioning his face to lick the wetness her pussy was squirting.

She tried to keep her head lifted so she could watch as Charles ate her just as well as any fellatio she'd had with experienced men. With each shot of sensation, she had to rest her head back, but still clutching her nails into the back of Charles' head, letting him know he was handling business properly. Every now and again, he'd raise his eyes up to meet hers. At times, her eyes would sensually roll up in her head, making him take his tongue even deeper inside of her in a circular motion while licking the walls clean of any pudding. When he knew she climaxed, he stopped to turn her over on her stomach. He didn't know why, but he had an overwhelming desire to lick her ass. He wanted to kiss her ass cheeks because her ass was beautiful to him. Then he wanted to bury his face in between her ass cheeks while teasing the door of her pussy with his tongue before stroking it up until it found her asshole. When Tapioca's body tried to run away, he knew he was doing good. Minutes later, his dick was good and hard, deep inside of Tapioca's pussy. He was hoping she didn't stop him for a condom, and to his surprise, she put up no resistance.

Charles was thoroughly enjoying Tapioca and enjoyed her even more when she pulled his wet dick out of her pussy to guide into her asshole. His orgasm felt so good to him, he thought he was having a convulsion. He was feeling so good, he hated to pull apart from Tapioca long enough to order room service and eat dinner.

After dinner, they cuddled like a couple in love, while feeding each other the strawberries and chocolate dip they ordered from room service. They had a pillow fight, tickled one another, and even danced. He was enthralled when Tapioca taught him the many ways to have fun with the ice from the champagne bucket. She attentively listened to all of the stories Charles was willing to share about his life and his work, unlike he was able to do with his self-centered wife. Then they watched television in each other's arms until they fell asleep.

Charles awoke with the morning light, while having the best dream of his life. He reached over on the pillow beside him which was empty. However, the wonderful sensation coming from his loins caused him to look in that direction only to find his love giving him head. She didn't have to work too hard to get the erection she was aiming for before she climbed on top of it, taking him inside of her. She moved her hips to a sensual rhythm. Charles couldn't remember the last time, if ever, he had been awakened to good loving.

When Charles could no longer take the teasing her vagina was dancing on him, he flipped Tapioca on her back, holding her ankles apart up in the air while thrusting in and out of her, occasionally making a rhythm of his own. He was determined to make Tapioca's pussy speak his name over and over again. He looked into her eyes with each thrust as she seductively licked her lips while caressing her breasts, intermittently rubbing his testicles that would slap against her pussy with each stroke. Their eyes spoke the words neither could cohesively say from their mouths. He rested his sweaty chest against her breasts as he took her tongue into his mouth, intensifying his strokes, grinding his pelvis against her clit, which brought about his explosion and caused hers in turn.

"Boy, you sure got me working up an appetite."

"Well, this is a good reason you should be waking up in my bed with me instead of a hotel room. I could have fixed you a hot delicious breakfast instead of this mess," Tapioca said, holding up her cold piece of toast brought up by room service.

"Spend the night with me tonight," she said out of nowhere as her eyes lit up. "I love falling asleep in your arms and especially waking up with you. I have never felt this way with any man before." She got up from the table and went to retrieve her overnight bag. She opened it and pulled out a bag of oils. "I brought this last night to give you a nice massage. I wanted to make you feel good."

"Oh, you certainly made me feel good. No doubt about that," Charles laughed.

"No, I wanted to take my time with you, and then you with me. I wanted to rub the flavored oil all over your body and then rub our bodies together before we licked the oil off each other."

"Wow! Sounds like delicious fun."

"Say you'll stay with me, Charles. We could have so much fun together. We can make our private movie together, and you can watch it over and over again…when *she* ain't treating you right. Let me show you how a man is supposed to be taken care of."

Little did she know, she was singing his song. Just the thought of him being able to have his own private production with Tapioca Pudding from next door excited him. That was more delight than his fifty-year-old heart could stand. He knew he was taking a major risk by staying with her, but the prize was too great to turn down.

"Okay."

"Okay? Okay, you'll stay with me, or okay, that's enough now shut up?"

Charles' eyes smiled as they looked into Tapioca's hazel-green eyes. He stood from the table, taking her into his arms, and then kissed her. His kiss told her that he was in love with her. If she didn't know it before, she knew at that moment.

"Thank you, thank you, thank you. You won't regret it. I will make you feel like the king you are. King Charles. That's what you'll be to me from now on."

Charles smiled, liking the sound of her words. "You already make me feel like a king. Now I want to make you feel like my queen," he said, then thought, *Even if it is while living a lie.* He kissed her some more. "Come on, we better get ready to get out of here. I'm sure with all the bed thumping and bumping, along with the screaming, moaning, and groaning, they wouldn't consider letting Bob Johnson stay another night," he laughed.

"That's okay. I'll just take Bob Johnson home with me where we can be as loud as we want to be."

"Hmm, sounds good to me," he said before guiding her to the shower, where she bathed him with her tongue. He loved how she held her head under the water as she sucked him and didn't worry about her hair.

When they left the hotel, he walked her to her car, kissing her as if it would be the last time. He didn't want to leave her, not even for a little while. He was in love and didn't care who knew it. Even better, she seemed like she loved him, too. He'd deal with his marriage on another day, but on that day, he would be King Charles and she would be Queen Tapioca.

7

After leaving Tapioca, Charles decided to show his face in his architectural firm. He hadn't done so in some time. Now that he was in love and on top of the world, he was feeling inspired. Charlotte wanted Charles to find some inspiration, and she'd be happy to know he finally found some. She just wouldn't be happy with the source of his inspiration. All of his colleagues even noted how happy he looked for a change. When he left his office, he met up at a sports bar with two of his buddies, Arty and Larry.

"Okay, what gives?"

"What do you mean?"

"So now me and Larry have to play guessing games? You look happier than when you first met that nutty wife of yours."

"I don't know what you're talking about," Charles said, trying to hide his joy.

"So what ever became of that young girl you mentioned at the cookout? Do you ever see her at her pool? I'm sure with this heat, she'd be skinny dipping on a regular," Larry asked.

"That's probably why he's looking all extra happy. I know I would," Arty laughed.

"Cut it out! I just had a pretty good day at the office, that's all."

Charles hated lying to his friends. He wanted to tell the world how good Tapioca's pudding was.

"So have you seen her again? I'd like to come and sneak a peek, too. Lord knows I could use something pretty to look at. I bet she got titties like POW!" Larry demonstrated by extending his hands from his chest.

Charles could feel his anger about to take over. He didn't appreciate the thought of Larry, or any other man for that matter, ogling over his young lady.

"Okay, that's enough. Don't talk about her like that."

Larry and Arty looked at each other and then at Charles before breaking out into laughter.

"You hit that?!" Arty asked.

"NO!" Charles said an octave higher.

Larry laughed. "We're your boys. You can tell us the truth, you know."

"I am not hitting it."

"Well, I hope Charlotte was the one who put those scratches on your neck," Arty said, pointing. "Then again, we know her ass is still in Japan. Otherwise, you wouldn't be out this evening with us *hoodlums*. So that would be a long reach to get to your neck."

Charles tried to quickly conceal the scratch marks left by Tapioca that he forgot about.

"Look, ain't nobody trying to run up in your business, but you just better be careful," Larry warned. "You don't shit where you sleep. She could be one of them psycho, fatal attraction bitches. That's all you need for Charlotte to get wind of."

Charles gave up his denial. "I don't care. I don't give a shit about Charlotte finding out. I think I love her."

"Love Charlotte?" Arty asked.

"No! Love Tappy."

"Tappy? What the fuck is a Tappy? You got a new dog?" Arty asked, with Larry sitting in anticipation for the same answer.

Disgusted, Larry sat back in his seat, and then he leaned back towards the table. "Look, it's all good that you're getting your tool greased, but love? That's not good."

"You don't understand." Charles was coming to life, ready to bubble over. "Tapioca is beautiful. She's intelligent, and she wants to make me her king. Who wouldn't love that? She is sexy-gorgeous, and she cooks for me. My own wife won't cook for me. If you saw her, you'd understand."

"Charles! Snap out of that love shit! When I was doing that fat-booty girl from Jamaica, now she was sexy-gorgeous. But, you didn't see me getting all gooey. When Art was boning that Asian chick, you didn't see him catching feelings. Besides, didn't you say once before that the girl is white? You don't do white anymore, remember? Remember all that shit you talked about your Nubian sisters being tossed to the side because brothers don't know how to be men anymore?"

Charles sat back frustrated. He was kicking himself for agreeing to meet his longtime friends. "She's not white. Well, not exactly. She looks like she can pass for white."

"Then she's white!" Arty laughed. "She got a big booty? If she has one, that's how you'll know she's a sister."

"Well then, I guess she's a sister," Charles shot back proudly.

"My man!" Arty said, holding up his hand for a high-five from Charles, but got one from Larry instead.

"Damn, she got an ass like that? Now I really gotta come by your crib and check out the view."

"Don't even think about her, Larry. Have some respect here. I said I love this girl."

"Man, if her ass is all that, I'd love her, too," Larry laughed.

"So is she a white girl? Didn't you say she had blonde hair or something?" Arty asked.

"She's bi-racial. She has strawberry-blonde hair and hazel-green eyes. She has the cutest pink freckles on her face. She's gorgeous from head to toe and inside out…"

"And I bet you got deep inside to find out. Pink freckles, huh? That means pink titties, right?" Larry continued to pick. "How old is she?"

Charles wasn't too comfortable disclosing her real age. "She's thirty-four, and her breasts are not of your concern."

"Breasts? What happened to tits, ta-tas, hooters, or something?" Arty asked before Larry could respond to Charles.

"Damn, she's old. I kind of pictured her being a young twenty-five-year-old with a fat ass and big, nice, firm titties. Thirty-four means cellulite and sag."

"Breasts, Larry. They're breasts," Arty teased.

"Hate to disappoint you, Larry, but she's none of that. She's perfect."

"Just be careful whatever the case. You're still a married man, and you know that gold-digging wife of yours will have everything you own, including your pair of lucky drawers from college."

Larry burst out laughing. "That's Charlotte."

"Ha ha! Funny! Anyway, I've got a hot date tonight that I need to get home and get ready for."

"My dawg!" Arty said. "Sitting here trying to play like he's all innocent. Welcome to the club, player! That means hit it and keep it moving. And make sure you keep Jimmy wrapped up."

Larry and Arty fist bumped one another.

Charles didn't dare let his friends know he adamantly had no intentions of using any condoms with Tapioca. He wasn't interested in their lectures.

"Whatever! I'm out. I'll make my own club—The Charles in Charge Club."

"Doesn't sound like you're in charge while you're in love, or should I say lust," Larry said while shaking his head, annoyed by his friend's blindness. "Do you, man, but just be careful."

"I will," Charles replied, getting up to leave and leaving a twenty on the table for his drink.

*****

Later that night, Tapioca made him feel like every bit of the king she promised. First, she fed him a meal fit for a king, then prepared him a nice bath before his sensual massage and hours of lovemaking in front of the three video cameras she had set up for their private movie. She allowed Charles to take close-up shots of her masturbating and squirting while he lent a hand on occasion. He had her in every room of her 3,400 square-foot home and even on her pool table after they played a game. To end the night, he took her outside to her swimming pool so he could always remember this moment each time he looked out of his window. As the sun started to rise with them still getting it on out by the pool, they decided it was time for them to retire to her bedroom for rest.

When he awoke, he decided to wake her up the way she woke him up the day before. They spent the entire day together making love, cuddling while watching one movie behind another, and eating. Charles finally left at one o'clock the next morning, long after Mrs. Vanderbilt's spying eyes would be awake and able to catch him leaving from Tapioca's house. And not one time was he distracted by Charlotte's twenty-one calls to his cell phone throughout the day.

8

The more Charles looked at the kitchen faucet that Charlotte oozed over when buying the house, the more he hated it. He made up his mind that Charlotte would no longer wear the pants in his home. After all, Tapioca declared him a king, and at the very least, he would be king of his castle; not Charlotte.

Something about good sex has a way of making a man feel more like a man, he thought.

He went around the home making notes and taking measurements for all of Charlotte's favorites he was about to replace with a trip to Home Depot.

As he strolled around Home Depot thinking about his personalized movie he would watch when he got back home, he saw a familiar face. He looked at the man smiling at him.

"Do we know each other from somewhere? You look awfully familiar to me."

"Jonathan. Jonathan James. My wife Karen and I were at your wife's birthday party last month."

"Oh, okay. Good to see you again," Charles said, still feeling as if he may have seen the same guy more recently.

"So I see you're doing some home improvements, as well," Jonathan said, looking into Charles' cart.

"Yeah, I'm trying."

"Karen had to fly to New York a few days ago and left me with a laundry list of chores to complete before she returns in two days."

Charles couldn't help staring at Jonathan, trying to place where he may have recently seen him.

"I'm sorry for staring, but did I just see you somewhere within the past few days? I'm trying to recall if I've ever seen you while I was out running, but can't say I have."

"You don't remember seeing me the other morning? You were leaving the Doubletree Hotel with Strawberry. I was having an early lunch right next door at the bistro. I saw when you were looking around and then right at me. I didn't think it would be cool to call you out. Trust me, I understand," Jonathan chuckled.

"Understand what?" Charles quizzed, wondering just how much was witnessed.

Jonathan laughed. "Nah, I ain't mad at you. I understand. That's one sweet strawberry."

"Strawberry?" Charles asked, perplexed and hoping Jonathan wasn't alluding to what he thought.

"Tappy. I call her Strawberry since she got those… Whew! You know." Jonathan held his chin as he smiled, having a flashback of his own. "I tell you, that is certainly one sweet piece of… Strawberry. And she can burn in the kitchen, too. Shit, I look forward to my wife taking her little business trips. She wants to be Miss Independent. I say go right ahead. All these women want to be all independent and leave their husbands unattended. They need to get with the program and handle business."

Charles could hardly believe his ears. Then he became further surprised when his memory delivered the fact that Jonathan was the image he saw closing Tapioca's blinds just a few nights ago.

"You're sleeping with Tapioca?" Charles asked, still not wanting to accept it.

Jonathan was taken aback and laughed. "Puuf! Man, you say that like you're surprised. Strawberry is the neighborhood treat. We get to have a good time, and she doesn't make waves for anybody like a lot of these bitches out here nowadays always trying to out me to my wife. Hell, even old man Vanderbilt gets a taste of that Strawberry, and he had a stroke."

Jonathan laughed, but then got serious when he saw the distressed look upon Charles' face.

"You really didn't know? I thought that's why you were doing her, too, because that's what she's all about. That bitch likes to fuck. I know you weren't taking her serious, were you? Man, that's what happened with the dude that lived in your house before you. He got it real bad and was willing to leave his wife for that ho. Wifey wasn't having that shit. She was gonna kill our Strawberry dessert."

"How do you know she's been with the other guys?" Charles' cracked voice asked, almost ready to cry and still not wanting to accept Jonathan's disturbing words.

"We talk. Just like you and I are talking now. Everybody knows what time it is, and no one gets their feelings all caught up like the other dude did. This way, we stay happy while Strawberry takes care of all of us."

"How many are 'all of us'?"

Jonathan shrugged his shoulders. "I don't know. I say about six or seven. Nah, make that eight or nine, including both of us, and that's just from the neighborhood."

"Do you not see anything wrong with sharing one woman between a bunch of men? I can't believe what I'm hearing."

"She's a porno ho. That's what porno hoes do. They like to fuck. They are insatiable. Trust me, you by yourself don't have enough dicks for that girl. You need to see her movies. You can tell when them girls like it or don't like it. She gives us all the Strawberry we want, and unlike a hooker, we don't have to pay her. She even brings us treats. Slap a rubber on my joint, and I'm good."

"Well, I can assure you that things will be different from here on out. I will not be sharing Tapioca. You may have been at her house a few nights ago, but that's the end of that. Spread the word," Charles said buffed up, no longer caring about his wife finding out. He was in love with Tapioca, and whatever she used to be, she didn't have to be ever again.

Jonathan looked at Charles as if he were stupid, then broke out in a roaring laughter.

"You can't be that stupid, can you? My dick was in her mouth this morning right after she brought me breakfast. Her exact words, 'I brought you something good to eat for breakfast in exchange for your big black dick for my breakfast.' Damn, that shit's making my dick hard right now just thinking about it." Jonathan briefly fondled his manhood. "Then you're standing here trippin' like you don't have a wife of your own. Hell, she has to share you, doesn't she? And while we're standing here shooting the shit, I know Scott Talbert was on his way to her crib to tap that ass. Scott lives two doors down from me. We crack some brews and swap Strawberry tales."

"I don't want to hear anymore. You're obviously saying these things because you want her to yourself."

"Are you kidding, dude? You really think you are it? She's fucking Mr. Vanderbilt's old ass, and he's crippled and partially paralyzed. She sneaks in there when she knows the missus will be gone just to fuck the old man. That's probably how she figured out your wife was gone. She told me she likes leaving her pussy juices on his face to drive the old lady crazy. She also said the old man be happier than a mutha. She claims his tool still functions just fine."

Charles pushed passed Jonathan, leaving his cart in the middle of the aisle. He could hardly breathe. He wasn't going to entertain any more of Jonathan's lies. He knew it had to be all lies, because he couldn't understand why the man would share such incriminating information. He also couldn't understand how Tapioca would be able to sneak into the Vanderbilt's home to have sex with an old crippled man, when his wife is the neighborhood spy.

Charles went directly home to look out of his window. He saw nothing. Then he went and rang Tapioca's door. No answer. His anger grew as he imagined Scott Talbert in bed with Tapioca. When he was about to walk away, he saw a white Beamer pulling up. Just when he figured it was one of Tapioca's men, a blonde version of Tapioca, only wearing a tougher looking face, stepped out of the passenger side.

Before she could get all the way to the door, she yelled out, "My sister in there?"

This was obviously Vanilla. She spoke with a more urban dialect that one in their neighborhood might have very well found intimidating.

"Uh… Uhm… I don't know. No one answered."

Charles was astounded by the striking resemblance of the two women, though Tapioca had a hint more melanin in her complexion and a rare pinkish version of strawberry-blonde hair, not the yellow blonde of her younger sister. Vanilla had light brown freckles, while Tapioca had pink freckles. He could only remember one time in his life having been so intrigued by a white woman, but Vanilla would certainly be at the top of his list. Just her presence caused his loins to ache and his anger to be forgotten. Even her toughness was attractive, despite its intimidation.

"So who are you? You banging her?"

"Uh… Uhm… Oh, I'm a neighbor. I'm up the hill," he answered.

Vanilla looked Charles up and down. "If you say so. You got a stuttering problem? You stutter a lot."

"Uh… Oh, no…. No," Charles stuttered again.

"Yeah, okay," she laughed. "You got her number so I can call her? She pissed me off, and I deleted it from my phone."

Charles realized at that moment he never had Tapioca's phone number. "Uh… No."

Vanilla went and banged on Tapioca's door. Still, there was no answer. "Uh… You got a bathroom I could use?" she stuttered, mimicking him. "I figured I better stutter so you'd understand me better," she laughed. "I've been holding this piss in for the longest. I'm about to pee on myself. Damn traffic! That's why I hate coming out here."

Charles didn't know what to say to the sexy but rude young girl. "Well, I guess…"

"Cool!" she said, cutting him off before he could say another word. "You mind if I squat at your place until Tappy gets back? She's probably in there fucking. That's why she ain't answering her damn door. Bitch!"

Charles' jaw tightened.

"I really don't want to have to ride all the way back up here again. My friend picked me up from my hotel and gave me a ride. She needs to get back to her job she left only to give me a ride."

Charles was nervous by the thought, but agreed since he figured there could be no harm. After all, he was angry with Tapioca, not her sister.

"Sure. As long as you don't mind that I have some work I need to be working on."

She smiled. "Not at all. You sound pretty decent when you ain't stuttering. Let me go tell my friend she can go."

As Vanilla turned to walk away, she tussled to pull down her skirt that was not going to go any further than the inch beyond her ass cheeks it extended. To keep himself from becoming aroused, Charles tried not to look when she bent into the driver's window to give her friend some money. She returned carrying her pocketbook as the friend pulled off.

"Lead the way." She held out her hand in the direction of Charles' house.

"Maybe you should have had your friend drive you up the hill. It's going to be a tough climb in those heels."

She quickly kicked her feet out of the five-inch heeled sandals and said, "Ain't nothing but a thang." She then picked her shoes up and walked barefoot. "What I really need to do is learn to drive so I can drive my damn self around instead of calling fake-ass friends that only want money to take me where I need to go." She laughed at her own joke as they hiked up the steep hill. "So I don't think I caught your name. You just told me the 'neighbor up the hill.' You could be a mass murderer for all I know."

Charles thought she was a little late to be trying to find out.

"Charles. I'm Charles."

"Vanilla. Everyone calls me Nilla. I'm Tapioca's wicked half-sister," she laughed. "That's what she tells everyone. Truth is, she's the wicked one."

"Why do you say that? You two don't get along?"

"We get along. She just acts funny sometimes, and I ain't got time for that shit. That's my sister and always will be. I think we get along better now that I live in P-A. I always got the impression that my sister found me threatening. That's her problem, though. I think she's worried about me knowing too much and telling too much."

Charles wanted to know what those things were, but he knew Nilla would never tell him.

"This is my house right here," Charles said, pointing to his house.

"Damn! That's nice. Really nice. I like this. Only two houses on top of the hill. It reminds me of climbing the mountains of life. The higher you get, the less people you'll find at the top."

Charles chuckled. "Hmm, never quite looked at it like that. Maybe now I'll begin to appreciate this house."

He opened the door, allowing Vanilla entrance. Before closing the door, he looked back to see if Mrs. Vanderbilt was anywhere lurking. Instead, he saw Mr. Vanderbilt at his favorite window. Again, Jonathan's words played inside his head, causing him to slam the door.

"Bathroom?" Vanilla asked.

"Oh, it's right behind you. Have you eaten?" Charles asked.

"No..." Her voice trailed off when she rushed behind the bathroom door.

Charles went to the kitchen to find something quick to prepare for them to eat.

"I could grill up a couple of chicken breasts with a salad, if that's okay with you," he said when she found him in the kitchen.

She looked around the large kitchen in awe. "This kitchen is dope! And you have a grill! That's what's up!" she said, mesmerized as she rubbed her hand along the black granite top island. "Oh, you must not have heard me. I said I could wait for Tapioca. She loves to feed me. That's why my ass is so fat now, because of her." She patted her behind, drawing Charles' attention to the lusciousness of it.

"You're not fat. You look great."

He let the words slip. He didn't want Vanilla to know that she was by far, the hottest looking version of a white woman he had ever personally been in the company of. He couldn't put his finger on it, but he was turned on by Vanilla. He wanted to know if Vanilla Pudding tasted better than Tapioca Pudding.

She blushed at his compliment. "Well, since you put it that way, I'll take you up on your offer. Besides, there's no telling when Tappy will bring her ass home. I probably should have let her know I was dropping by today." Vanilla walked around admiring the kitchen. "This is really nice. You mind if I check out the rest of your crib? I don't want to be creeping around when your wife gets home from work. Then she'll be trying to kill a bitch."

"No, don't worry. She's in Japan on business. If anything, she'll probably kill me for having anyone in her quote-unquote house. Take your time."

Vanilla went off on her exploration, while Charles prepared their meal.

"Is that my sister's house you can see from that one window with the nice scenic view?" she asked when she returned to the kitchen.

"If you're talking about my office window, then yes."

"That skanky bitch! I knew it! No wonder she ain't answering her door. I just saw some naked guy standing at her backdoor drinking something," she laughed.

Charles dropped one of the glasses he had just taken out of the wine rack and tried to hide his immediate rage. "Damn!"

"Oh, I'm sorry. I didn't upset you, did I? I never did ask what your relationship was with my sister."

"No, no, I'm fine. The glass just slipped from my hand. My wife will have a fit," he answered, trying to sound convincing with a chuckle while cleaning up the broken glass.

Vanilla studied his behavior. She could tell he was lying, so she decided to drop the subject.

"It smells good. I can't wait to taste it," she said with a hint of seduction, losing her tough-girl tone.

Charles looked into her eyes to get a read on her. Her eyes smiled back. His lips parted as if about to speak, but instead, he just smiled. Her eyes were hypnotic. They were familiar to him and had a hold on him. So much so, it caused Charles to drop yet another glass, breaking his trance.

"I am so sorry."

Charles fumbled once again to collect the shards of glass. "What are you sorry about? I'm the butterfingers today."

"I can just imagine the hell your wife will raise when she finds out that she lost two crystal stemware wine glasses. I'd be having a fit myself." She moved closer to him, taking the mini broom and dustpan from his hands. "Here, let me get this. You finish dinner."

Charles could feel the electric warmth transmit when her hand touched his. Her fragrance filled his nostrils. She was beautiful. She was young, and she was sexy. She pretended not to notice Charles watching her every move as he prepared their plates and set them at the table. Vanilla grabbed two more glasses from the wine rack, rinsed them, and set them on the table.

"I just thought about it. Are you legally able to have a glass of wine?"

"Well, don't think about it. I go to all kinds of parties and drink champagne or whatever. It's not like I'm driving anywhere."

"So I take it you're not legal then?"

"I turned twenty in May."

"You know how much trouble I could get in for giving alcohol to a minor?"

"A minor?" Vanilla said, offended. "Under the drinking age maybe; a minor, not. I have my own big house with a wine cellar. I'm not going to die if I don't have your funky-ass wine." She stood with her hands on her hips. "Come to think of it, I don't need your funky-ass food either. My sister is right down the road." She turned to leave the kitchen.

"Wait! I'm sorry," he pleaded, ready to cave into her wishes. "I'm sorry. Please sit. Have dinner with me. I just wasn't thinking right."

She turned back to face him with fire in her eyes. He patted the chair at the table.

"Please. I'm sorry. I didn't mean to offend you."

Vanilla rolled her eyes up in her head and twisted her lips. "Fine! I'll have your dinner since you already fixed it and all."

She walked over, taking the seat Charles was offering. Her sitting provided a distracting, ample view of her shapely thighs and a portion of her cookies when she crossed her legs. Standing before her, Charles poured the wine in the glass, spilling it from trying to peek through the glass table to see under her skirt. The red wine spilled onto her white skirt.

"OMG! OMG! Oh my freakin' gosh! My skirt!" she yelled, jumping back, half upset and half laughing. "I guess you really didn't want me to have any wine."

Charles quickly handed her a cloth to blot the wine that heavily stained her skirt.

"I am so sorry. I should have known better than to pour wine after dropping two glasses." He was embarrassed. "Please forgive me. I'll get you something to put on, and I'll get your skirt cleaned up for you while you eat."

He quickly rushed off to get her one of his robes. He couldn't believe how powerless he felt around the young, beautiful woman that was thirty years his junior.

She took the robe to change into. "Are you sure you can get out a red wine stain from a white skirt?" she asked skeptically.

"I'm going to damn sure try. I am so sorry about this."

"Stop trippin'! It's a skirt. If you can't get it out, I'll borrow something from Tappy to wear back to the hotel. Can you put it in a soak or something so we can eat? The whole point was to eat together, right?"

"I guess, but that was before I created this disaster." Charles pulled the seat out for Vanilla again. "Here, have a seat and eat while I go try to Shout out the stains."

She handed him her clothes. "I got my top there, too. I saw a couple of splatter stains on the white areas. You can't see it on the black parts."

Charles tried not to get excited by the thought of her nudity underneath his bathrobe. He wished he had given her one of his shirts instead, but he didn't know she was removing her top, as well. He never saw any hint of panties when he was checking out her ass while they were outside. He definitely didn't see any when she crossed her legs.

As Charles was returning to the kitchen from his laundry room, his doorbell rang. He knew it had to be nosey Mrs. Vanderbilt wondering why the woman was still in his…'Charlotte's' home. He snatched the door open to give her a piece of his mind. Instead, there stood Tapioca with a smile.

"Hey, my king. I wanted to drop this off to you and see if you'd be up to making another," she said, handing him a DVD.

He took the DVD hesitantly. "What are you doing here?" he asked, suddenly looking around for Mrs. Vanderbilt.

"Can I come in, or do you think the battleaxe is going to come ringing again?" she laughed. "She's not even home. She's supposed to be going to play bingo or something." She stepped closer to his guarded door that he barely opened. "You gonna let me in?"

"Uh… No, I can't. I'm busy. I'm having dinner."

She laughed. "And?! I can feed you, if you'd like."

Charles wanted to ask how she knew Mrs. Vanderbilt's whereabouts when the two don't speak to one another, but he was more concerned with getting Tapioca away from his door before she learned that her sister was naked in his kitchen. He didn't want to have to explain the freak accident, because he would not have believed it himself had it not happened to him.

"I need you to go. I will talk to you later."

Able to hear the sound of running water coming from his kitchen, Tapioca looked into Charles' guilty eyes. "You have company? And that's not your wife? And you don't ever wanna wear a fucking condom?"

"Please, just go. I'll talk to you later." He could see a combination of anger and hurt forming in her eyes.

"Oh, it's like that now? But you love me, huh?" She shook her head and turned to walk away, but then turned back to say, "Go be with the bitch. Two can play this shit. Just keep watching."

His heart sunk. He wanted to run after her. He couldn't call out for her because he was afraid Vanilla would hear him. He wanted to believe all he had heard about her were lies. He couldn't understand her hostility if she supposedly just had a naked man in her house.

Why is she being so unreasonable? he thought.

After he closed his door, he continued to watch as Tapioca walked directly to the Vanderbilt's home and went in almost immediately. It was as if the door was left open for her. Mr. Vanderbilt was like the lowest of the low hit below the belt. More annoying, his dinner was innocent; he just wanted to protect the relationship and privacy of the two sisters. He was beyond furious at this point. He put the DVD down on the table in the foyer and returned to the kitchen to play host to his guest for the evening.

"Gee, your food is cold now. I figured I'd eat slowly while waiting for you. Hell, I've already washed the dishes, and I'm on my third glass of wine," she said, holding up her glass. "This is really good. I hope you have some more, 'cause I think I drank it all. Well, the part you didn't spill." She was obviously tipsy already.

"I can eat it cold. I'll just put it in my salad," Charles replied, taking his seat across from Vanilla. "You can finish the wine. I probably don't need any, no how."

He tried hard to be cordial, but inside, he was seething. As his mind raced at how he could get back at Tapioca for unjustly trying to punish him, he looked down through the glass table and saw the robe on Vanilla partially opened below the waist, exposing her nudity. She talked and laughed about something, completely oblivious to her exposure that was arousing Charles, who occasionally laughed with her while pretending to be listening.

"Would you like some more wine?" he asked when she drained her glass of its last drop.

"You trying to get me drunk? I'm already nice," she laughed.

"No! No, I was just trying to be a good host. I saw your glass was empty."

"Well, if you want to be a good host, you think you could find me something else to put on. This damn robe is too hot. It's the dead of summer, man. Geesh! You trying to cook a bitch," she laughed again.

"Sure, I can get you something," he said, standing from the table.

"And while you're at it, get that wine, too."

Charles picked through his collection of t-shirts trying to find the one he felt would complement Vanilla's sensual curves. He figured since Tapioca wanted to play games, then he'd at least have the perverse pleasure of watching her sexy sister prance around to his satisfaction. He found a lightweight t-shirt, which wasn't too long nor had any prints on the front that would obscure his view of her breasts. He wickedly smiled to himself as he envisioned her wearing it. He collected another bottle of wine and returned to the kitchen with the items in tow, but not before once again peeping out of his window to the Vanderbilt's house.

Vanilla held the shirt up to her and laughed. "I guess I better not sit down. Otherwise, my stuff'll be hanging out."

"I'm sorry. I could get you another shirt. A longer one," he said, disappointed.

"No, this is fine. I was just joking."

Charles was relieved when she went into the bathroom to change. He took it a step further and turned the temperature down on the thermostat. *A colder house makes for harder nipples,* he thought. He wanted to see some young, hard nipples like the ones in his porno movies, and her being Tapioca's sister was an added bonus.

When she reappeared in the kitchen, his loins awoke at the sight of her in his shirt.

He handed her a fresh glass of wine that she didn't need. "Here, take this. I'm going to go work on that stain in your skirt. Make yourself comfortable."

"Comfortable?! Your home is like one of those places where they bury rich people. There's no place to get comfortable besides your bedroom. You don't even have a television to relax and watch other than in your bedroom. What's up with that?"

"My wife. I usually watch television in my office when she's home. She thinks televisions are distracting me from being creative or either they will make my friends want to hang around too much."

"Are you serious? She's a silly bitch! How could you have a wife like that? Trey would have left my ass ages ago if I was tripping like that. Trey, that's my boyfriend or should I say my baby's daddy," she said, proudly gushing. "You should meet him. He'll tell you a thing or two about being the man of the house."

Charles thought about telling her they've already met, but just smiled instead.

She continued, "No fucking way should a house like this not have a fly room with televisions all over it. You better find your balls and man up in your house."

"So where is your man right now? He's not looking for you? You know I don't need you getting me into any trouble."

She laughed in between big sips from her glass. "Trey's at home with the baby. I came to see Tappy about more money. I don't know why she wants to put my life on a fucking budget. Bitch!" She took another swallow from her glass. "That bitch had the nerve to be fucking my man. She wants to fuck him, then she's going to cough up more dough."

Charles was once again stunned by Vanilla's candor.

"I guess she thought he wouldn't tell me how she seduced him when he came to her fucking cookout. She never could keep her hands off of him. She always tries to claim he's the one hitting on her."

"You don't seem all that angry about it. Why?" Charles asked, amazed.

"Please! I'm not going to be tripping over a piece of dick. Trey makes porno movies. My sister makes porno movies. They made a movie together, but after it was all said and done, he chose to be with me, not her ass. She can't stand that shit. So, no, I don't be tripping. I just laugh at her dumb ass. No matter how hard she tries, he knows where home is. And no matter how much pussy bitches want to throw his way, he knows where to find the best pussy. I don't have to be all mad 'cause bitches want what I already got. My momma ain't name me Vanilla Pudding for nothing. Everybody knows vanilla pudding tastes better than tapioca pudding any day."

She laughed hysterically at her own joke. Charles tried to laugh along with her, but that only made him want to taste for himself and vote.

"Anyway, let me get this skirt cleaned up. I don't want to hold you up too late and then your sister disappears on you."

"Well, if she does, I'll just have to crash here or you will have to take me back to my hotel… Nope, I'll have to crash here 'cause I need to see the bitch about my money."

A part of Charles wanted her to stay, just as long as she'd entertain him. On the other hand, he didn't want to be caught up in their web of drama. He hated to have to say it, but her relaxing in his marital bed was strictly Charlotte's fault for not allowing them to have a comfortable family room with a television.

"If you'd like, you could watch television in my bedroom. Unfortunately I don't have too many comfortable options to offer."

"Can I bring the wine? I promise I won't spill any. Spilling is your thing." She laughed again at her own joke.

This time, Charles laughed, also. "Sure."

He led her upstairs where she bounced on the bed instead of Charlotte's chaise lounge before getting comfortable. While he was turning the television on for her, the last porno movie he had been watching automatically came on. He tried to quickly turn it off before she realized what was on.

"Ooh, a freaky one," she laughed.

He changed the television from the DVD to the cable channel and handed her the remote. Then he went to the laundry room to tackle the wine stain. The Shout and Oxi-Clean seemed to do the job. He ran her clothes through the washing machine and then went to check on his uninvited houseguest. She was curled up under the covers watching television in the dark. As his eyes adjusted to the darkness, he noticed the t-shirt she had been wearing was now at the foot of the bed. He wondered to himself what she could be wearing underneath the covers. He couldn't tell if she was asleep or not, until she yelled out, "Oh hell no!" to the Lifetime television drama she had on.

"You okay in here? Figured I'd come in and check on you. See if you need anything."

"It's like super cold in here. I hope you don't mind, but I had to climb underneath your covers. A bitch is over here getting real comfortable," she laughed.

"No, that's fine. I told you to make yourself comfortable."

"I also hope you don't mind me peeling off that t-shirt. I love Egyptian cotton sheets, and that t-shirt was strangling me."

"I can find you something else," he offered, hoping she'd decline.

"Nah, I'm good under the covers. What's the worse that could happen? You'd catch a glimpse of tits? From what popped on the television when you turned it on, you don't need my tits to see. I'm good, though. I could move over if you want to get comfortable."

"I'm fine. I'll just sit right here." He sat on the edge of the side of the bed.

Vanilla laughed at his awkwardness and moved over away from him. "Here, get up here and get comfortable. You're going to make me feel bad watching you all uncomfortable and stuffy." She pulled her arm from underneath the cover and patted the empty space on the bed beside her. "Shoot, as cold as it is in here, I could use your body heat near me."

Charles removed his shoes and rested his feet on his bed.

"Could you pass me my glass? I can't reach it now."

He got up to get her glass, which was almost empty, and poured her some more. He wanted her drunk. He wanted to touch her, and he wanted her to want to be touched. Wine had a way of persuading people of the things they didn't know they wanted.

As she sat up to take the glass from his hand, the covers fell from her breasts, exposing a beautiful set of double-D's. Even with the darkness, he was still able to see hardened light brown nipples. Vanilla made no effort to cover them as she drank her wine. Charles was throbbing between his legs. He could not stop looking. After guzzling the wine down, she handed the empty glass to Charles. She suddenly kneeled in the middle of his bed as the covers dropped completely off of her.

"I have to pee." She crawled off the bed, almost falling off. "Oh damn!" she laughed. "I guess the wine is going to my head now."

Charles grabbed her before she could fall forward onto the floor. His hand conveniently caught her breast by accident, though he was glad for the cheap thrill. She didn't seem to have a problem with it. He was aroused by how her neatly trimmed, light brown pubic hairs laid. He wanted to touch them. She made her way to the bathroom and back. When she returned, he helped her climb back on the bed.

"I'm going to go check on your clothes. Can I get you something from downstairs?"

"No, I'm good. Just hurry back so you can get comfortable. You need to relax some. You're so uptight."

Charles laughed. "Okay."

He went and put the clothes in the dryer, then stopped in his office to check some things. He couldn't resist looking out of his window. His timing could not have been worse. He saw Tapioca giving Jonathan head on her lounge chair. He stood watching for a while until Vanilla called out for him. Again, he tried to contain his anger, but he became more determined to fuck the sister of Tapioca if for no other reason than to even the score.

"What's taking you so long?" she asked when he returned to the room. "Get comfortable and watch this movie with me," she almost demanded, briefly reminding him of Charlotte.

Charles looked at his prey and debated if he'd go for it or not. He stripped down to his boxers. Vanilla looked somewhat surprised, but said nothing. He crawled underneath his covers near Vanilla, but not touching her. She backed her body up near his, causing him to turn on his side towards her. She then snuggled into the contour of his body, pressing her behind against his quick erection. As he wrapped his arm around her, cupping her inviting breasts, she continued to rub against his hardness that was ready to come out of his boxers. She moaned as his fingers slid down past her navel to stroke her pubic hairs. He felt a thin scar apparently from a c-section. She slightly parted her thighs to allow his fingers to explore further. He pressed harder against her backside as the sensation shot through him. Reaching behind her, she peeled off his boxers.

"Are you sure?" he asked, knowing she wouldn't object at that stage. He no longer found this girl intimidating, but was ready to show how intimidating he could be.

"Touch this pussy and see for yourself," she answered with a sly smile.

He did and was convinced. She was super wet. The further he dug, the wetter she became. She was extra tight, which turned him on more than anything.

He got up to turn on the lamp on the nightstand. He wanted to see her pussy before he tasted it.

"You need the lights on?"

"This feels so good, I have to see it. All of you. You are beautiful."

She smiled as she turned her body sideways on the bed to allow him to inspect her tightness. She spread her knees apart and fondled her own breasts.

"How's that for you?"

Charles didn't speak. Instead, he inserted three fingers inside of her while his thumb tickled her clit. He looked into her eyes, commanding her attention.

She gyrated her hips, intensifying the feeling and causing her to juice up more. Charles moved his fingers in and out while his eyes stayed on her eyes that fought to stay open. He knew he had her when her eyes rolled in her head and her back arched up from the bed. Her breasts called his mouth and he answered. Her body was quivering from the sensation. By the time his mouth reached the opening of her cave, he pulled his fingers out of her and gave them to her mouth to suck on. Charles sucked and slurped, enjoying all of the pudding Vanilla was squirting. When he was done, he came up to kiss her mouth.

He pulled her body to the edge of the bed where he stood and parted her legs to enter her. His dick was ready to explode as he pressed himself deep inside her young, tight pussy. That time, his eyes rolled in his head. He was glad he was able to hold on without letting go.

First, he stroked her slow. Then he stroked her hard and fast, turned on by her breasts' movement with his strokes. He turned her on her stomach so he could admire her pleasantly plump ass. He bent to plant kisses on it before lifting her on her knees and reentering her from behind. Vanilla tried to bite the pillow to contain her screams, but it was useless. Charles knew he had a nice-sized dick, and he wanted to hurt Vanilla's tight pussy with it. He was angry at Tapioca and would make himself feel better by beating up on her sister's pussy.

He touched her asshole as he debated if he'd boldly go for it, but she pushed his hand away. When he tried again, she moved it again, indicating her asshole was off limits. Right then, Vanilla lost the unknown battle to her sister. He wanted her ass, but Vanilla wasn't having it.

Before he came, he stopped so she could take him in her mouth. She didn't have the skills of her sister, but she served her purpose. He came in her mouth, but she wouldn't swallow. That also turned him off. At that moment, he knew he'd do whatever he'd have to do to get back in Tapioca's good graces. He'd just have to find a way to not let her have time for the other guys, especially not Jonathan and Mr.

Vanderbilt. He did enjoy how Vanilla used her large breasts to get him up for the next round.

With the rising of the sun, Charles was ready to send Vanilla on her way. She woke up groggy and unaware of her surroundings. Charles had already showered and was dressed for his run.

"Did you fuck me while I was drunk?" she asked in disbelief, realizing she was naked in Charles' bed.

Charles nonchalantly answered, "Nope. I just let you lay here and sleep it off."

"Why am I naked then? Why am I sore down here?" she asked, pointing between her legs.

He looked into her green eyes. "The truth?"

"Yes, the damn truth!" she spat as if she'd hurt him.

"I came up to check on you and saw you doing yourself with the empty wine bottle. I tried to take it from you, but you kept trying to grab at me. I let you be until you fell asleep. Then I came back to check on you and removed the bottle you fell asleep with between your legs."

Vanilla looked horrified, while Charles remained straight faced as he told his lie.

He continued, "Now, your secret is safe with me. So, it's up to you who you tell your business to."

"Oh my God! Please don't tell anyone about this. Oh Lord, if Trey finds out about this... Even if Tappy finds out I slept here, she'd tell Trey just so she could be with him."

Vanilla started crying. Charles callously watched the young girl come apart based on his deception. He felt it was for both of their own goods. After Vanilla quickly dressed, Charles drove her back to her hotel, convincing her not to go see Tapioca. Otherwise, she'd think they had slept together. Vanilla agreed and took the ride back to her hotel.

9

Tapioca opened her door to find it was Charles ringing her bell.

"What do you want?"

"I told you I needed to talk to you."

"What happened to the other bitch you had last night? Go talk to her."

"Tapioca, I can't believe you're acting like this. I saw you with Jonathan James last night after you went in the Vanderbilt's house, and that was after Jonathan told me you were doing Scott Talbert."

Tapioca tried to keep her embarrassment from showing as Charles spoke.

"If you would have given me a chance, I would have told you that my wife's nephew was here. I couldn't exactly let him see you. He's a teenager. He'd add his own twist to your presence."

Tapioca looked at Charles' eyes. She was ashamed. "I am so sorry, Charles. Oh my goodness, how could I be so stupid?" she said, while stepping back to allow Charles inside. "Flowers?"

Charles pulled the dozen of roses from behind him and handed them to her. "I want you to ride with me to San Diego for a week. No intrusions or interruptions."

Tapioca pulled her face from the flowers she was inhaling. Her face lit up. "Really?! When?"

"Now. Maybe we can ride into Mexico, too. I just want to romance you for an entire week while I be your king."

Tapioca looked down sadly. "You're not angry at me for what I did yesterday?"

Charles gave a half smile. He was fuming, but if he could have the opportunity to have Tapioca all to himself without any of the other jokers being able to touch her, that would make it all well with him. He also wanted to get Tapioca away before her sister's drunken memory returned.

"I'd be lying if I said I wasn't angry, but as long as we promise to leave them behind, I can get past it. No more Jonathan, no more Trey, no more any of them."

"What happens to me when your wife returns home?"

"You don't think it's quite bold of me to come here not caring who's watching, with flowers in my hand, asking to take you on a romantic getaway? Tappy, I don't give a shit what Charlotte has to say anymore. If she wants a divorce, so be it. I know what I want, and that's you."

Tapioca looked like a kid on Christmas morning. She jumped up on Charles, wrapping her arms around his neck and her legs around his waist. She kissed him deeply. To her, this was as if he asked her to be his wife.

"Yes, yes, yes! Let's go to San Diego! Can we make it two weeks instead?"

"You can stay with me for the second week. I have a company to run that I haven't been doing much work for lately."

"Stay with you? In your house with Mrs. Vanderbilt watching?"

"Let's give her an eye full to watch then. No more sneaking. I want to be with you, and that's that. So, one week in San Diego and one week here with me. That way, I can sneak in a little work in between a whole lot of lovemaking."

Tapioca's eyes answered, giving her approval. She kissed Charles for the first time as if he were her husband.

He patted her on the behind. "Come on, let's get going."

When she finished packing, Charles loaded her bags into his car, and they rode up to his house to get his bags. He saw Mrs. Vanderbilt watching as he pulled into his garage.

Before he could leave, he had a strong urge to have sex with Tapioca in the bed he had just finished screwing her sister. A part of him was still angry, and somehow that would make all of the transgressions wash away. Tapioca seemed more turned on than he ever saw her before by having sex in his marital bed. She just didn't have a clue as to the real reason that moment was so monumental for Charles. Nonetheless, he appreciated every minute of it. They made love over and over, never making it out.

The next morning, Charles was in his gym working out, while Tapioca prepared him breakfast before their road trip. His workout was continuously distracted by his memories of the previous night's hot sex he had with Tapioca on his weight bench and other equipment in the gym.

Tapioca stopped by a window near the front door when she noticed Mrs. Vanderbilt outside of her house looking in the direction of Charles' home every so often. Tapioca decided to remove the bathrobe belonging to Charles that she had been wearing while fixing his breakfast. She tried to find some reason to keep herself in plain view of Mrs. Vanderbilt so there would be no doubt that she was sleeping with Charles. She wanted Mrs. Vanderbilt to get word back to Charlotte. She felt the sooner, the better. She wanted Charlotte gone from Charles' life, and Mrs. Vanderbilt would be the key. She walked past the window several times until she noticed Mrs. Vanderbilt's full attention focused on the window Tapioca was near. Tapioca moved closer to the window so Mrs. Vanderbilt would know she was nude. When Tapioca heard Charles coming, she stepped back a bit towards the foyer table.

"Is this the video I dropped off the other night, honey?" she asked, holding up the DVD.

"Yeah, that's it."

She set it back down when Charles was close enough for her to grab hold of. She wrapped her arms around his sweaty body.

"You didn't want to watch it? Or did you want to make some more?"

She stood on her toes to kiss Charles. She made the kiss extra passionate knowing his hands would start rubbing her body. She guided his mouth to her breasts, which he savagely sucked as if it were the first time. Tapioca kept lowering her body until the two of them were lying on the cold marble floor in the foyer. She managed to peep over Charles' shoulder to see Mrs. Vanderbilt standing in the middle of the street for a better view into the window.

Tapioca pulled Charles' shorts down to his thighs and spread her knees apart, allowing him to fuck her right where they lay. She came harder knowing an audience was watching.

Her mind also went on a journey to two nights prior when she sat on Mr. Vanderbilt's face while he licked her pussy. Since his stroke a year and a half ago, he couldn't do all the things he used to do to her, but she'd be eternally grateful because he was the first one in the neighborhood that ever tried to make her feel welcomed. The stroke left him sixty-five percent paralyzed, but in the course of a year, he had made enough progress to move around on his own. She was shocked when she got the phone call six months ago from him asking her to come visit him. The missus had no idea of the progress of his recovery. Tapioca liked to think of herself as part of his recovery. He had enough of an erection for her to ride him. Each time he had an orgasm, she noticed his increased ability to use certain muscles. She also felt his eating her pussy was helping his speech because he was learning to use his tongue again.

When Tapioca noticed Mrs. Vanderbilt practically standing in front of Charles' house watching, she pretended it was the first time she had noticed her.

"Oh my goodness, Charles, she's watching us."

Charles turned towards the window and quickly tried to pull up his shorts when he saw Mrs. Vanderbilt. All of Tapioca's wetness was inside of his shorts. Mrs. Vanderbilt hurried away when she noticed she was caught watching the pair.

"Damn her nosey ass!" he said, getting up and then helping Tapioca up. "Let's hurry up and get out of here. We should have been gone."

Tapioca wickedly smiled when Charles walked up the stairs. She looked out of the window and saw Mrs. Vanderbilt still watching from her own window.

10

The time spent behind closed doors was ecstatic. The time spent out in public was a different story. Everywhere the couple journeyed, people would either give them disgusted stares or boldly ask if Charles was Tapioca's father. Tapioca didn't know which was worse: the group of young white guys who said, "Those niggas are taking all of our women. They need to stick to their own kind," or the many black women who blatantly said, "White bitches always got their claws in our good men." Neither of them could believe the level of racism that still existed in this day of age. Homosexuality was better embraced than interracial relationships. It was harder on Tapioca, who considered herself bi-racial, although she barely appeared to have a hint of African American.

The day spent in Mexico was no better. Racism was there just the same. By day five, Tapioca didn't care what anyone thought or had to say. If anything, she'd give them something to talk about. Every time she'd see someone staring, she'd give him a big kiss and let everyone else be bothered instead. On their last day when they went to the beach, she practically had sex with him out in the open. She sat straddled on his lap and grinded on his erection until she reached an orgasm. Her bikini remained on the entire time with the crotch area moved to the side. Charles smothered her bulging breasts with kisses when she buried his face with her bosom. That was the most fun they had in public. That's also where they received the most derogatory comments.

Charles became worried as they traveled back to their neck of the woods. Sex with Tapioca was wearing him out. She could never get enough. Jonathan's words about Charles not being enough dick for her rang in his head over and over. He didn't know how he would keep her satisfied enough to keep her all to himself. He thought about checking with his doctor for one of those sex enhancement pills. He never had a need with Charlotte around.

Despite all of his concerns, by the end of their second week together, he looked at Tapioca as the wife he always dreamt of having. She didn't talk down to him. She went out of her way to keep him pleased. She cooked every morning, afternoon, and evening. She cleaned the house while he did his work. She watched porno movies with him and would try to please him in the manner shown in the movies if she knew it turned him on. She even offered to call in a second woman to please him if that's what he'd like. As tempting as the offer sounded, she was plenty enough for him.

In less than a month, he'd eaten more pussy, had more blowjobs, and performed more anal sex than he ever had before. He felt like he'd had more sex than the ten years total he spent with his wife. He was in love more than he could remember ever loving Charlotte. Additionally, Tapioca was supportive of his work and his taking care of business. Not one time did she make waves when Charlotte called to berate him for one reason or another. At the end of the third week together, he was rehearsing his "I want a divorce" speech for his wife. Ironically, by the third week, Charlotte had abruptly stopped calling him altogether. He didn't know if that was a cause for worry or not.

"Honey, did you move our DVD from the foyer table? I was hoping we could watch it tonight instead of watching those other people," she asked, coming into his office where he barely looked out of the window anymore.

"That sounds really nice. I forgot all about it. It was near the door before we left, remember?"

"I know, but it's not there now. I just thought about it when I saw Mrs. Vanderbilt pulling off."

Charles patted his lap for Tapioca to sit on. "That's strange. We didn't take it with us, did we?"

"No."

"Well, I guess we need to start working on a new video," he said, kissing her.

Minutes later, the video was no longer a thought, and he was eating her pink pussy on top of his large mahogany desk.

*****

Three more months had gone by, and as far as Tapioca was concerned, that was her home and not Charlotte's. She'd been with Charles without a break for almost four months, and they were getting along perfectly. She hung out on the campus with him on the days he had to teach classes, followed by dinner out or a movie where they would behave fresh with one another. At least twice a week, he was having flowers delivered to the house for her. She'd be surprised each time she opened the door to find another delivery. She was glad when she heard Charles tell Charlotte on the phone that the marriage was over and she could stay in Japan for all he cared.

They became so open with their relationship, Tapioca would go out at times to get the mail or newspaper for him. They'd go everywhere together. She'd even ride with him to his firm. He introduced her to his best friends, Larry and Arty, after he confessed her true age. She couldn't ask for more except she was missing the variety in her sex life. She missed the perverted eroticism of sleeping with William Vanderbilt. She missed the arrogance of Jonathan James, the taste of Trey in her mouth, the quick humping from Scott Talbert, the hairy testicles of Jerry Peterson, the penile enlargement of Dan Winters, and the pelvic pounding of Keith Coswicki, the neighbor whose wife had just put their house on the market to keep Tapioca away. Instead, she just about traded all of that for the sake of love.

Tapioca stood gazing out of his office window as he worked at his drafting table. As she watched the sun positioning itself for the evening, her eyes occasionally wandered to her poolside, and she reminisced about all the great times she had there. For Charles' love, she would sacrifice it all, though.

She could never figure out what it was about Charles that caused her to fall so deeply. There was a deep, unexplainable connection. She liked that Charles was an important man, and he didn't make her feel bad for never having gone to college. He appreciated everything about her, not just her body. He made sure everyone treated her with respect, and he didn't seem the least bit fazed by their age or racial differences.

"Sweetheart, I'm going to have to ask you a huge favor today," Charles said with a cracked voice, breaking her concentration on the other men she had left behind for Charles.

It was obvious something was wrong, and he had been a little distant for the previous two days. He seemed suddenly distracted in bed for those two days, as well. Typically, he was very pleasing to Tapioca, but then that morning, he kept losing his erection, which was a first. Tapioca was hoping his favor would be to find a replacement dick for the lame sex he had just given her that morning.

"Sure.. What'cha need?" she asked, turning from the window while twirling a loc of her hair.

He closed his eyes and took a deep breath. "I need for you to stay at your house tonight. Charlotte's on her way back from Japan, and I just need to square things away when she gets here. I don't think it would be a good idea for you to be here when she arrives."

Tapioca could hardly believe her ears. She walked to his desk to be sure she was hearing him correctly.

"Are you kidding me?! Why do I have to go? Didn't you tell her ass that you want a divorce already? Why is she even coming here?"

Charles stood up and took both of Tapioca's hands into his before kissing them. "I did tell her, but legally, this is still her home in the United States. I'm sure she's not going to just go away quietly. We need to sit down and talk like two reasonable adults, and I know she won't be reasonable if she sees you here."

"We've been together in this house for the past three months. This has been my home, not hers. Now you want me to go? Why can't that bitch go stay in a hotel somewhere? I don't want her here, Charles. I don't want her near you. I don't want her touching you."

"That won't be happening," he laughed. "That should be the least of your concerns. I know you've been here with me all of these months, and after Charlotte and I talk, we'll still be together. I just need you to do me this huge favor tonight."

"Just tonight?" she asked, searching Charles' eyes for an answer.

"Hopefully so. Everything is going to depend on how she acts. I'm sure she's not going to make things simple, and I don't want you caught up in the crossfire."

"Why can't you stay with me at my house then? I'm okay with that. You know I'm not going to be able to sleep without you."

"Let me just get through this one night. If I see she's going to be difficult or anything, then I'll come stay with you until she's gone."

Tapioca grabbed a loc of her long, curly, strawberry-blonde hair to twirl and twisted her lips to each side. "Promise?"

"Absolutely. Lady, you need to realize that I love you and am not going to just let you slip out of my life. Oh no! You are here for keeps," he said, leaning forward to kiss her.

"Oh, Charles, I needed to hear you say that. I love you so much, too." She kissed him again. "Okay. I'll do this for you. Should I take my things?"

"Uh, yeah, I guess that would probably be a good idea. I don't know if she'd try to destroy stuff or not, so better to be safe than sorry.

Don't worry, I'll help you take the stuff down the hill."

"I can just load it in my car and drive it down."

"I still want to help you. I helped you bring it, so I can help you carry it back."

"On one condition."

"What's that?"

She lifted one of her knees on his desk and pulled Charles' hand underneath her skirt. "I need make-up sex," she said, kissing his lips tenderly.

"Make-up sex? We didn't have a fight," he said, returning her kisses in between their words while feeling her wetness.

"No, you need to make up for that not-so-good fuck you gave me earlier. I take it your mind was focused on this conversation."

"Ooh, you know me so well, don't you?" he asked, pressing his finger inside of her.

She moved her hips around, holding his neck tightly and reaching for the hardness inside of his shorts. He lifted her onto the desk, laid her on her back, spread her knees, and entered her forcefully as she liked it. That time, he was able to satisfy her. He was still distracted by the fact that during his last conversation with Charlotte, she told him that she was returning home to reclaim her marriage and was willing to do whatever she needed to do to keep him. He had yet to figure out how he would deal with his dilemma.

As much as he cared about Tapioca, he didn't know if he'd want her around for the rest of his life, mainly because he constantly feared her sleeping with other men the first chance she'd get. This would be their first time apart in almost four months, other than a time or two when he made a quick trip to the grocery store to pick up a couple of items she needed to cook with.

Inside his heart, he loved Charlotte and wanted to love her for life, but their relationship was becoming unbearable, and Tapioca's presence made it look worse than he had realized before. He didn't know if he'd be willing to let Tapioca go if Charlotte was willing to change for the sake of the marriage. If he had a say, he'd want Charlotte to be like Tapioca was to him, and that would make him want Charlotte and only Charlotte. His problem with Tapioca, he couldn't trust her beyond his seeing her. He cringed just at the thought of whom she'd be sleeping with for the one night.

That day, Tapioca intentionally kept Charles preoccupied with sex because she was hoping Charlotte would show up and see them together. She wanted to come face to face with Charlotte to tell her to get to stepping. No such luck. By six o'clock that evening, Charles was packing her up and sending her home. Alone.

11

Tapioca tossed and turned that night, fighting the temptation to go to Charles' house. This time it was her who stayed camped out near her back windows and door to catch a glimpse of her man. She didn't see his office light on the entire night and didn't know what to make of it. She waited by her phone for him to at least call her. The wait was killing her. She even called him, but no answer. By four o'clock the next afternoon, she could stand the wait no longer. She found a sexy, revealing halter top to complement her revealing miniskirt. Although there was a crisp fall chill outdoors, she figured it would be just right to harden her nipples and make her nemesis see what she was up against and hate herself.

As quickly as she reached the top of the hill, she spotted Mrs. Vanderbilt watching in her window. Tapioca figured the old woman didn't have anything else better to do before going to bingo at seven. She wondered how the mister was getting along for the past couple of months since she hadn't been taking care of his needs while being closely guarded by Charles. With nearly twenty-four hours having gone by, which was almost her longest record without sex, she was already planning in her mind of taking care of the old man when Mrs. Vanderbilt left. That is, if Charles didn't hurry up and take care of her insatiable appetite. Since Mrs. Vanderbilt was staring so hard, Tapioca flipped her middle finger to the old woman. The woman just shook her head and moved from the window.

Tapioca was feeling herself as she approached Charles' door. She rang the bell. After a minute, she rang the bell again before turning the doorknob. It was locked, so she rang over and over again.

"May I help you?" Charlotte calmly asked when she opened the door wearing a bathrobe and a towel on her head.

"I need to see Charles. Could you let him know I'm here?" Tapioca said arrogantly.

Charlotte looked Tapioca from head to toe and then into her hazel-green eyes. "Oh, you must be the skank from down the way."

"Whatever! Just go get Charles. Let him know his 'skank' good pussy is here."

Charlotte gave a mischievous smile. "Yeah, I saw your skanky ass in that video with my husband. My dear neighbor sent it to me all the way in Japan."

Tapioca was confused. She remembered neither of them knew what happened to the video, but never did they think someone came into the home and took it out.

"Whatever!" It was her quickest comeback line to keep from showing that Charlotte rattled her. "Well, since you saw it, now you know what he wants and who he wants. Now, could you go and let my man know I'm here. You should be packing your shit right about now anyhow. He told your ass he wants a divorce."

By that time, Mrs. Vanderbilt was standing in her doorway watching the two women. Charlotte waved her hand and Mrs. Vanderbilt waved back.

"Wait right here," Charlotte said politely.

"Thank you!" Tapioca rudely responded.

Charlotte went in and closed the door. When Tapioca noticed Mr. Vanderbilt watching from an upstairs window while Mrs. Vanderbilt stood watching from downstairs, Tapioca whipped out her two breasts from beneath the halter top, then turned and mooned them. She fixed herself while laughing as she waited for Charles to come to the door.

She was about to ring the bell again, when the door opened. Charlotte was fully dressed in a warm-up suit.

"Where's Charles?!" Tapioca demanded.

Charlotte pulled a shiny, silver .22 caliber from behind her and held it sideways, placing it against her bosom without pointing it at anyone.

"I'm going to tell you this just this one time, and hopefully, we'll never have to have this conversation again. If you ever bring your trashy ass around here or my husband again, you will be a dead trashy ass. Obviously, you didn't get the memo, but there won't be any divorce. Charles and I have decided to work on our marriage, and while he sowed his wild oats with you for a minute, that's all behind us now. You are yesterday's trash, bitch. So, now, I highly suggest you skip your trashy ass back down that hill before the garbage truck comes for your ass, and don't you come back up here again," Charlotte said collected and composed in a scary way.

Tapioca studied the gun and then called Charlotte's bluff.

"Bitch, you obviously don't know where I'm from. You don't scare me with that shit. I know your punk ass is hardly thinking about going to jail and being some dyke's bitch. Now, I said I want to see Charles, and I want to see him now. And as far as I'm concerned, he's my man, and I will fuck him when my twat gets good and fucking ready."

She stood with her hands on her hips as if daring Charlotte. She didn't flinch or back down. She was in love and willing to fight, if need be, for that love.

Charlotte hadn't anticipated Tapioca's boldness. She was the one uncomfortable with the direction things were about to head. She certainly didn't want to go to jail, even if for only a night, because of a man who blatantly disrespected and violated their wedding vows. Charlotte tried to change her tune to reasonable.

"Look, I don't see any point in having to fight over my own husband. I am asking you as nicely as I can. Please leave my husband alone. He has already decided he wants to work on our marriage and has no more intentions of being with you. He went to his office, and when he returns, I will have him call you so he can tell you himself. Now, please leave here and don't come back, 'cause I will use this gun if you force me to."

Tapioca stepped closer, provoking Charlotte. Charlotte turned the gun towards Tapioca, and Tapioca smacked it, causing it to fall to the ground behind Tapioca. Charlotte got nervous, not knowing if Tapioca would grab the gun. Charlotte grabbed Tapioca by her halter top, while pushing her as hard as she could at the same time. As Tapioca fell backwards to the ground, Charlotte quickly grabbed the gun and ran into her house, locking the door. Tapioca yelled and kicked from the other side. As Charlotte's shaking hands were about to wipe her tears, she realized she had Tapioca's halter top in her hand. She laughed through her sobs. She could imagine Tapioca standing topless in the cool, almost night air. Charlotte turned her attention to the yelling outside.

"That's why your husband drools over this pussy, bitch!"

"You wish he'd want a tramp like you," Mrs. Vanderbilt yelled back.

Charlotte thought about putting Tapioca's top outside for her to cover herself, but then thought against it since she brought her mishap upon herself. She had no business wearing something like the nylon fabric Charlotte held in her hands to her home to disrespect her in late October, looking like she was dancing in the strip club.

As she hid behind the safety of her own door, Charlotte heard Tapioca yelling near the window on the side of the door that allowed her to see a shaken Charlotte sitting on the floor.

"Keep the blouse, bitch! I hope you got a kick out of seeing these titties Charles loves sucking on, just like I know your pussy was getting wet while you were watching our video. You scary looking bitch! You need to wax that damn mustache off of your face."

Tapioca kicked the door again before boldly walking away, making no effort to hide her nudity.

Charlotte cried all over again just for the fact that she had to go through that experience. When she returned the night before, Charles was cold and distant with her. Mrs. Vanderbilt sent the video to her months ago, and Charlotte decided then that she was done with the marriage. She planned to hold onto the video for leverage in her divorce and would leave Charles penniless. As time went on, she became emotionally stronger and decided she would not lose her marriage without a fight. She decided she'd do what she must to get her husband back and realized that wouldn't be happening with her in Japan.

She cringed at the thought of having sex with him that morning, but vowed to do what she must to get her husband back. As painful as it was, she watched the video countless times before returning home so she could see what it took to please her husband.

Having been orally sexually molested as a child, Charlotte had never allowed a man to go down on her nor had she ever went down on a man beyond her sexual abuse. Since she promised him that she'd do whatever it took to save their marriage, she cried in silence as Charles' first test for her was to let him go down on her. She was so distraught, she couldn't enjoy him. She thought of sharing her deep, dark secret of being molested by her babysitter's husband, which also factored in her decision to never have a child, but she didn't know if it would push her husband further away. Also on his list of demands, he told her that he wanted a child or two, and she needed to spend more time at home rather than Japan. The truth was, she chose to spend more time overseas when Charles continued to pressure her for a baby as she approached thirty-eight. She really worried what would happen when Charles found out she had her tubes tied two years prior.

She had hoped Charles would fly to Japan for a few days just so she could give him a small dose of sex to keep him from being unfaithful to her. For some reason, it had never occurred to her that Charles would choose a near white woman to be unfaithful with. His porno movies she discarded had all black women as the actresses.

She just knew their neighbor Karen James would be the one. She was a scorned woman seeking to pay her own husband back. Charlotte watched how Karen kept her eyes locked on Charles while at her birthday party. So, Charlotte enlisted the spying eyes of Mrs. Vanderbilt to ensure that Karen kept her distance. She went as far as leaving a key for Mrs. Vanderbilt to barge in if Karen was in her home and Charles refused to answer the door. She never in a million years expected to see her husband co-starring in a disgusting movie with a girl half his age. In her initial anger, she cursed Mrs. Vanderbilt for mailing the unexpected surprise, but later called to apologize. That's when she learned that Tapioca was living in her home. Her first instinct was to hop on a plane and kill the two of them instead of going through a divorce. The thought of prison didn't sit well with her, though, which rattled her when Tapioca mentioned it as if inside of her mind.

The night before, Charles callously explained to Charlotte why he was in love with the young girl and no longer in love with her. Charlotte felt her world crumbling and could hardly breathe as she listened to him. After he fussed for over an hour, Charlotte reasoned he just had a lot of pent-up anger that had to be released, because shortly after that, he softened up and kept apologizing. Two hours into the conversation, they cried together and then fell asleep while holding each other.

By morning, he was telling Charlotte that he may not have been in love with Tapioca, but just turned to her as a crutch through his anger. That was all Charlotte needed to hear. She begged him to never call or talk to Tapioca again because she would lure him back in her web. Charles agreed, particularly after Charlotte conceded to allow his redecoration projects done in her absence to remain. That was a small concession for Charlotte, but the oral sex seemed like more than she could handle. To keep her marriage, she'd just have to suck it up. Literally.

12

Tapioca arrived back in her home and cried like she had never cried before. She had never been so humiliated in her life. She wanted to believe that Charlotte was lying, but Charles hadn't made a single attempt to call or see her, and he hadn't answered any of her calls. The more Tapioca cried, the angrier she became. Charles would be sorry he messed over her. She would also find a way to pay Charlotte back.

Tapioca looked out of her window just in time to see Mrs. Vanderbilt leaving for bingo. Mr. Vanderbilt is just what she needed at that moment. She went and cleaned herself up before heading to the Vanderbilt home. William Vanderbilt was too happy to see her, and that made her feel instantly better.

"Big Willie, have you been a naughty boy?" she asked after entering the house with the key he gave her long before his stroke and walking into his bedroom where he sat in his favorite chair watching television.

"I've been a real bad boy, Tappy," he answered with a slight slur.

"Well, I don't know if I'm going to let you have a taste of this," she teased, lifting her schoolgirl skirt and placing a foot on his armrest.

"Please let me taste it. I'll be a good boy," he begged, staring into her crevices and going along with their role playing.

"I'll let you touch it. If you can make it nice and wet, then I'll let you taste it. And if you be a really good boy, I'll even let you put your big, giant cock inside of my hot, wet cunt," she said with extra emphasis on the word "hot".

"Okay!" he answered excitedly, reaching out his fingers to gently touch her freshly shaved pubic area.

At first, he touched it as if he were afraid of it, but then, his thumb found her clit and concentrated on pleasing the area. Slowly but surely, his fingers touched the mouth of her wetness.

"Can I taste it now?"

"Nope! You have to make it wetter."

She tried hard to focus on William making her feel good, as her mind continually drifted towards the window that faced the home she practically lived in just the day before.

"Make it wetter, you bad boy."

William massaged the outside of her vagina along with her clit until it started making popping noises, indicating its wetness. Then he stuck a finger inside of her, which brought her attention back to him and away from the window. His finger went in and out a few times before he added another finger. The feeling was getting good to Tapioca. She finished opening her tight, half-buttoned blouse to reveal her bare breasts. She bent enough to let them touch his face.

"Here, suck my tits."

His mostly toothless mouth caught hold of a nipple and teased it with his tongue. As she moved her hips with the rhythm of his finger strokes, she got as wet as she could stand. She pulled away from him.

"Come and lick this wet pussy."

She went to his bed and laid back, holding her legs up and apart. She played with herself as William struggled to get out of his chair and undid his pants while making his way to the bed. He climbed on the hospital-type bed onto his back. His penis was standing in the air. Tapioca lowered the head of his bed and sat on his awaiting tongue. He sucked all the juices from her as she helped him to fondle her breasts.

Tapioca was feeling good. She pressed her body down more to

make his tongue go deeper inside of her. When she stopped him so she could inch her hips down to meet his hips, she looked out the window again and noticed Charlotte standing and watching out of her window. She wondered if Charlotte was able to see into the window. Tapioca was hoping she would see and tell Mrs. Vanderbilt.

Tapioca put one breast at a time into William's mouth as she slid a condom onto him before climbing on top of his dick. First, she rode him extra slow, creating long strides along his shaft. Then she moved faster before slowing the pace again. William fondled and squeezed Tapioca's breasts as if they were extra large marshmallows.

For a minute, Tapioca forgot about Charlotte in the window. When her attention was drawn back to the window, she realized Charlotte was still watching. Tapioca decided to give her an eyeful for the next fifteen minutes. As she was on the verge of an orgasm, she heard the front door open and close. Charlotte was still at her window.

Mrs. Vanderbilt was up the stairs and coming at Tapioca in a matter of seconds. Obviously, Charlotte must have called her.

"Get out of my house, you Jezebel! How dare you come in here!" she screamed. "WILLIAM!"

Tapioca just laughed and stayed on top of William, who was still holding onto Tapioca's breasts. "Bitch please! Can't you see we're busy?"

Mrs. Vanderbilt seemed like she was about to have a heart attack, but then she looked around for something to hit Tapioca with. She picked up a hardcover book to swing. Tapioca jumped off of William, leaving mounds of cum on his still erect penis. She hopped off of the other side of the bed, keeping a safe distance from Mrs. Vanderbilt.

"Get out of here! Get out of my home!" she yelled repeatedly.

"William, I'll see you later." She dug between her legs and smeared her wetness on his lips, further inciting Mrs. Vanderbilt who chased behind her with the book in hand. "I left some of my pussy on Willie's big dick and lips for you to taste. I'm sure you've been wondering what

Tapioca's pudding really tastes like," she said as she was going out of the bedroom door.

As she nonchalantly left out of the Vanderbilt's home, she saw Charles' car pulling into his garage as the door was closing. Tapioca thought about going there and giving him a piece of her mind, but Charlotte remained watching like a hawk. Tapioca hadn't forgotten how close she had come to getting shot. Instead, she went back down the hill to her own home, pissed off because Mrs. Vanderbilt blocked her orgasm.

As she approached her house, she saw Trey standing at her door writing a note.

"Hey! What are you doing here? When did you get in town?" she asked as she got nearer.

"Oh good, I was just about to leave you a note. I needed someone to talk to. Figured you were the best person."

"Sure, come on in," she said, unlocking her door and letting them inside. She was all too happy to see him at that moment.

"Where are you coming from? You look a mess."

"Trust me, you don't want to know," she laughed. "Make yourself comfortable. I need to take a quick shower. You know where I keep the Remy. I'm gonna probably need a hit off of that joint I know you have on you."

"Damn! That bad?" he asked, going straight to her liquor cabinet for the bottle of his favorite drink: Remy Martin.

"That bad," she answered before disappearing upstairs.

She was hoping Trey would join her in the shower and finish what she didn't get to finish with Mr. Vanderbilt. She was hornier than before and planned to have him handle her problem before he left. If she had to smoke some weed and drink with him to get that dick, then so be it. She certainly couldn't wait to pay Charles back by parading every man that she could in front of him. She would force him to watch each of them as they fucked her.

Trey didn't join her in the long shower she lingered in with hopes that he'd eventually show up. When she went back downstairs, she saw him out back smoking with his drink. She stepped outside with just her robe on.

"Have you eaten anything?" she asked.

"Yeah, I got something before I came."

Tapioca took the joint he was smoking from his hand and took a toke.

"Damn, you were serious."

She took his glass and drunk from it.

"Girl, you better slow down. You're gonna be toasted in a minute."

"Hey, that's fine with me," she said, taking another toke before passing it back to him. "It's been a rough day."

"You wanna talk about it?"

"Nah. Besides, you came here 'cause you had shit to talk about."

"Well, you might not like what I have to talk about," he said, passing the marijuana back to Tapioca and taking his refreshed drink from her hand.

"Oh lord! What's going on now?"

"Your sister."

"What about my sister?"

"After the last time we were together, I've been thinking about breaking up with her. You know I've been feeling your ass from the giddy. I know you ain't trying to be tied down with my ass, but I be wanting you like a muthafucker. You know I got a kid to think about, but then I figure I could still be a good father to my son and don't have to stay in a relationship with Nilla."

"That's true. I think you're a really good father and always will be."

"See, that's my problem," he said, swapping the drink for the weed. "She's about to have another baby, and now I really feel stuck."

"Are you serious?! When the fuck did that shit happen? How'd I miss that one?" Tapioca laughed in disbelief.

"Four and a half months. Four and a half more to go."

"Dammnn! I can't believe that shit! A baby-making machine. Hell, these past few months I've been trying to get pregnant, and here my little sister is about to have her second child. Ain't this a bitch!" she laughed.

She had never told Charles that she was trying to get pregnant by him so she could keep him. She wanted to fuck Trey, but the whole "new baby" thing was a turnoff. But then… Tapioca spotted a shadow hiding in Charles' office window. She tried not to look, because she didn't want him to know she was aware of his presence.

"Okay, so what should I do? Should I just leave her pregnant, should I at least stick around until the baby comes, or am I supposed to man up and stay with her for the children?"

"Nigga, please! I'm sitting here fucked up, and you asking me about some serious shit," Tapioca laughed as she stood up from the patio chair. "Hell, I'm horny as hell and need some dick. I ain't trying to hear about my bitch sister who only calls me for more money. I say fuck the bitch! Leave her ass if you ain't happy. Shit, from now on, I'm about making me happy. Fuck all that other shit."

Tapioca opened her robe and stood in front of Trey. However, he wouldn't bite. He wouldn't touch her. She sat on his lap trying to arouse him, as she continued to drink his Remy.

"You better slow down, girl. You ain't gonna be able to walk in a minute."

"Please, I ain't no punk," she laughed.

As she attempted to stand again, she almost stumbled, but he grabbed hold of her, catching her by her waist. She giggled.

"Okay, let me get you inside. You out here falling all over the place."

He helped her up to her bedroom where she pulled off her robe and climbed on her bed, immediately stimulating herself. Trey stood and watched her. He was enjoying the show. He watched as the juices poured from her.

"Fuck me, Trey. Fuck me. Put that big black dick right in this wet pussy. You see how wet this pussy is? Come on and taste it. Let your black tip touch my cunt. Uhm, this feels so good. Come on and touch it," she said, enticing him.

He groped himself when he could no longer stand the temptation. He came near the bed and bent to kiss her breast nearest to him. Then he let his hand join hers. She moaned uncontrollably as if she were about to climax. He rubbed harder while hungrily sucking her nipple. She freed his manhood from his pants and squeezed while stroking it, causing a clear discharge to escape the head. Tapioca lifted herself just enough so she could lick the escaped wetness.

"OH! OH! I'm cumming! Fuck this pussy, baby! Fuck it! Uhmm! Uhmm! OHH!"

The more erratic her body jerked, the harder he rubbed her clit while her fingers were inside of herself.

"Uhmm! OH! It feels so good!" Then she released her nut, tightening her thighs with both their arms stuck in between. "You know I want this dick, Trey," she said, lifting her head enough to suck the head a few times. "That was just the hors d'ouvre. Your long-ass tongue is the appetizer, and this dick is the entrée."

"I can't," he said, pulling away from her mouth.

"You what?"

"I can't do this."

"What the fuck do you mean you can't do this? You need to handle this shit, Trey!"

"Tappy, I only came by to talk. Right now, I need Tapioca, my friend, and nothing else. I'm so stressed the fuck out right now about shit... I just can't right now."

"So if I help you talk, then you'll give me some dick?"

"I said I can't. If I'm gonna be with Nilla, I can't be doing this here shit with you. You ain't trying to be with me, and I'm about to be a father again."

"Please! You sitting here trippin'. Besides, how you know the baby's yours? You sitting here depriving both of us for a baby you don't even know if it's yours or not. You over here fucking me and you know Nilla's back in P-A getting her swerve on, too"

Trey moved away from Tapioca. "You know what? Fuck you! I'm out! Find one of your other dicks, you ho!"

"What?!" Tapioca tried to figure out if Trey was serious before she laughed. "Trey, stop playing! I know you ain't getting all bent out of shape just because I said that baby probably ain't yours…"

"Yeah, whatever, bitch!"

Trey flew out of the room, down the stairs, and out of the door. Tapioca called out his name, figuring he couldn't have been serious. He didn't return, and Tapioca just laid there as the room and her world turned.

13

"Hello."

"Hi, I'm trying to reach Tapioca Pudding."

"This is she."

"This is Dr. Beaumont's office calling to remind you of your appointment for your annual tomorrow at ten a.m."

"Oh damn! Oh, okay. Thank you. I almost forgot. By chance would you have any openings today? I think I may be coming down with something and don't want to end up too sick to go out tomorrow."

"If you can be here in the next forty-five minutes, I could get you in. We just had a cancellation this morning."

"Great! I'll be there," Tapioca said before hanging up.

She didn't know if she was hung over, getting depressed, or really coming down with something.

*****

After leaving her doctor's office, she stopped off to buy groceries. Since she had been with Charles, she had no need. Now with two days of no phone calls and him choosing Charlotte over her, she was going to have to find a way to get some of her men back.

Anywhere Tapioca would go, there were tons of men trying to pick her up. She could tell her doctor was getting a thrill from doing her physical examination. The way he'd touch her breasts was more sensual, and if she didn't know better, the balding old man seemed to inhale deeply while giving her a pap smear. Not only that, she heard he rarely performs EKG's but always administers Tapioca's. After the way he touched her at her previous examination, she swore she would shop around for a new doctor but hadn't gotten around to it. As much as she enjoyed all men lusting for her, being touched by her doctor felt more like a violation than a pleasure.

During the past two and a half years, she had limited her sexual encounters to her male neighbors. She liked that they were married and didn't try to complicate her life. She didn't care if they talked about her with one another. She found it flattering and was just happy they were talking. She received more of a thrill sneaking into their marital beds and sexing the husbands of the women who despised her simply because she was single. They treated her like a low-class leper rather than reciprocate the neighborly friendship she tried to establish with them. They had also laughed at her name, saying, "No one likes the dessert tapioca pudding, so that's all the more reason to hate Tapioca Pudding, the person."

One day, she attempted to visit the neighborhood church. One neighbor, who was also a member, asked her why she was there and suggested she find another place to worship. After that, she had no more respect or regard for any of her neighbors and gave up on trying to exist in peace or go to church. Instead, her mission had been to violate each of their marriages and make their husbands lust for her. Starting with the queen-bitch of the neighborhood's husband, Mr. Vanderbilt. Soon, the thrill was like a drug rush, and she'd be on the prowl looking for her next prey. The sex became an addiction that she was ultimately willing to give up for Charles' love.

Her multiple sex partners in the neighborhood kept her busy enough to turn down opportunities from men outside of the neighborhood. She also felt it was safer than taking chances with strange men. She liked the fact that the men were aware of her relationships with the others and didn't try to put any pressure on her to be exclusive. Charles was different, though. She couldn't explain the connection she felt with him. Nevertheless, he made his choice, and he'd have to live with it.

"There's my strawberry. That stuck-up prick finally let you out of his sight?"

Tapioca turned away from the bell peppers she was picking out in the produce section of the store. "Jonathan! How are you?"

"Been missing my strawberry kitten. Karen went out of town a few days ago, but you were stuck up under the prude. Heard his wife's back in town. Guess the honeymoon's over, huh?"

"Whatever! Fuck both of them. They deserve each other," Tapioca snapped, turning back towards her peppers to hide her hurt.

"Hey, this is me you're talking to. You know you can keep it real with me. I was just trippin' about how you cut everybody off for old dude. Damn, we couldn't get a pancake, dinner plate, loving, or anything. Just cold turkey cut a brotha off. But, I miss you. Ain't had good lovin' since."

That made Tapioca smile. She needed her ego stroked, and maybe stroking Jonathan was just what she needed. Especially after how Dr. Beaumont sensually touched her during her vaginal examination that she tried not to get turned on by.

"How about some dinner tonight at my place?"

"Any other time that would be great, but the wifey will be home tonight. An afternoon snack might work as long as you're offering."

"Uhm… I don't know. You know how I feel about snacks when I don't have a main course to follow it up," Tapioca said seductively.

"You know how bad I want a bite of that sweet strawberry," he said with seduction of his own and stepping into her space.

Tapioca could feel her nipples harden. "Damn, I have a few errands to run. I was going to just drop this stuff off and go. It'll be almost dinnertime by the time I get back home and cleaned up. Besides, I need for you to do more than bite the strawberry."

"Hell, I got no problem with you kissing the prince."

"Not what I was talking about. I need the prince to kiss the strawberry," she responded, stepping even closer to him.

She was close enough to feel his body heat. He let his hand touch her hip.

"No, no, no, no, no! Please tell me this isn't what was fucking my husband?"

Jonathan tried to quickly step away when they spotted Charlotte. "Talk to you later," he said to Tapioca before quickly departing.

"First, I see you all over Mr. Vanderbilt. Then, I see you outside of your house with another man only moments later. Now, you're standing in the middle of the grocery store trying to screw yet another married man. You can't find any single men your own age? No wonder they call your nasty ass the town whore.

"Your mother, bitch! You need to stay the fuck out of my business and worry about your own man. And since Charles told me how unskilled you are in bed, I will gladly give you some extra videos to go with the one you've already been watching so you can take tips from it. Maybe he might really end up wanting your ugly ass. You know, I have the names of a few places you could go to get that hair waxed off of your face. It's not ladylike."

Charlotte laughed. "Yeah, okay. Oh, my husband's wanted this ugly ass all night long and some more this morning. I don't know what lie he told you, but I keep my husband quite happy, tramp! That should be obvious since he kicked your ass to the curb for the hairy face and all."

Tapioca tried to hide her hurt. "Just get the fuck out of my face, bitch." She turned to leave with her cart.

Realizing she hit Tapioca below the belt, Charlotte grabbed her shoulder from behind. "Oh no, I haven't finished with you yet. You're not going to just walk away from me, you classless bitch."

Without thinking about it, Tapioca turned and punched Charlotte between the eyes with every ounce of hurt energy inside of her. Charlotte, who hadn't anticipated such, flew backwards, falling into the banana stand. Ironically, everyone watching ran to Tapioca's aide, asking if she was all right.

When a manager came to see about the commotion, Charlotte yelled, "Call the police! I want her locked up!" Charlotte had a cut between her brows from the ring on Tapioca's hand.

Tapioca stood crying, shocked from what had occurred in addition to the hurt of Charlotte's words. She had never in her life hit anyone that hard and realized that all of her hurt and anger was in the one punch.

When the police came, they asked Tapioca if she wanted to press charges on Charlotte since she was the aggressor and both the cameras and the witnesses' statements proved Tapioca had defended herself after Charlotte attacked her.

"Oh, this is ridiculous. I can't believe you're asking that home-wrecking tramp, who slept with my husband and hit me, causing a cut on my face, if she wants to press charges. I'm the victim here. Are you asking her because she's white? Is that it?

"You don't know shit about me, so get off of that white shit," Tapioca yelled back before the police officers admonished her. "Yeah, I want to press charges, and if I can charge her with a hate crime, I wanna do that, too."

"Hate crime?! I hate you for sleeping with my husband. Adultery, now that's a crime," Charlotte screamed as the police put handcuffs on her in front of everyone watching.

Some spectators went as far as to applaud while they took her away. Tapioca felt bad about sending Charlotte to jail. Where Tapioca was from, that was something you just didn't do. People got shot and still wouldn't tell. Then she thought Charlotte did it to herself. She ought to be lucky Tapioca didn't tell the police how she pulled a gun on her the previous day.

Tapioca's whole day was wasted filling out paperwork at the police station. It was nighttime when she left. As she was being escorted by a police officer back to her car, she noticed Charles driving to the station. She wanted to call out to him, but figured it was best she didn't with the police there. Seeing him again made her glad she got a good punch off of Charlotte. Even better, there was a large lump that formed on her head.

Her young heart had never experienced such hurt as the hurt she was feeling without Charles in her life. She was just happy to be in his company. It made her happy to please him. Instead, he chose to be with a woman who caused him nothing but grief and misery. Before all of the mess in the store, she was planning to go to Charles' office to confront his cowardness. She felt at the very least he owed her an explanation.

Once again, she went to bed without eating and cried herself to sleep. She awoke to the sound of her doorbell. When her eyes focused on the neon numbers, she saw it was 1:15 a.m. and knew it had to be quick-humping Scott Talbert. Obviously, Jonathan must have gotten the word out that she was no longer in Charles' shadow. Scott would often sneak around to her house on the nights he'd go to the bar and get drunk. He wasn't so bad to have around on the sober days his wife would be away and he could take his time, but on that night, Tapioca was in no mood to entertain a drunk, particularly since he had never been able to satisfy her when he was drunk. If anything, he'd make her hornier, and she couldn't stand that.

She peeped out of her bedroom window to see him as he rang the doorbell persistently. In her heart, she wanted it to be Charles coming to say what a huge mistake he'd made choosing Charlotte, and then they'd live happily ever after. After twenty persistent minutes of ringing, he finally gave up. However, he rang long enough to ruin any chances of her going back to sleep anytime soon.

She attempted to watch some television while curled up with a cup of chamomile tea. Every channel she'd turn to, someone was happy in love. Everywhere she'd look, she saw the good times she and Charles had shared on the occasions the pair would hang at her house for all of its recreation compared to the lack of at his house.

She grabbed a fleece throw and went out back to lounge beneath the stars in the chilled still-night air. She laid on the cushioned lounge chair trying to empty her thoughts, but knowing Charles' window stood above her only enhanced her suffering. So, she collected her blanket to go back inside. Just as she was about to go, she saw the office light come on. Charles appeared in front of the floor-to-ceiling window waving his arms. She stood trying to figure out if he was trying to get her attention, but then decided he must have been angry with her hitting Charlotte and having her arrested. She stood trying to figure out what he was trying to communicate to her, but then suddenly, he flipped the light back off. That angered her once again.

Finally at 4:45 a.m., she fell back to sleep but was up at seven. She went through the refrigerator to find the ingredients for one of her breakfast pies. She was tired of grieving and felt it was time to get back to living. She chose Dan Winters to be the recipient for the morning. With his penile implant, she loved the feel of his thick twelve inches inside of her. She only wished he had some tongue skills. Technically, he had no skills, but as long as he provided the stiff dick, she'd handle it from there.

She returned home less than fifteen minutes after dropping the pie off, feeling unfulfilled. As she approached her home, she noticed the mail bulging from her box and grabbed it to take inside. Her phone was ringing as she entered. She quickly set the mail down to answer it.

"Tapioca Pudding?"

"Yes," she answered out of breath.

"This is Dr. Beaumont's office calling. The doctor asked that I give you a call to see if you could stop in this morning to discuss your results."

Tapioca's heart sunk as she took a seat. She knew that wasn't a good sign. She had only seen him the day before, and it typically took two weeks just for him to tell her everything looked well.

"Uh…sure…I guess."

Then she wondered to herself if the nasty doctor just wanted another feel of the pudding. That thought made her feel better as she convinced herself nothing was wrong with her, just the doctor.

"Sure. Let Dr. Beaumont know I'll see him just before noon," she said, no longer worried.

"I will let him know," the secretary answered.

*****

As expected, Tapioca needed to undress for another pelvic examination. She started to object, but instead, she decided to play along with the old man. She didn't understand what the purpose was for the nurse to be in the room, because it certainly didn't discourage his perverse behavior. In fact, the nurse would be any and everywhere else in the small room rather than watching Dr. Beaumont inappropriately fondling his patients.

He looked directly into Tapioca's eyes as his stout fingers tickled her clit before entering her. This time he allowed more fingers as he pressed around her lower abdominal area. *That's a new one*, Tapioca thought to herself. His nurse scribbled onto the chart when Dr. Beaumont called out, "Eight or nine," just before pulling his fingers out of Tapioca.

"Push back before getting up, and you can go ahead and get dressed. I'll be back shortly to talk to you," he said, while peeling off his useless one glove he used for the examination. He smelled his bare fingers on his other hand that had touched her, then placed those fingers to his lips before licking his lips.

The nurse collected the chart and left the room with Dr. Beaumont.

Fifteen minutes later, he returned alone with the chart.

"I'm going to send you upstairs for an ultrasound. I just want to be certain of how far along you are since you had an irregular cycle before."

"Huh?" Tapioca asked, genuinely confused.

"The pregnancy. I figure you to be somewhere between eight and nine weeks. I just need to make sure. Your hormone level is a bit higher and more suggestive that you'd be a bit further along, but on physical exam, your uterus presents smaller."

Tapioca looked at him with a blank stare as she tried to process his words. "Pregnant?" was all she could manage to say. She had wanted a child of her own ever since Vanilla gave birth to her nephew almost two years prior, but since it had never happened, she assumed she was incapable of becoming pregnant. She was really trying with Charles.

"Oh, you didn't know? I thought my nurse said she told you?"

Tapioca shook her head in disbelief.

"Yes, you're expecting. I know at your last exam a year ago you inquired about your ability to conceive with an abnormal cycle. Are you okay with this or do you need to discuss alternatives?"

"Alternatives?" she asked, again confused. "What the hell is an alternative? Either you're pregnant or you're…" Suddenly, she thought about what he meant. "Abortion?! Are you crazy? I wish I would kill something growing inside of me!" she scolded.

"Well, there are other alternatives, such as adoption."

"Hold up! Why would I want to carry a baby just to give it away to some strangers? This is my baby. I'm carrying it, and I'm keeping it. I'm insulted that you'd think I'd consider a quote, unquote alternative."

"I'm sorry. I didn't mean to offend you. I know you're still young, and I didn't know if you were quite ready for such a big lifestyle change. Do you think the dad will be okay with your decision?"

"Who the hell cares what he…"

Tapioca stopped mid-sentence when she thought of who the father could be. She had just slept with old man Vanderbilt and Dan, but they couldn't have fathered her child.

"Charles!" she said elated.

"Excuse me?" the doctor asked.

"Nothing." Tapioca hopped off of the examination table and grabbed her bag. "Is there anything else? I really have to get going," she said, excited over her opportunity to reclaim her man and permanently push Charlotte out once and for all.

"Wait a minute! I need you to head upstairs for that ultrasound and then come back down to see me. I need to figure out how far along you are for sure so we can have a good due date for you, as well as get you started on your prenatal vitamins."

Tapioca already had a hand on the doorknob. She couldn't wait to give Charlotte her walking papers. She just wished Charles could be there for the ultrasound. She knew how much he wanted children and would be beyond thrilled.

"Fine! Let's get this over with. I have things to do."

14

"How did you let yourself fall for this young girl?"

"Ed, if you saw the ass and tits on that young, fine thing, you'd understand how ole Charlie done fell so hard. Oh, she'll make you drool if you see her."

"Hey, don't talk about her like that! Show some respect!" Charles scolded Arty, his longtime friend.

Arty was the closest thing Charles had to a brother. They had been friends since middle school. Arty was the more outgoing one, and most of the girlfriends Charles ever had was because of Arty's aggressiveness. Charles was always stronger in the books, so he was able to help Arty stay grounded enough to go to college and now own a real estate development company. Edward came into the picture during high school when he was a junior and Charles and Arty were freshmen. Larry came while in college with Edward, but the four ended up in the same school and have been the best of buddies ever since.

"Anything is an improvement to that evil wife of his," Larry crooned in. "I can't believe how she did you, Charlie. And now she decides she's going to be a 'good' wife? I'm not buying it. I say boot her ass to the curb."

"I already told you, it's not that simple," Charles said, frustrated by the situation with his wife and the pressure from his friends to leave her.

"I still don't understand how in the hell she got hold of the DVD of you and the young girl when the movie was in your house. You sure she didn't sneak in from Japan and take it?" Edward asked.

"No, she's just evil like that. She's sneaky!" Larry answered before Charles could. "She's probably got her meat on the side over in Japan or wherever she's been hiding out. That's why she ain't trying to give you any loving, and you know damn well she ain't trying to be saddled down with your kid. She's too selfish to give you a baby. Her sneaky ass is probably sneaking birth control pills just to make sure she doesn't give you a kid. If she does come and say she's pregnant, you better get a test. With her evil ass, it might be a Japanese kid."

"Damn, Larry, tell me how you really feel about my wife," Charles laughed, shaking his head. "As long as Charlotte has that DVD somewhere, I'm going to have to stay put. I've worked too hard for everything I have to just give it away to her and her heckling sisters like that."

"So what's the difference in her having the DVD when you had the girl practically living in your house? So what she has a DVD. Tell her to have a good time watching it while you go bury your face between them tits and make a new DVD," Arty said, laughing at his own joke.

"Y'all make this girl sound like the hottest thing on this side of the Mississippi. She can't be all that," Edward stated, taking a swig from his bottle of beer.

"She's all that and then some," Larry answered. "You know who she reminds me of?"

"Who?" the men asked in unison.

"Remember at Eddie's bachelor party when we had those girls? There was this one hottie who had that same colored hair. I think she was white, but I'll never forget that ass on her."

"Damn, you getting me hard with that trip down memory lane," Edward said. "I remember the shit I saw that girl doing to herself. Uhm, uhm, uhm, uhm! I'm still mad I didn't fuck her. I was trying to be all faithful before getting married."

As the guys reminisced, Charles zoned out, having his personal memory of the girl. He remembered how she did a perfect split on him, which resulted in him losing his soldiers in literally a matter of seconds. The experience was so quick that the girl got pissed and went on to some of the other guys that were willing to pay her. Charles' feelings were hurt and he tried to blame it on the alcohol, but when he screwed the next woman, the results weren't too much better. He tried to forget that day ever existed. His ego was so bruised by the experience that he seldom drank any hard liquor since then.

At that moment, it clicked in his head why Tapioca had immediately grabbed his attention from the first moment he caught a glimpse of the back of her head. Though he never shared it with his friends, for many years, Charles had secretly wished he'd run into that woman who took joy in mutilating his ego and reputation so he could prove to her that his dick had plenty of staying power. After ten or fifteen years, he finally gave up on ever finding her, especially once he met Charlotte.

"Earth to Charlie. Earth to Charlie. Do you read me?" Arty snapped his fingers in front of a zoned-out Charles.

"Damn, man, where'd your mind wander off to?" Edward asked as soon as they saw Charles had come out of his trance.

"He was probably thinking about that sweet piece of ass he couldn't handle," Arty said.

The men burst out laughing. Charles just chuckled.

"For real, man, you okay?" Arty asked.

"Yeah, I'm fine. I was just thinking about Charlotte," Charles lied.

"Hopefully you were thinking about how to give her the ax," Larry said.

"I told you, we are going to work out our marriage. She's trying. Give her some credit. Who knows? Maybe one day we'll be able to celebrate a silver anniversary like Eddie. I don't want to be married two or three times like you two. Worse, Larry, you're all by yourself now after three marriages in fifteen years. And Arty's trying to catch up in his third marriage now, always forgetting he's married."

"I love my wife," Arty defended. "I ain't going anywhere. Three times is a charm for me. I got a good woman. Those other girls on the side just help me to appreciate my wife more."

Charles shook his head with a chuckle.

"And how about I just prefer my freedom," Larry also defended. "I love not having to answer to a woman. I love variety. I like being able to come and go as I please. And as for your wife, let's just say you need to cut your losses while you still can. Maybe if you hurry up, you'll be able to find a new wife that you can spend the next twenty-five years with."

"Please! I'm about to be fifty-one years old in a few days."

"Damn, you make that sound old. I'm fifty-one already," Arty said. "Larry and Eddie are about to make fifty-three."

"I made fifty-three last month, and all the ladies still want some of this," Larry said, holding his shirt at the shoulder. "That's why I need my freedom right now. Hell, I bet your wife ain't even going to give you any nookie for your birthday. You should have held onto the young girl until after your birthday."

The other guys nodded in agreement.

"I know one thing, though," Larry continued. "You need to figure out what you're going to do with your young neighbor. You know her and Charlotte will clash again. You should have left Charlotte's ass inside the joint at least until after your birthday."

Charles gave Larry a dirty look and Larry laughed.

"He's got a point about keeping them apart," Edward said. "You're not going to keep them apart forever. You said Charlotte caught you waving at the girl last night through your window after you had to bail her out of jail? You're lucky she didn't throw a pot of hot grits on your ass."

"And don't forget about the big knot on her forehead," Arty chimed in, laughing.

"Yeah, that too. Do you really think that young girl, who you were sticking nonstop day and night for like four months straight, is just going to suddenly not have any more feelings and go away?"

"Charlotte told me that she saw her with the old guy across the street from me, and she saw her out of my office window the other night with some other guy that same night. She seems to be doing okay to me. Besides that, I left a note in her mailbox three times asking her to meet me so we could talk. She hasn't responded, so I guess she's doing what she wants to do."

"The old guy? A note?" Larry asked, surprised. "Hold up! Did I miss something here?"

"In the mailbox?" Edward cosigned, missing the part about the old guy. "How tacky is that? Just because she's young doesn't mean you have to pull some juvenile move. Why not just call the girl and say what you gotta say?"

"Because I don't know if Charlotte is tracking my calls. The last thing I need is for Charlotte to start monitoring my calls. She wanted me to call Tapioca the other night to let her know we were done."

"So why didn't you?" Edward asked.

"Because he knew he wasn't done," Arty answered for Charles. "There ain't no way you could tap an ass like that and then not want to tap it again. Especially not when you have to compare it to Charlotte."

"Would you all just lay off of my wife?! I've made my decision. I'm staying with my wife, and we're going to work through our problems together. Yes, I care deeply for Tapioca, but that chapter is closed, and she'll have no other choice but to accept it."

"I want to know about this 'old guy' shit. Older than you 'old guy' or what?" Larry persisted.

Charles was too embarrassed to say and decided to back off of it. "That's just what Charlotte said. You know she'll say anything at this point."

The men accepted that.

"Well, let me ask you this. If Charlotte didn't hit you with that DVD, would you still be trying to work out your marriage? I mean, just a couple of weeks ago, you were saying Charlotte didn't have a chance in hell, but as soon as she called you letting you know she was coming back with that video in hand, you barely laugh at anything. You're clearly unhappy."

"I have to agree with Larry on this one. Charlie, I would have your back if you were working out your marriage because that's what you want to do, but she blackmailed you. She's a bully. How happy can you be, being bullied to stay in a loveless marriage? That woman doesn't have a concept of what love is. You deserve to be happy," Arty said.

"Art, Eddie, Larry, I know you all care about what happens to me, but I really need to handle this my own way. Everything's going to all work out in the end. You'll see. Charlotte and I will be fine, and Tapioca will get on with her life once she sees I am totally committed to my marriage. Charlotte and I are even talking about having kids, so you guys can stop worrying about me. Yes, Tapioca is a fascinating young lady, but she is yesterday. I just have to move forward now. I was hoping to sit her down face to face and tell her, but if I don't, she'll get the hint and go on doing what she's been doing. I stopped by her house after I left the office and put one last letter saying it's over in her mailbox right before I came here."

"So you're going to suddenly give up watching her through your window?" Edward asked.

The tough questions were starting to annoy Charles. In reality, he was having a difficult time with the entire situation. He didn't know how or if he'd ever get over his love for Tapioca. He knew in his heart, the love he had for Charlotte would never come close to the love and deep connection he found with the young Tapioca.

He had hoped to see Tapioca one last time to at least kiss her lips one final time. He knew when he had made love to her the last time that it would in fact be his last. He couldn't bring himself to tell her the truth of how Charlotte blackmailed him into staying married to her. He knew the hell that Charlotte would cause them, and he felt he was doing Tapioca a favor by letting her go. He also didn't want to be around on the day Tapioca found out he had slept with her younger sister. He didn't know if or when Vanilla's memory of that night would resurface, and he felt it would damage the relationship he had formed with Tapioca. To be proactive, he'd just as well stay with Charlotte. Especially since she finally consented to the oral sex and giving him children. She was on opposite ends of the oral sex Richter scale compared to Tapioca, but it was a start.

"I might even move my office to another part of the house. I can spend more time at my other office until I get her out of my system."

"If you say so," Larry said dryly before the men laughed.

Charles was just happy for the opportunity to be at Larry's house to play poker. It was a treat that he'd been missing out on for a long time under the old Charlotte regime. The new Charlotte had to agree to his weekly outings with his longtime friends. And since his birthday was coming in a few days, that's how and where he chose to celebrate it. One thing he did agree with was that his birthday would have been much better spent with Tapioca than Charlotte.

15

"Hi, Susan. I'm looking for Charles. Is he here today?" Tapioca asked Charles' office manager when she arrived to share her good news with him.

She was overflowing with joy from the news that she was carrying his baby. She could think of no better birthday gift to give him. According to her ultrasound, she was twelve weeks pregnant, which made the baby Charles' without a doubt in her mind.

Susan wasn't too fond of Tapioca because one, she looked too white and Susan was against interracial dating, and two, because of the significant age difference. Nonetheless, Susan could tolerate Tapioca any day over Charlotte. While Tapioca bragged about Charles' "wonderful work," Charlotte would constantly spew negativity about his work and the authenticity of his architectural firm that had her living large in an eight-million-dollar home. Susan also hated Tapioca's name. She couldn't imagine anyone in their right mind naming their child after pudding, even if their last name was really pudding.

"Sorry, Tapioca. He was here earlier but left. I think he said he was going to celebrate his birthday early playing poker tonight."

"Oh, that's cool. I know how much he loves to play with the guys. Anyhow, could you leave this on his desk for me," she said, handing Susan a brown envelope containing her ultrasound pictures and a card.

"Sure thing," Susan said, taking the package from her hand.

*****

Tapioca stopped by the mall to pick up some new clothes. She was going to be someone's mother and had to start dressing the part. She couldn't wait to start showing so everyone would know. She also couldn't wait for Charles to return to his office and see the pictures of their baby. She thought of going to tell Charlotte, but then decided she wanted Charles to know first from her instead of Charlotte. She also couldn't wait to share her good news with her sisters. She hoped now she might have more in common with her youngest sister, which would help them become closer since they would both be mothers.

She stopped at her mailbox on her way in and noticed an envelope with her name but no address or postage marking. After she showered and got comfortable, she was about to open the envelope along with her other mail, when her doorbell rang. She swung the door open without checking, figuring it would be Charles.

"Jonathan? What are you doing here? I thought your wife just came back?"

Jonathan quickly pushed himself into Tapioca's house and closed the door. "Yeah, she is home, but I had to sneak away for a quick piece," he answered, while opening his pants and pulling Tapioca's arm to take her into the family room.

She jerked her arm away from him. "Uh-uh! Candy shop is closed, honey."

"Yeah right! Please! Get over here and stop playing. I don't have that much time, I told you."

His pants were down to his thighs, and his full erection was in his hand as he tugged at her nightgown. He ripped a condom open with his teeth and slipped it on in a single swoop using his one hand.

"Stop, Jonathan! I told you no. No more. I'm done!" she said, pulling away from him again.

This time, he snatched her arm more forcefully. "Fuck that shit! You can close shop tomorrow. Tonight, I need some strawberry."

Again, she snatched away from him and moved quickly towards her back door to get away from Jonathan, who was scaring her at that point. She knew Jonathan liked the rough stuff, but he didn't seem to be listening to her when she told him no.

Jonathan followed behind her, snatching her by the back of her hair as she almost made it out of the door. Tapioca's scream got cut off as her head jerked back. He wrestled her to the ground while she tried to fight him off of her and protect her baby. He completely ripped her gown off and wrestled her legs open until he was fully positioned between them, having his way with her as she cried. When he was done, he kissed her lips as if they had just finished making love.

Tapioca laid balled up naked on the floor by the door, crying for well over an hour after Jonathan left. She didn't know what to do. She knew no one would ever believe her if she called the police to report the rape. Any other day, she would have appreciated the pounding of Jonathan's long cock banging up against her cervix, but it was something about carrying Charles' baby that made the act a violation. Then she cried about the thought of Charles possibly having seen her with Jonathan since her back door was within his window's view. She hoped he was still playing poker.

*****

"I get sick every time I see that nasty bitch fucking yet another man."

"What are you talking about, Charlotte?" Charles asked when Charlotte greeted him coming into the house from his poker game.

"The nasty, trampy, white girl you were sticking your dick in, amongst other things. I just saw her on her floor with Karen James' husband. That's who she was all over in the grocery store yesterday.

She is nasty, Charles. I'm sorry. I know we agreed not to talk about her, but this is ridiculous. Do you know how difficult it is for me to get the images of you and her out of my head? But then to see her with everything attached to a penis… Ugh! How disgusting. I think we're going to need to get an AIDS test. I'm sorry. I know I also agreed to perform for you, Charles, but I can't do it until I know you have a clean bill of health. I'm not willing to die for that whore."

Charles could feel the vessels in his head about to explode. He looked forward to coming home and being with his newly submissive wife, only to find she had a new reason to withhold sex from him. He was equally disturbed to hear about Tapioca being with Jonathan again. He was glad he dropped that letter off. While he drove home, he had second-guessed himself. He thought of going by her mailbox and taking the letter if she hadn't already gotten it. He thought maybe he was being premature by cutting Tapioca off, not really knowing how long Charlotte could wear sheep's clothing before it tarnished.

"We can make an appointment sometime next month since it's about time for your annual physical. I just can't live like this."

"Next month?! My birthday is in three days. We can go get whatever tests to make you happy tomorrow. Furthermore, we can use a condom so you feel more comfortable in the meantime. I can't believe you'd want to punish me because you saw her screwing another man. I don't know why you were watching her anyway," Charles fussed as he looked at an unfazed Charlotte.

"It makes no sense to go tomorrow. If you did give me something, it's too soon for it to show up. Therefore, we can wait and go next month. Secondly, you know I'm allergic to latex. And you're questioning why I was watching the bitch? Why did I have to catch you watching her just last night with your face damn near pressed through the window trying to get her attention? I wanted to see exactly what you be waiting to see, and now I know. How could you want to be with a woman that you have watched many other men have sex with? I guess if you can watch that nasty porno stuff that corrupts your mind, then, of course, you'd want to watch everyone in the neighborhood dicking the child. What I want to know is how could you want to be with a white woman, Charles? Do you see how nasty they are?" Charlotte said with tears in her eyes and a cracked voice that made Charles feel bad.

"She's not white; she's bi-racial. And I think it's very unfair for you to generalize women based on their nationality or race. I have known some African-American women who were not the most honest."

Charlotte stared at Charles for the longest before she spoke.

"You're really in love with that girl. I can't believe you. You're standing here putting down your own people to defend that trashy whore. When I look at her, she's a white bitch, one that has no business with my husband or consuming my husband's thoughts. I am going to say this one time, Charles." She spoke with her hands on her hips and venom in her words. "It's going to either be her or me, and if you choose her, you can kiss the shirt on your back goodbye, because I will leave you with nothing for you and your whore. Do you hear me? NOTHING!"

Charles stood in the room off of the kitchen, as that was as far as he was allowed in from the garage before being confronted by Charlotte, who left him standing holding his ailing head in his hand.

16

Dear Tapioca,

It pains me to write you this letter in such an impersonal manner. I left a couple of notes asking for us to meet and talk face to face, but you didn't show up, which was probably for the best.

As you now know, I have decided to reconcile with my wife. I would have preferred to explain to you in person, but there's probably no good enough explanation for you to accept. You're a wonderful young lady, and I will always cherish the time we spent together. But, at this point in my life, I must get my priorities in order, and right now, my marriage is my priority. I'm sure this situation is going to be quite uncomfortable for all, to say the least, but I'm hoping we can be cordial with one another since we will be neighbors. Additionally, I'm going to have to ask you not to bother my wife anymore. Your lashing out at her will not change things for you and I. If you're going to be angry, please be angry with me and not my wife, who is just a victim in this affair. I wish you the best.

Regards,
Charles

Tapioca laid in her bed as she stared at the words on the letter, reading them over and over again. She was convinced Charlotte must have written the letter, because Charles would never be so heartless. She felt raped twice in the same night. At least the water helped soothe

the first raping, but she couldn't imagine what she could do to help her cope with the finality of Charles' piercingly harsh words. She felt degraded, and although she'd been with many men, she felt like a worthless, expendable piece of meat for the first time. A piece of meat about to give birth to the fruits of that heartbreaking affair.

She wanted to just go to sleep and never awake again, but she had a baby to consider: Charles' baby. Dr. Beaumont's words played over and over in her head. *Alternatives.* Perhaps she needed to consider her alternatives rather than raising a child that would never know its father as she never knew hers. She was the daughter of a whore, was a whore herself, and would probably give birth to another generation of whores. She cried herself to sleep while holding Charles' words to her bosom as she considered the alternatives she'd look into the next day.

Upon waking, her head was heavy and gave the feeling of a hangover. She looked at her swollen eyes in the mirror. She hardly recognized herself. When she walked downstairs to open her blinds that allowed a spectacular view of Los Angeles even in the daytime, her attention was drawn to the figure standing in Charles' office window. When she saw his attention appeared to be in her direction rather than the wonderful Hollywood Hills view, she held up her middle finger until he turned and walked away.

How dare he, she thought to herself. *If he thinks he's going to be able to just watch me whenever he chooses, he has another thing coming.*

Tapioca picked up the phone to get the information for the luxury retreat she had visited a few years ago. She would stay there for as long as needed to get over Charles. She decided she would return and put all of her love and energy into her baby and not focus on Charles being a part of their lives.

After she reserved her spot at the retreat, she called around until she was able to find a house sitter to watch her home while she was away. She was able to find a friend of her former porn colleague. The sitter was twenty-six years old. Tapioca felt she would be better than the twenty-one-year-old alternatives she was offered. Tapioca knew she was a very attractive woman, but when the statuesque 5'10" goddess showed up at her door, Tapioca felt inferior. Her complexion was like golden honey, and her slanted, light brown eyes gave the woman the ability to draw anyone looking into them. Her lean waistline didn't show an ounce of fat from beneath her cropped t-shirt. Even with the loose fitting USC gym sweats, it was obvious the woman had a well-chiseled ass. Her breast weren't as large as Tapioca's, but still, their fullness was enticing.

Upon sight, Tapioca's gut was to tell the woman, "Never mind," because she knew this woman would have Charles drooling, and Tapioca didn't want that. Then she thought about her purpose for leaving, which was to help put distance between her and the father of her child. On second thought, she couldn't wait for Charlotte and the rest of the neighborhood wives to catch a glimpse of the goddess-type woman who would have them all clutching their husbands tighter.

"Madison, thank you so much for doing this for me on such short notice. I really need to get away quickly."

"I should be thanking you. This house is spectacular, and this view is to die for," she answered, already looking out of the back door. "I can only imagine what the view must be like from the house up there," she added, pointing to Charles and Charlotte's home.

"Yeah, I'm sure it's pretty nice," Tapioca said, unenthused. "Well, let me show you around so you can get comfortable. I want you to be totally comfortable here, but just no parties. And I'd appreciate if you limit your guests in my home to no more than two. If anything goes missing or gets broken, I don't want to hear, 'I don't know who did it'."

"Five years ago, that was me. Believe me, I've had my one bad experience with the friends over. I currently am not dating, so I won't be having any boyfriends over. Actually, I'm working on my second novel, and this really works out for me while I work on that."

"Oh really? What's it about?" Tapioca asked, pleased with having a real author staying in her home.

"It's a psychological thriller about this man living a dual lifestyle. Eventually the two worlds clash, and he becomes desperate and will do anything to protect his secrets."

"WOW! Sounds exciting! I can't wait to read it."

"Well, it's going to be a while. I'm only up to the introduction. I like to write poetry in between."

"You are the busy one, aren't you?" Tapioca laughed, temporarily forgetting about her pain.

"I write music, as well. I've done pretty well with that. Had a few top 40's. My family always tells me I should perform them myself the same way Jill Scott did."

"I am so impressed right now. I can't believe you're a house sitter. Why? You could have your own mansion somewhere up in the Hills."

Madison laughed. "Hardly. I am an artist in every sense of the word. I need freedom to create. I can't be tied down. I love the different sceneries that come with house sitting. Just my being here, I can imagine the wealth of art that I could produce in here. I definitely will be painting this landscape before I leave."

"You paint, too?" Tapioca's amazement had yet to cease.

"I draw. I make clothes. I play the piano and guitar. I sing, studied ballet and contemporary dance, paint, and write," Madison boasted.

Tapioca thought to herself that her only talent was fucking. Sex was her art as she was very creative in finding ways to please her men. She felt inadequate. The more she listened, the more she realized she didn't have any real skills or talents. She wondered what she'd be able to teach her son or daughter. Suddenly, she didn't want to hear any more of Madison's accomplishments.

"Well, let me show you around so I can hurry up and get going. I'm sure you're anxious to get cracking on your art."

"Yes indeed," Madison answered, then followed Tapioca around the house.

Tapioca left her list of instructions before she hit the road to her secret luxury retreat where she would not be disturbed.

17

"I'm coming! Hold on!" Madison yelled out as she headed for the persistently ringing doorbell. "Can I help you?" she answered, not so polite.

"Where's Tapioca? I need to see Tapioca," Charles said frantically.

Madison looked at Charles as if he were a juicy steak to a poor man. She changed her abrasive tone. "I'm sorry, but she's not here."

"Where is she? I need to find her."

"Tapioca left three days ago. I'm her house sitter. From what I understand, she's going to be gone for a while."

"Where did she go? I have to find her. It's urgent," Charles said, pulling the envelope from his pocket that Tapioca left at his office a few days ago. "I have to see her now before it's too late."

"I'm sorry. I didn't catch your name."

"Charles. Charles Webb. I live at the top of the hill."

"Really?!" Madison said with more enthusiasm than she should have. "Well, I'm Madison. Nice to meet you."

Charles was not interested in all of the pleasantries. He needed to find the woman possibly carrying his child. He had been so busy with his brand-new pool table Charlotte let him purchase for his birthday, he hadn't been to his office to pick up the package his office manager Susan told him Tapioca had dropped off until that day. He was in no rush to go pick up a letter filled with what he expected to be hateful comments in response to how he had treated her. Instead, he found a greeting card showing a stork carrying a baby and that read "Congratulations". Also inside of the larger envelope were pictures from Tapioca's ultrasound. Both were inside a larger birthday card. He was no medical professional, but he immediately knew what the black and white pictures were, and he knew the card with the stork on it along meant he was finally going to be a father at fifty-one years of age.

He didn't know how they'd manage financially if Charlotte were to divorce him and take everything, but he knew that child would mean more to him than life itself. He knew one thing, and that was he had to find Tapioca before she aborted his child because she believed he no longer loved her. The moment he saw the contents of the package and cried like a baby inside of his office, he knew he was madly in love with Tapioca and would walk away from everything for her love. A child was the seal on their love and fate that they were meant to be together. He was going to be a father. The one thing he begged his own wife for, for many years, and more recently, she cut off his ability to touch her altogether.

"Could you please tell me where to find her?"

"I can't do that," Madison told him, getting annoyed by the fact that Charles hadn't taken a second look at her in a sensuous way. He paid no attention to cleavage busting out of her button- up shirt.

"Well, could you call her and tell her I need to see her?" Charles' eyes filled with tears as he spoke with urgency.

"I can't do that either. She didn't leave me anything other than a contact number for her sisters in New York and Pennsylvania. She distinctly said she didn't want anyone to know where she was going or when she'd be back."

"Oh hell!" Charles punched the frame of Tapioca's door, startling Madison. "I'm sorry. I didn't mean to scare you. I just need to find her." Charles pulled out his wallet and dug out a business card. "Here, this is my card. If you find out anything, please let me know as soon as you find out."

"Okay, but don't hold your breath. She doesn't want to be found."

Madison took the card, taking mental note of Charles' tantalizing fragrance he passed on the card. She watched as Charles quickly walked away. She didn't know who Charles was to Tapioca, but she knew she'd have Charles scratching that itch deep inside of her long before Tapioca returned.

*****

"Charles, who is that bimbo down there sunbathing and it's cold outside?"

"How the hell do I know? You're the one watching out of the window," Charles snapped at Charlotte, who insisted on keeping him company inside his office while he worked.

Charles had been in a bad mood for the past five days, ever since he learned of his expecting a child but could not find Tapioca. He thought of hiring a private investigator, but he changed his mind when he thought about Tapioca laying up somewhere with another man.

He noticed the beautiful Madison attempting to seduce him through the window, but he was not interested. He only wanted to find Tapioca. He wanted to go back and ask Madison if she heard anything, but he knew she was trouble. He needed to find Tapioca before he announced to the world that he was about to become a father. Also, he needed confirmation before he dealt the final blow to his farce of a marriage.

"She must be some kin to the white girl, because she's just as trashy. I'm sure she has got to see one of us in this window looking at her fool behind."

"Why don't you go down there and ask who she is? You're so interested in who she is and what she does. Just go down there then. I'm trying to work here."

"You don't have to be so nasty. I was just trying to make pleasant conversation with you. I've noticed you've been on edge lately. You need to get over yourself and stop acting like I've done something to you, when it was you frolicking with the whore."

Charles looked at his wife with pure disdain. He needed to find that videotape and get Charlotte out of his life. He knew Charlotte would never live down his relationship with Tapioca and certainly would never accept his possible child on the way. He had about all he could stand of the woman and her constant insults she was always dishing out.

"Charlotte, please leave my office. I am trying to work here," he said calmly after silently counting to ten.

"Work? That mess you scribble can't be work. That's why I told you to visit Japan. Now that's work. I think all you want is for me to leave out of here so you can watch the bimbo bitch down the hill. What, you wanna fuck her, too?"

"No, I already fucked her!" Charles lied to hit Charlotte back.

Her shocked expression was priceless. It took everything in him to keep from laughing. That certainly shut her up. He decided to lay it on thicker.

"Now that girl can suck a mean dick. You might want to tap on her door and ask for personal lessons."

Charlotte couldn't speak. She stood frozen for several minutes before she bolted out of his office sobbing. Charles felt overcome with guilt. He felt even worse for lying on the innocent woman.

His apology went out the window later that evening when the doorbell rang while the couple was having dinner. Charles let Charlotte answer since he knew it had to be the meddling Mrs. Vanderbilt.

"Charles! Your bitch is here, and you better come and handle this before I do," she yelled from the door as Charles was heading into the foyer area, surprised to see a confused Madison.

Charles felt guilty seeing the woman, as if he had actually slept with her.

"Bitch?! I'm sorry, did I do something to you?" Madison asked with her hands on her hips, practically daring Charlotte to repeat herself.

"I don't have time for this shit. Charles, get her away from my house," Charlotte said, walking away from the tall woman standing outside of the open door.

Charles hadn't noticed how attractive the woman was when he saw her days prior. She wore a mustard colored sweater dress that hugged her curves perfectly. The chilled evening air caused her nipple to protrude, bringing to his attention that she was not wearing a bra. His eyes scanned lower where he noted no panty or thong lines. Her long, golden legs that extended from her dress that stopped mid-thigh turned him on, and the strappy multi-colored sandals that were wrapped up her calves completed the sexiness in her sexy outfit. Finally, he looked back up into her golden eyes that smiled at him taking inventory of her assets. At that moment, he wanted to wrap her long legs around his waist, while pressing her against the wall and fucking her.

"I...I'm sorry about that. She saw you and thought I... we may have hooked up."

"You told me you fucked her!" Charlotte yelled from the doorway of the kitchen after hearing Charles. "Didn't you just tell me you fucked her? And now the bimbo boldly shows up at my door looking like a ten-cent ho!"

Charles stepped outside of his house and closed the door behind him when he noticed the disturbed look on Madison's face. "I'm so sorry you had to catch that."

Madison flashed a beautiful smile. "You told your wife we slept together? Why would you tell her something like that?"

"Long story, but in short, she already accused me of it. So, I told her I did to shut her up."

"Wow! I'm flattered I was part of the conversation," she chuckled. "Anyhow, I was on my way out, and I received a phone call. I've got some good news and some bad news. The good news is Tappy called and I let her know you were frantically looking for her. The bad news is she said she'll be away until the spring. She wanted to make sure I'd be okay staying for six months. I told her I didn't mind at all. Unfortunately, she still would not say where she was staying. She just said she'd be in touch."

"Six months?! Are you kidding? What the hell!" Charles said, expressing a combination of anger and hurt. As Madison spoke, his mind tuned her out while he calculated the twelve weeks from the ultrasound photos plus the six months. "That's nine months!" he randomly blurted out.

"Nine months? What's nine months?" Madison asked, confused.

The thought made Charles feel better about his concerns of Tapioca getting an abortion. He knew it meant that she was planning on returning with their child in tow. The thought was bittersweet. He wanted to be with her and take care of her as she carried his only child. He wanted to feel the baby's kicks and feed her all the foods she craved. He wanted to go to her medical appointments and hear the baby's heartbeat. He wanted to see his son or daughter born and cut the cord. But, then, he thought of all the stress and aggravation his dysfunctional marriage would cause the pregnancy, and he quickly decided it was best for her to be where she was at.

"What do you mean nine months? That's only six months," Madison repeated.

Charles caught himself. "Oh yeah, I meant to say six months. Please keep me posted."

Madison looked at him as if she wasn't buying his explanation. "Yeah, okay."

When she turned to walk away, Charles noticed the awesomely sculpted ass on her.

"By the way, very nice dress," he boldly complimented, forgetting about his wife on the other side of the door.

Madison slightly turned and flashed a smile. "Glad you like," she replied, then walked to her waiting car that she drove up the hill rather than having to walk up in her four-inch sandals.

Charles watched her walk all the way to her car. Madison was glad she managed to hold his attention. The truth is she had no place to be and had only put on the dress hoping Charles would be enticed. After she drove to a drive-thru for a burger, she went straight back to the house.

Charlotte threw water from her glass into Charles' face the second he re-entered the house. "And you wonder why I won't have sex with you? You disgust me! Don't you ever lay your finger on me again."

"Whatever, Charlotte. I've been cut off, remember?" he said, wiping the water from his face as he brushed past her in a fury.

She stayed on his heels. "Then you ask why I refuse to give you oral sex? That's why!" she said, pointing towards the door as if Madison were still there. "You obviously don't realize just how much you have to lose. I'm not going to take much more of this nonsense. If I didn't have to go back to court because of your white girl, I would have put a gun right between this bitch's eyes and sent her ass fleeing. Then she'd know never to bring her behind around here again."

"Oh, now you're some gangster with a gun?" he laughed. "I don't get it. You have a problem with the one because you insist she's a 'white girl', although she's not. Well, this one is black. Does it sit better with you if I were fucking her since she's not white?" Charles amused himself and walked away before Charlotte could answer.

"Where is your respect for this marriage, Charles? I'm your wife. What happened to the vows you made to me?" she asked, hanging on his heels.

"You destroyed those vows when you single-handedly decided when we could and could not enjoy our marital bed. How is it you got to decide if I would be able to relieve my loins? First, you withhold sex from me, your husband, and then you want to make sure I don't relieve myself by destroying any sex video I own."

Charles decided to bait Charlotte in order to find the video of him and Tapioca so she wouldn't have it as evidence for a judge to watch and then gain sympathy when it came time for the divorce settlement.

"And don't think I don't know your uptight ass is watching the video you've been holding hostage. I can tell you watch it almost daily."

Charlotte turned flushed, letting Charles know the video was at least in the house.

"For your information, I left the nasty thing in Japan. Speaking of which, I will be leaving after my court date and gone for three weeks. That'll give you plenty of time with your whores."

Charles shook his head in disgust. "So you had no intentions of trying to fix this marriage, did you? You've barely been back a month and already have your next trip planned. Why didn't you just stay there? No, you had to come back and try to ruin any chances of me possibly being happy. You came back promising to change and do what was necessary to fix this marriage. Yes, I was with the girl, but for the sake of fixing our marriage, I was willing to walk away from her."

"That's a damn lie! You were the one unwilling to fix this marriage. I had to threaten you with a damn video to get you to agree to work on this marriage. All you've been doing is trying to play me to get your hands on that videotape. Don't think I haven't noticed how you've been snooping through my belongings and trying to say things to trick me into saying where the video is. Well, let me put you out of your misery. The hard copy is in Japan. I have the video saved on my laptop. I have it in my email files, and I have a copy in my office downtown. I'm not sure how stupid you think I am. I knew I wasn't the best wife. That's why I was willing to make some concessions for the marriage. But, despite my efforts, you feel you don't have to do anything to save this marriage. You're out there in the streets with those no-good friends of yours; you turn my beautiful home into a piece of classless junk. And now you're trying to press me for the whereabouts of the video of you and your whore. Guess what? You'll never get your hands on it, so I'd highly suggest you get your act together and do right by this marriage."

Charles was livid. There was no way he'd ever get those videos away from Charlotte's hand. Knowing Charlotte the way he did, the video would be viral with the press of one button. He didn't know how much ass kissing he would be able to tolerate. She was right. He had no interest in fixing their marriage anymore, particularly with the expectation of a child with a woman he did love.

"What else should I be doing, Charlotte? What else do you want from me? You want me sexually deprived. You want to continually berate my trade that has provided this house that you just had to have. You limit the time I can spend with my friends. Then you want to continually leave me with no form of human companionship because you need to be in Japan more than you need to be with your husband. So I ask, what else do you want from me?" he questioned, looking into Charlotte's diverting eyes. "You don't even know what you want, so you can't answer that, can you? Can you even say why you want to save this marriage? Can you?!" he yelled.

Tears streamed down Charlotte's cheeks. Without answering, she turned away from Charles to collect the dishes from the counter. After several minutes of silence, Charles realized he was not going to get an answer. He returned upstairs to his office to retrieve the ultrasound pictures that he looked at a minimum of three times a day since receiving them.

He wondered where Tapioca was and what she was doing. He wondered if she was alone. His heart grieved when he thought about the harsh letter he placed in her mailbox before she left. He wondered if his letter was what drove her away.

After returning the pictures to their safe place, he went to stand near his large window to get lost in the breathtaking view of the city, but his mind drifted to the first time he caught a glimpse of the strawberry-blonde bombshell. He smiled at the thought of how he became so fixated on her without ever seeing her face. He had fallen in love before knowing what she looked like or anything about her. He felt a throbbing between his legs while thinking about the first time they were together. Then his heart sank as he looked at the open blinds of Tapioca's house and reflected on the many occasions he had endured watching her with other men. The thought of her screwing old man Vanderbilt the day after her leaving him was unsettling. Anger set in when he thought about the day before Tapioca's leaving and Charlotte telling him that she saw Tapioca having sex with Jonathan…while carrying his child. Then he wondered just how many men's dicks were banging on his unborn child's head.

Charles punched the wall beside the window with the side of his fist. He was about to turn to walk away, when he saw movement inside Tapioca's house. His eyes stayed focused, not sure what he expected to see. He waited and waited and waited.

At last, there she was…standing as naked as the day she entered the world. She stood at the back door eating a bowl of something, while gazing out at the bright lights that Charles had just been admiring moments before.

He was mesmerized. His face was pressed against the window, wanting a closer look of the au natural beauty Madison had on display. After a few moments, she walked away, not returning. Charles spent the next hour by the window, waiting to see Madison again. However, she didn't return that night.

The next night, he was prepared with his binoculars when Madison stood eating a bowl of cereal in a negligee. He loved the silhouette of her body underneath. This became his new nightly ritual, just as it became Madison's nightly ritual to provide the incognito expedition of standing nude or next to nude while eating a bowl of cereal before going to bed. Charles became all the more fascinated when he realized that out of the two weeks he had been watching her, he hadn't seen one man or woman with Madison. He also loved watching her stand outside painting during the days.

By the third week, he was hoping she'd find a reason to call him. He knew she wouldn't come back to the house after how Charlotte behaved.

18

Charles was exceptionally glad when the judge gave Charlotte probation, but allowed her to return to Japan for her job. Charlotte told Charles that she would be back in three weeks, but Charles hoped she would stay gone longer. As quick as Charlotte's flight took off, Charles was making his move.

"Hi. I was just stopping by to see if you heard anything new lately," he said when Madison answered the door.

"No, I haven't heard anything since I told you a few weeks back. I've definitely been learning she was quite the popular one around these parts. I don't know how many people have come here looking for her, wanting to know when she'd be returning," Madison spitefully shared with Charles to make him aware that he wasn't Tapioca's only game in town. Charles' face was unable to hide its disappointment. "I'm sorry. Did I upset you or something?" She tried to play coy.

"No, no... I'm fine," he said, trying to quickly recover with a nervous chuckle. "Yeah, she was very popular." There was an awkward silence between the two as Charles thought of what he could say next to help him get closer to Madison. "So I noticed you're an artist. What kind of things do you paint?"

Madison smiled, glad he found a way to keep the conversation going. "I could paint anything. I do it for relieving stress. I've been drawing and painting since I was a little girl."

"Well, you're certainly not little anymore," Charles laughed.

Madison just raised her eyebrow at his corny come-on line.

"I'm sorry. I was out of line."

"No need to apologize. If you'd like, you can come in and take a look at some of my work." She paused as she opened the door wider. "Oh, I forgot about your wife. I'm not trying to get you in any trouble. Maybe some other time."

"No, no! I'd love to see. My wife just left for Japan. She knows I love art. I particularly love sculptured pieces," Charles shared to prevent losing out on his opportunity to spend time with Madison.

He was already turned on by the oversized men's shirt she wore. He loved the way the buttons revealed just enough cleavage to make you want to see more. Her erect nipples were also turning him on. Her lower buttons, unbuttoned, revealed enough thighs to take the imagination on a sensual journey. He was horny and didn't have any hopes for relief from his wife or Tapioca. He was a man with needs, and Madison would more than do for the occasion.

"I don't have any sculptured pieces here to show you. Sometimes I model for my sculpting class. It's invigorating, but in a classy way. I believe the human body is a beautiful thing. It is art. I love painting the woman's body. I have painted many of those, but people are always offering to buy them as quick as they're done," she told Charles, while leading him into the den where she had a collection of her works.

Charles looked around at her paintings and drawings. "These are absolutely beautiful. Is this one you?" he asked when he came to a painting of a nude woman.

Madison blushed. "Yeah, that's me. I know you're probably wondering who paints themselves nude."

"I am just amazed at the realness of the picture. It's almost three-dimensional. How did you do this? It's amazing. All of these are amazing."

"I stood in front of a mirror and painted myself. It's simple. I captured myself and then added on my background." Madison flipped through some of her canvases. "Thought you might find this one interesting."

Charles became embarrassed when he saw a painting of his house and him standing at his office window just as he did in reality. She managed to capture the scenery behind his house perfectly.

"Was I that bad? I stood long enough for you paint me?" he laughed. "And what's that in my hand?"

She laughed. "I added a telescope. Figured it would tell more of a story. And no, I didn't mind your standing there at all," she said, switching to seductive. "It made me feel less lonely."

"You lonely? Come on! You're far too beautiful for that."

She shrugged her shoulder and turned away to conceal her hurt of being lonely.

"Are you serious? I would think a woman as stunning and sophisticated as you, not to mention talented, would have a line of guys vying for her heart."

"Uh…not quite. Someone forgot to give all those guys the memo," she laughed. "I think I house sit just to convince myself that I volunteered to be alone. It's been almost eight months since I've been with a man. I'm starting to think I need to become a nun."

Charles felt his dick go "BOINK!" at the mere mention of her unwanted celibacy.

"Did you make up your mind one day that you were going to be celibate or what? How did that come about?"

"Believe me, I never signed up to be celibate. It's crazy. Guys don't seem to want a woman who is single and available. I don't get that. I think they think something must be wrong with me. I think some guys probably think I'm one of those guys who had their sex changed, based on my height."

"Please! There is nothing masculine about you. You are drop-dead gorgeous. If anything, men might find your beauty intimidating."

"Why thank you. That was very kind of you to say."

As Madison bent over to pick up a smaller picture from the collection on the floor, her shirt hiked up enough to give Charles a peek at her kitty. He went and stood directly behind her, leaving about a half of inch of space between himself and her ass.

"What are you doing?" she asked, putting him on blast as she returned to an upright position with him on her ass.

Charles stepped back, embarrassed by the rejection. He wanted her…bad.

"I'm sorry. I don't know what came over me," he answered in a whisper as he tried to clear his throat. "Well, I guess I better be going now. I'm sure I have some work to get done."

Madison tightly closed her eyes as she contemplated going for the gusto. She wanted him to touch her, but she didn't want the troubles that went along with the married man who obviously was involved with the owner of the house she temporarily resided in.

She turned to face Charles so he could see she had undone the buttons to her shirt, which revealed her nakedness beneath it. Charles' eyes lit up like Christmas. His hands gently caressed her face before taking it in his hands to kiss her lips. His hungry mouth devoured her waiting breasts. She held the back of his head as if her life depended on her holding on. He peeled the shirt from her shoulders so he could see her without any barriers. He enjoyed what he saw. She removed his shirt, revealing his sculptured chest. She could see that he took pride in his body. She slowly undid his belt as she stared into his eyes. Her stare was hypnotic as were her hips. He ran his hands up and down them as she opened his pants.

"Whoa! Didn't expect this," Madison chuckled at the sight of Charles' hard nine inches that emerged.

He immediately became insecure, not knowing if her reference was a compliment or dissatisfaction.

"Now this is art!" she said, while moving her fingers back and forth on it before fully gripping it in her hands. "You mind?" she asked as she bent to take it into her mouth.

It was in her mouth before Charles could object. His ego was restored as her tongue alternated between teasing his tip and sucking the head. Charles felt his knees ready to buckle from under him when his entire dick made its way into her mouth. It came without warning, and she showed no mercy. She was on her knees before him, with her long nails pressed into his buttocks as her throat sucked his dick. Charles held onto the back of Madison's head almost as tight as she was holding onto his ass. When he came to a point where he was about to erupt, he stopped her, although he really wanted her to swallow his fluids. Since this was their first time together, he couldn't trust himself to perform with a quick comeback if he were to let go. He had a difficult time stopping her and getting her to let go.

As he helped Madison back to her feet, his eyes suddenly made contact with Tapioca's eyes in the large painted picture hanging on the wall behind Madison. He felt conviction trying to muscle out his horniness. He tried to move Madison so he didn't have to look at the picture or feel Tapioca's eyes boring a hole through him. He was losing his erection and the battle. Everywhere he looked, he began seeing himself with Tapioca in that particular spot. Then it occurred to him that he was in her house about to fuck her house sitter, while she was somewhere trying to protect their child from the stress of his marriage.

Madison lifted a foot on the chair and took Charles' hand between her wet legs. That helped him to refocus on Madison for the moment, and minutes later, he had her legs wrapped around his waist with her pressed up against the wall, just as he had imagined. He pounded inside of her in that position until his legs and back began to weaken. Then they moved to the sofa and then the floor.

"Man-o-man! That was some workout," Madison said when she finally caught her breath as she lay in his arms on the floor. "You are definitely a pleasant surprise. I don't know why I expected less from you," she laughed.

"You weren't too bad yourself," he laughed back. "That was a damn good workout. You have some interesting art. I enjoyed it very much."

Madison looked over her shoulder at Charles, trying to figure out what he was talking about. Then he patted her hip to confirm that he was talking about the sex and not her paintings.

She laughed. "Yeah, I like your art, too."

"I'm laying here as if I don't have some work I need to be doing. You feel so good next to me, I hate to move."

"This does feel good. You already know it's been a very long time for me. I just hope this won't be our last time."

Madison pressed her ass against Charles, hoping to arouse him for another round before he left her.

"We'll see. Can't make any promises. I didn't expect this," Charles answered, not rising to the subtle request for another round.

He kissed the back of her neck and got up from the floor. Then he held out his hand to help her up.

"You need a towel or something to wash up with?" she asked, being the gracious hostess.

"No, I'm going straight to my house. I'll just hop in the shower before getting back to work," he answered as he put his clothes on while trying to avoid Tapioca's watchful eyes.

He also avoided looking into Madison's eyes since he wasn't sure if he wanted to sleep with her again. He didn't want to hurt her feelings, but he was horny and she was convenient. Nothing more than that.

19

"I have an announcement to make," Charles said to his three best friends while they were assembled at Larry's house to watch the opening round of NCAA Basketball.

"You're finally getting a divorce?" Arty said, and the others laughed.

"Well, that's probably inevitable. Hell, I might need a place to stay when she gets through with me."

"Uh-oh! That can't be good. You sure don't look like a man about to lose it all. As a matter of fact, you look almost happy," Edward commented before taking a swig of his beer.

"You still doing that clingy house sitter? The bitch sounds like a fatal attraction," Larry asked.

The other guys nodded in agreement.

"Oh, I know what your announcement is. Charlotte finally decided to give you some," Edward joked.

"Or maybe Fatal Attraction decided she has a friend and wants a threesome."

The men laughed as if that was the funniest joke ever told.

"Can I talk before halftime is over?" Charles asked, pretending he was angry. When the guys got quiet, he said, "I'm going to be a father. I have a little girl on the way."

Charles' friends looked at each other before erupting into laughter. They laughed so hard, they cried. Charles remained serious.

"Man, you're serious? 'Evilene' is finally giving you a kid?" Larry said, then paused for a thought. "Hold up! I thought she wasn't giving you any?"

"That's how them women be when they get pregnant. They don't be wanting anyone to touch them," Arty added. "I remember when my kids' momma was pregnant. She wouldn't even let me look at it."

"Not Charlotte. Tapioca," Charles proudly corrected. "She's due the end of next month. She sent me the pictures of the baby. They were in color, and you could actually see her face. It's a girl. She's beautiful."

The guys sat and looked at their longtime friend in shock. They were still trying to figure out if Charles was joking, but he seemed too serious and convincing to be lying or joking.

"Why y'all looking at me like that? I have the pictures to prove it." He stood up and produced the envelope of new photos Tapioca sent to his office, along with a note that simply read, "Your daughter."

Edward took the envelope and pulled out the three pictures, passing them around after he looked at them. The men were speechless, while Charles stood there smiling, glad to finally share the good news he kept from his friends for five months.

"Is this some kind of joke?" Arty finally asked.

"That's my daughter. After fifty-one years, I'm finally going to have my own child. You don't understand how much this means to me," Charles pleaded, trying to convince his friends to support his joy.

"I want to be happy for you, Charlie, but that girl is too young, fast, and loose for you to have to be tied to with a child. You talk about my being married twenty-six years now, but don't think it was easy. Trying to raise those kids was hard work, but both of us were mature minded to work together to get it accomplished. I don't think that young girl has the mental capacity to raise a child with you. Hell, Eddie Jr. is older than she is. She should be having my grandchild, not having your child.

She could be your daughter having your granddaughter."

"Alright, Eddie, now you're talking crazy! Girls younger are having babies. I love that girl, and I'm happy she's giving me the single most important thing to me."

"Well, it better mean a lot to you, 'cause you know Charlotte's gonna own everything you got when she finds out," Larry chuckled.

"I've got one question for you," Arty said to Charles. "What is it about this girl that got you so wide open? Why her? What do you have in common with her? If she couldn't give you sex, what will you have left?"

Charles sat and thought about Arty's questions. The truth is he didn't know why he loved Tapioca. He just knew he did. He knew he enjoyed her presence when she stayed with him. He loved watching her sleep. He loved bathing her while she was a chatterbox. He felt an overwhelming need to protect her even though she didn't know she needed protecting. He had an unconditional love that went way beyond sex. No matter what wrong she'd done, he still loved her. The more he thought about it, the more he realized he loved Tapioca as if she were his very own daughter, with the added benefits of a sexual relationship.

"I just love her. That's all there is to it. And it's not about the sex, because that other young girl doesn't make me feel anything for her."

"If you love the girl so much, then what you doing screwing the house sitter right there in her house? How long you gonna keep boning her ass? Until your baby momma comes back home?" Larry asked.

"You know what I think," Arty interrupted before Charles could answer Larry. "I think your fixation on that girl goes all the way back to Eddie's bachelor party. I think that young girl takes you back to that time, and you think you can just fix that two-second slip up you had with the raspberry-blonde girl who had everybody laughing at you that night. I think you just feel the need to redeem yourself and try to prove you can keep up, even though that was twenty-six years ago."

The men looked at Arty as if he may have been on to something, but then Edward and Larry broke out laughing.

"Okay, Dr. Phil," Larry said in between his laughter. "Think you've had enough beer, Art?"

"Please, I don't have anything to prove to anyone. I saw the young lady, was attracted to her, and we hit it off. It's as simple as that," Charles snapped. "Ain't nobody trying to hear that nonsense."

"You know, as crazy as it sounds, Arty may be right. Think about it. Once upon a time, you didn't give a damn what color the booty attached to the giving pussy. You'd take what you could get, but after that girl dissed you at my bachelor party all those years ago, you vowed to hate all white or white-looking girls. They had to be purple-black for you to give them the time of day. Now this girl comes along who supposedly has the same color hair and looks white like the woman from the party, and you're all over it like you're chasing some ghost. Explain that," Edward stated.

"There's nothing to explain. She happened to be a single young lady who came at me first. She was attractive, I wasn't getting any from my wife, and the rest is history. I didn't go looking for her. I didn't pick out that museum-looking house, and I didn't send my wife away, leaving me alone."

"If that's the story you tell yourself, then it's okay with me. The way I know it, you've been sex-starved your whole marriage. I even tried to set you up for some action a few times, but you were busy being Mr. Faithful. I don't care why you got the girl; I just hope she keeps the pipe properly greased for you," Larry said.

"So what are you going to do when the girl finds out you've been tappin' the house sitter's ass in her house and in her bed?" Edward asked. "You know she's going to find out."

"Hopefully, she'll forgive me. I'm sure she'll understand," Charles answered.

"Why are you still sleeping with that girl? That's the part I can't understand. You say you don't have any feelings for her and you hope she's not catching feelings, but you're still sticking her," Arty pointed out.

"That is strictly sex for me. I enjoy sex with her. There's nothing else to it. We've talked about this, and she says she's okay with the arrangement we have for as long as we can have it."

"If the other girl loves you so much, why is she running from you while she's supposed to be carrying your seed? Maybe she doesn't know who the father is," Edward said.

Charles' eyes looked as if he could kill Edward for suggesting such a thing. "There would be too much stress for her while carrying the baby. Charlotte already tried to fight her while she was pregnant without knowing about the baby. Then the neighbors give her a hard way to go, and finally, me. I gave her a cold letter the day before she left, telling her I was going to be with my wife and not her…"

"Do y'all realize there is only three minutes left in the game?" Arty cut Charles off to inform the guys.

"Aw man! What the hell?!" Larry shouted when he saw the time on the large television screen. "Sitting here talking about babies and pussy…"

"Now ain't nobody talk about the punanny," Arty laughed. "We've been talking about some soap opera story mess. But, I'm happy for you, Ole Charlie. You deserve this. I hope your daughter turns out to be beautiful and happy and looks like her momma and not her daddy," Arty said, standing to hold up his bottle of beer for a toast.

The guys stood and joined his toast, then hugged Charles.

"And whatever you do, don't let her mother try to name her after another flavor of pudding. It's bad enough her mother did that to them kids," Arty laughed, and the others agreed.

It made Charles feel better to know his friends would accept his woman and his child. He loved his friends because they were real talk and still respected the other. The biggest fallout they ever had in all their years of friendship was when Larry tried to warn Charles about marrying Charlotte. Charles got offended by Larry's comments about his bride-to-be, but before long, Charles was agreeing with Larry and the two made up. However, it was too late because he had already married her.

Charles could hardly concentrate on the game because his mind was swinging back and forth like a pendulum. One thought was about his baby, while the other thought was about the sex he was going to have with Madison when he left from Larry's place. He didn't dare tell his friends that Madison had made several references to him being her man. He didn't dare correct her and tell her that she didn't stand a chance at winning his heart because he didn't want to lose the good loving she gave so frequently and freely.

He had gotten so bold that he'd sneak down to the house and have sex while Charlotte was up the hill in the house still depriving him sexually. With Madison, he hadn't made a single attempt to touch Charlotte nor ask for any. Of course, that only made Charlotte more bitter than she already had been. He didn't understand why she wouldn't just leave and never come back since she was so miserable with him. If it weren't for his name on the mortgage, he would have left already. He couldn't wait for Tapioca to return with their daughter so Charlotte could see her and flip out. He already made up his mind that he'd spend all the time he wanted with his child, and there was nothing Charlotte could do about it.

The guys' loud cheers and celebration brought his mind back to real life. The game was over, and thankfully, the television kept showing a last-second shot from half court that won the game. Charles celebrated late after seeing the replay.

20

When Charles arrived at his office the next day after a joyous, full night of sex with Madison, his office manager Susan handed him an envelope that had been delivered by messenger.

"This came for you today. I wasn't sure you were going to make it in today."

"Yeah, I figured I could get more work done if I came in. Too many distractions at home."

"Your wife is working from the house, also?"

"She's home today working my nerve first thing this morning," he said, shaking his head as if Charlotte had no right to raise hell about him spending the night out and returning home after the delicious breakfast Madison served him along with some morning loving.

Charles was getting fed up with all of Charlotte's empty threats of divorcing him and leaving him penniless. That morning, he told her she could go and have all that a judge would give her. Then came the crocodile tears. It was the same routine, and he was tired of it. At that point, he figured he might as well live his life as if he were single since he didn't have a true marriage any longer. It had been months since he had been able to touch his own wife and his getting tested for every disease at his annual physical didn't help any. He didn't care anymore, and at fifty-one, he was planning on living his life on his terms from then on.

Madison was slowly but surely helping Charles get over his obsessive love for Tapioca. He still had love for her, but being with Madison made him feel like he didn't want to be tied down or committed to any one woman anymore. He thought about seeing Madison whenever Tapioca returned and any other woman he found attractive. Additionally, he thought of having sex with his neighbor, Karen James, just to piss Jonathan off, who he greatly despised.

His good friend Edward was right when he said there was a time when Charles did not discriminate when it came to the woman's nationality. The only requirements were to have a nice, sexy body and been born a female. After the bachelor party fiasco, Charles' confidence dropped tenfold. He felt as if he had become cursed for not respecting women prior to that time. After a while, he would reject women making passes at him for fear of another disaster. Instead, he focused on work rather than sex, but eventually became lonely. Of course, with his luck, he'd marry a woman who had no qualms with bashing his already deflated ego…not only sexually but professionally, as well.

For the longest time, Charles didn't think he was capable of satisfying a woman. Then Tapioca came along and changed all of that for him. She was a porno queen, and he was able to satisfy her. That was a major ego boosting. Madison also made him feel like he was the hottest thing happening. Now he was getting his confidence back up and was ready to test bigger waters. He also was glad he was able to satisfy without the help of any little blue pills or other sexual enhancement pills. With his hair beginning to gray, he thought of shaving his head bald since so many younger girls liked a bald head these days, but Madison told him that she preferred it graying rather than bald. He was thankful to still have his own hair covering his head, unlike most men his age. He was even prouder of his chiseled physique that had women of all ages and nationalities turning their heads to take a second look. He attributed his chiseled body to Charlotte since he would constantly use working out in the gym as therapy for the stress and lack of sex.

"I don't mean to be up in your business, but I don't know how you stay married to that lady. She is not a nice person. I can only imagine what your life is like trying to work from home with her there."

Charles laughed at Susan not holding back. "Trust me, I ask myself the same thing every day."

"Charles, you deserve to be happy. Life is too short, and you're not getting any younger. I remember all the times you talked about having a family. Now I cringe at the thought of you having a family with that woman. Keep wasting time with that marriage, and you're going to lose out on any hope of ever having a family. All of the women will be menopausal and going through the change of life like me."

Charles was smiling like a Cheshire cat. "Come here, I have something to show you," he told her as he walked into his office, closing the door after making sure there were no spies. He pulled out the envelope that held the pictures and handed it to Susan.

Her eyes widened as she looked at the baby in each picture. "Oh my goodness! How?! When? Oh my goodness, goodness! Your wife is expecting?" she asked, already knowing the envelope came from Tapioca Pudding.

"Unfortunately not. Now no one knows about this yet, so I don't want you saying a word to anyone."

"Charles, you must be so excited. Congratulations! When are you expecting?"

Charles couldn't stop smiling. "I am so excited, and thank you. She should be here next month. I can hardly wait."

"Wow! This is amazing. It's a girl, I take it?"

"Yep! That's my baby girl."

"Is it that young lady I met last summer?"

"That's her."

"How is your wife taking the news, or have you told her yet?"

Charles laughed. "Yeah right! No, she doesn't know yet. When the time is right, she'll know."

"Next month? I think the time is now, unless you're trying to wait on the paternity test. You are getting one, right? You know momma's baby is poppa's maybe."

"Well, I hadn't really thought about it. The time is right. I'm pretty certain that's my daughter."

Susan put her hand on Charles' shoulder as she looked up into his eyes. "Look here now. I know you're all syked up about being a daddy, but instead of being *pretty certain*, be totally certain. Get the test. That way, you will never have a doubt in your mind. Hell, my own daughter had to test two guys before she found the third guy who was the baby's daddy. I thought if that happened to one of my sons, I would have to kick the girl's ass."

Charles laughed as he turned to walk to his seat behind his desk. He didn't want to hear any doubts about his daughter's paternity. At the same time, he knew with Tapioca's lifestyle he probably needed that test more than anyone.

"I guess you're right. It can't hurt. Well, of course, I'd be devastated if I learned she wasn't my daughter, especially because I want her to have my last name. I'd hate for my child to go through life with the name Pudding. It's hard to take a person seriously."

"Well, just wait until after that test. The name can be changed up to a year. Trust me, my daughter had to change the name of my grandson."

"Thanks for the advice, and please, please, please, not a word about this to anyone." Charles was ready to get rid of Susan so he could tear into Tapioca's newest envelope that had been freshly delivered.

Susan pretended to be locking her lips and throwing away the key. "Not a word." She headed to the door. "Get to work, dad," she said just before opening the door and leaving.

Charles opened the envelope and found a very pregnant photo of

Tapioca. She was glowing in the picture. He noticed the colorful mountain scenery in the background, letting him know she was somewhere in the southwest. Although she was beautiful, she was fat. That turned Charles off. He liked a fat ass and fat tits, but not a fat woman. Tapioca's picture was making Madison more attractive by the second. She was even making Charlotte with her mustache, facial hairs and all, more attractive. The more he looked at the picture, the hornier he became for Madison. He was totally disappointed with how Tapioca grew. He only hoped she'd lose the weight after having the baby, just as her sister Vanilla did. He had no intentions of touching her again until she did lose the weight.

He pulled out a letter from the envelope:

My Dearest Charles,

I thought with time and distance, my love for you would fade. As our daughter continues to grow inside of me, so does my love for you. I know you said you didn't want to be with me anymore, and I've been trying to accept that. It's just harder to accept while carrying our child.

I've been staying in Sedona in a stress-free atmosphere. I want our baby to be completely healthy, which is why I've decided to have the baby here. I just wish for you to be a part of the experience with me. I understand you have an obligation to your wife. I just pray you won't turn your back on us. I need your love. Our daughter needs your love, also. I will send you the address when I get closer to the time of birth. I hope you will be able to share in the arrival of our baby. I have enclosed a picture of me just in case you had any doubts if I was really pregnant. I love you and miss you. Hope to see you next month.

Oh, I almost forgot. If you get a chance, can you go by my house and get one of my bedrooms ready for the baby? I'll call my house sitter to let her know to expect you. Her name is Madison. Hopefully, she'll be pleasant to you, with the intrusion and all. She's a friend of my friend, so I don't really know her all that well. Again, I hope to see you soon.

Love,
Tapioca ~ Your Favorite Strawberry Blonde ;-)

Charles could feel a distressful electrical sensation buzzing in his head. He did not want to have a conversation with Madison about his expecting a child with Tapioca. In all this time, he failed to let Madison know he was intimately involved with Tapioca, and she never asked. Now, not only would she know they were involved, but she would know about the baby, as well. The revelation was likely to dampen his sex life with her.

Surprisingly, the news of the baby did not cut off his sex. If anything, it enhanced it. Madison even helped Charles set up the nursery for the baby. She went to the store to pick out the baby's furniture, while Charles got the room in order. The more easygoing Madison was, the more Charles found himself drawn to the young woman. He started thinking ahead of how he'd be able to continue his relationship with Madison once Tapioca returned to stake her claim, just as Charlotte had done when it was Tapioca on the scene.

For the next month, Charlotte quietly took a backseat to Madison and Charles' blatant affair, choosing to hang around more than ever. She would watch her husband in the arms of the other woman from the window in his office. She knew when Charles finished sowing his wild oats, he'd return to being the man she married and they'd grow old together as planned, the same way her sisters and parents had also remained in their marriages.

As much as she hated what was happening, she knew with eleven years together, this was a temporary phase Charles was going through. She felt it was a privilege to have a gorgeous husband that every woman wanted. She just had a hard time accepting him touching her while he was touching those girls, but she knew she was knocking on the door of him divorcing her. Therefore, something had to give soon.

21

"Baby, I'm going to miss you when you leave tomorrow. I wish you didn't have to go," Madison said, lying in Charles' arms after their lovemaking.

"I know. I'm going to miss you, too. Unfortunately, we knew this time was coming. You definitely will be seeing a lot of me in the future, though," Charles responded, kissing her neck.

"Ooh! I like that. You know I can't get enough of this beautiful, big dick. I wish we could live together. I love going to bed with you inside of me. I love waking up with you inside of me. I love kissing your lips with the rising of the morning sun, even before you brush your teeth," she laughed.

"It does feel pretty good, doesn't it?"

"It feels perfect. I love feeding you grapes."

"I prefer these grapes," he said, gently pinching one of her nipples between his thumb and forefinger.

"You so nasty!" she giggled while pressing her ass against his still wet dick as she anticipated their next round.

She turned her neck to position her face in order to receive his mouth on hers. His hand cupped her breast one at a time before sliding down past her navel to tickle her clit. She slightly parted her thighs, allowing him deeper access. He quickly rose for the occasion and pressed his way back inside of her from behind until he found her hot, wet blanket to keep his hard cock warm.

He liked to have died when he heard Madison say, "I love you, too," in response to his slipped words during the heat of the moment. He told her that he loved her. Yet, he did not love her. He just enjoyed and greatly appreciated her. Charles was so disgusted with himself for letting the words slip, even though it was a lie.

"Damn, I just remembered some stuff I have to get done before I hit the road tomorrow," Charles lied, looking for a quick exit.

She pouted. "Are you kidding?! You're spoiling the moment."

"Baby, I'm so sorry. It just hit me. You know I wouldn't go if I didn't have to," he answered, while quickly dressing without bothering to clean his body of Madison's juices that were still wet on him.

"You're coming back, right?" she asked with a hint of attitude as she got up and put on a robe.

Charles was halfway down the steps, trying to avoid Madison's instantly growing wrath. "I don't want to say yes and not make it back. I just remembered this design that was to be completed this week. I need to get it done and sent in to the office before I can leave."

Madison wasn't buying it. "Do I look stupid to you, Charles? What kind of cockamamie bullshit is that? You of all people are meticulous when it comes to your calendar and your to-do list, and now you want me to believe you *suddenly* remembered a project due this week? You're running up there to fuck that bitch before you leave, aren't you?"

Charles looked both nervous about being caught in his lie as well as confused as he wondered which 'bitch' Madison could have possibly been talking about.

"Who are you talking about?" he asked, still unable to process it.

"Your wife! Don't try to play dumb with me, motherfucker! How are you just going to lie to me right after telling me you love me? Or was that a fucking lie, too? Do you love me, Charles? Do you really fucking love me, or am I just a convenient piece of ass to you?" she asked, calling him out.

"Look, all this name calling and madness, I can do without. I have been nothing but honest with you this whole time, and now you want to act indifferent…"

"INDIFFERENT?! How dare you say I'm acting indifferent when it was you who lied the whole time, knowing you were about to have a baby with this slutty, mutt-looking bitch," she said, referring to Tapioca. "I accepted that shit as long as I knew you were going to be with me instead of her ass. I even tried to believe your ass when you told me that you were only going there for the baby and not to be with her. But, now you wanna run up out of here with some lame-ass lie about work you need to finish?"

"That is not a lie. As a matter of fact, before I leave, I will show you the design so you will know I'm not lying," Charles conceded, not knowing why or what design he would concoct to show as proof.

Madison quickly lightened up and smiled. "Really?"

"Yes, really."

Madison went and hugged Charles around his neck, kissing his lips. "Okay, I believe you. I'm sorry for doubting you."

"I understand. I did promise you the night and then had to cut it short. So, if you can forgive me, I can forgive you," Charles said, continuing his charade.

"I forgive you. I just get a little insecure sometimes because I don't understand why you won't just get a divorce from that ugly bitch. I know I shouldn't be tripping and all, especially since she clearly knows we're a couple now."

Charles cringed at her words of them being a couple. He kissed her lips with a peck.

"Alright, let me get going before I get in trouble with this job."

"Okay. I love you," she said in a singsong tone.

Rather than lie to her again, Charles kissed her, then patted her bottom and hurried out of the door.

Madison was in seventh heaven. That is until she spent the next three hours watching his home office window light that never came on, which convinced her that he had lied.

22

After a long night of tossing, turning, and crying herself to sleep, Madison was awakened at ten o'clock in the morning by the phone. She figured Charles was calling to let her know he hadn't left yet and wanted to see her before he hit the road. She answered without looking at her phone.

"Hey, baby."

"Madison?" a woman asked.

"Yes. Who is this?"

"This is Charlotte. I am Charles' wife, and I'm just calling to let you know that you better stay the fuck away from my husband. I've sat back long enough for the dumb shit, but I've had about enough."

Madison was sitting up in the bed at that point in shock.

Charlotte continued, "When my husband returns from his trip, we will be working on our marriage, and last I checked, three makes a fucking crowd."

"Try four, bitch!" Madison shot back, now standing to her feet, livid as she paced back and forth.

"Excuse me?

"You heard me! I said try four, bitch! I'm pregnant, and baby makes four."

"You lying little bitch!" Charlotte yelled into the phone.

"I got your bitch, bitch! You want to come here and see the beautiful nursery we have for our baby?" Madison taunted her. "He has such a hard time keeping his hands off of me when we're together. But then you should already know that as much as your sorry ass likes to watch us together from his office window. You're probably playing with yourself while you watch. A baby was inevitable. How about I put your ass on notice; when my man gets back from his trip, *your* ass is history. We just talked about us living together last night, and the way I see it, your sorry ass makes the fucking crowd, bitch!"

Charlotte ended the phone call as Madison laughed to herself, half pissed about Charlotte's call. Madison immediately tried to call Charles on his cell phone, but the call went directly to voicemail. She tried repeatedly, but then figured Charlotte must have beaten her to confronting him. The thought made her laugh to herself. She was disappointed because she hadn't gotten the opportunity to let Charles know that she really was expecting. She had just received the news that day from her doctor that she was pregnant.

*****

Charles kept his cell phone off during his ride, knowing Madison would be calling to raise hell about him not coming back to see her before he left. When he arrived home after leaving her, Charlotte wanted to talk about fixing their marriage again. They talked for hours. Charlotte insisted she was ready to do what she needed for the sake of the marriage. She ended up opening up to him for the very first time about her sexual abuse history, which played a major role in the problems they had in their marriage. She offered to get help coping with it if he was willing to give the marriage another chance. He didn't want to make any promises and only told her that he'd think about everything while he was away, including the sex he and Charlotte had before he left on his "business" trip. He was just happy to finish off his jollies without having to go back to face a scorned Madison, although he finished with Charlotte by pretending she was Madison.

It took everything in Charles to look happy to see his soon-to-be baby's mother. She was huge…huger than huge to him. Bigger than her photo she sent him. Her nose was spread across her face, and her lips were extra full. He had never been more turned off by a woman than he was at that moment. Her face was so fat, he couldn't tell if she was smiling or angry.

"We need to talk," she said as quick as he made it to the door, letting him know she was indeed angry.

He couldn't imagine what he could have done wrong from the time he left L.A. to the eight-hour ride to Sedona. He wished she would tell him that he could leave so he wouldn't have to lay with her for any amount of time. Every sensuous image he had of Tapioca from the past was gone and replaced with the hideous thought of moving layers and layers of skin in order to find her pussy. Actually, she wasn't that big, but to Charles, that's how she appeared to him.

"Hello to you, too. That's not the greeting I was expecting."

"You impregnate that bitch in my house, in my bed, and you're looking for a fucking greeting?" she yelled. "I have been here all of this fucking time trying to have peace and tranquility. Then I gotta hear about you and Vanilla's bullshit."

"Vanilla?! What the hell are you talking about?" Charles nervously asked, afraid his secret had been exposed that he was all set to deny.

"She got stupid shit going on, too, and still begging," she answered, causing Charles to somewhat relax. "But, I'm more interested to know about you fucking my house sitter. Let's talk about that shit, Charles. Please tell me how did she end up six weeks pregnant when I only sent you to my house to fix up a room for the baby last month, not six weeks ago."

"Tapioca, I have no idea what you're talking about. This little girl is the only baby I know about. Anything else is bullshit. I don't know who would tell you something like that or why."

"How about Madison told me about an hour ago when I called her to see if she knew if you had left or not. Since I couldn't seem to reach you by your phone, I called her for the surprise of a lifetime. She told me that she, too, was unable to reach you, and she wanted to let you know about the baby before your wife did, who called and confronted her this morning after you left. She claims she was intending to tell you last night before you left my fucking house, but you never returned."

Charles was so ready to run out and strangle Madison. He couldn't believe that she would be so cruel towards Tapioca. He also couldn't believe Charlotte would stoop low enough to contact Madison just after they talked about the possibility of working things out yet again. He was ready to strangle Charlotte as well for confronting Madison, which more than likely was the catalyst for Madison to tell Tapioca about their affair. He was really kicking himself as he mentally did the math and realized it was about six weeks ago when Madison last had a menstrual cycle. It was five weeks ago when Madison found out about Tapioca's baby.

As much as Charles' head was screaming for him to run, his legs would not cooperate, causing him to take a seat instead and put his head in his hands.

"Oh my Lord! Oh my Lord! You can't be serious, Charles. I was waiting for you to say it wasn't so. I wanted you to tell me that bitch was lying on you and you have never touched her, especially not in my house. So what the fuck, were you attracted to my house and not me? Does it even matter who's in the house? I don't even want to go back there now. I don't even want you here anymore. I have been so happy about your coming. Get the fuck out of here! I don't want you around my baby. You disgust me… UH!"

Charles looked up when he heard her groan. She was holding her large belly as she wet her pants.

"Uhh! My water!"

"Tappy?!" Charles stood up, unsure of what to do.

He put his hand on Tapioca's back, and she used the back of her hand to hit him in the nose with all of her might. Charles could feel the instant flow of blood come into his nose. He wanted to knock Tapioca out cold.

"I'm so sorry. Oh my goodness. What have I done? The baby's coming. Charles, help me," she cried in distress.

Charles didn't want to help her after the way she had just hit him, but he knew he was moments away from holding his very first child.

"What should I do? I don't know what to do," he answered frantically through his covered nose.

"My doctor's number is on the table. Grab my small suitcase and get me to the hospital," she replied, trying to be calm.

"But I don't know where to go. I've never been here before," he said while nursing his own wound.

"Just come on. I'll tell you…or use your GPS to find Sedona Memorial," she told him, peeling the wet maternity pants off of her to change into a dress and put on a sanitary pad.

By the time they made it to the hospital almost thirty minutes later, Charles was ready to put Tapioca out of his car along the side of the highway. She had hit him again while he was driving, cursed him, and then would apologize in between the contractions that were coming every three minutes and last a whole minute. He was glad the doctor was there waiting. It didn't sit well when he saw the doctor was a tall, young, very attractive man that Tapioca seemed to be quite fond of. The doctor was a smooth, charismatic brother, who was able to keep Tapioca calm. Charles was more annoyed when the doctor asked him to wait outside while he examined her.

"Is that your daughter?" a lady in the hallway asked Charles.

"Huh? Who? No!"

"Your niece? I don't dare say granddaughter. You look much too young," she pressed.

"Ma'am, please!" he said, irritated and wanting to get her to back off.

"Oh, I'm sorry. I just figured you were too old to be the baby's father. I didn't mean to offend you," the woman said, furthering offended him. "I thought you might have been expecting your first grandchild because you seem so nervous."

Suddenly, the reality of his life being tied up with a girl young enough to be his daughter hit him. He also needed to get to the bottom of the Madison saga. It was one thing to have a child with the one young lady, but two would be like eighteen more years of gasoline and fire. Eighteen pure years of hell.

Charles checked his phone and heard thirty-seven voicemails. Only two were work related, one from Susan reminding him to get the paternity test, and the other thirty-four from Charlotte and Madison. Charlotte was obviously upset in her first three voicemails as she insisted he call her right away. By the fourth, she was level-headed and told him that she spoke with Madison about the baby and said they would work through it and get custody of the baby, if need be. Charles could hardly believe how cool she was being about the situation. She almost sounded psychotic in a calm manner. Madison, on the other hand, was anything but cool. She went ballistic in the other thirty messages. She was definitely a loose cannon. He was beginning to fear for both Tapioca and Charlotte's safety. He decided he would go back after the baby was born to handle Madison so she wouldn't get out of hand more than she already was. He was glad the calls only seemed to go on for a two-hour time span. He figured his mailbox must have been full, preventing any more messages.

Two and a half hours later, a healthy Diamond Nichol Pudding-Webb was born. Charles cried like a baby, but his tears of joy were quickly replaced with anger when the good doctor seemed to hover over Tapioca and baby Diamond more than Charles was allowed to. Charles knew there wasn't a chance in hell that he was leaving the hospital without that paternity test. Particularly when he left the room to watch the pair through the door and witnessed the doctor kiss Tapioca on her forehead.

After providing his DNA swab, he left the hospital to go back to Tapioca's rented villa practically in the middle of no-man's land. He wanted to stay at the hospital, but with the baby in the nursery, it was pointless. Not only that, he hadn't had a chance to change his shirt from his nosebleed or wash up from the long trip.

While at the villa, he decided to search for some sign of Tapioca's affair with her obstetrician. He wasn't sure what he was looking for, but his search yielded more than he was bargaining for. Not only did he find a picture of the two together since she'd been pregnant, but he also found pictures of Jonathan James in that very bedroom, sleeping under the covers and obviously naked. He realized these young girls had too many games for his liking. The two of them were giving him all the more reason to stay with his wife and eliminate all of the childish games. When he went to search her kitchen, he found the biggest shock of them all--one to make him call his good friend Edward.

"You're never going to believe what I'm standing here looking at right now," Charles said when Edward answered the phone at two o'clock that morning.

"It better be important since you're calling here this time of night. How's your baby doing?"

"If it's my baby. You won't believe the shit going on here."

"A porno star? I'll believe anything."

"How about a porno star that is the daughter of the hooker from your bachelor party?"

"Huh? What are you talking about?"

"I'm standing in Tapioca's villa, and she has this picture held up on the refrigerator with a magnet. The woman is posing with her four daughters. This is the lady from your bachelor party twenty-six years ago. This is definitely her in this picture. The back of the picture says

Portia, Chocolate, Tapioca, Butterscotch, and Vanilla."

"Portia? I think I kind of remember that name. I remember someone saying, 'Who wants a portion of Portia,' but that's too much of a coincidence. You sure that's the same woman?"

"Eddie, do you think I'd ever forget her hateful ass...ever? I remember hating her ass that night, and I couldn't stop staring at her because I was hoping I'd run into her behind one day when she was alone so I could tell her about herself. I remember looking at her and thinking she was an evil bitch. Now I'm standing here looking at the same evil bitch trying to look like a damn mother." Charles spoke with venom in his voice. "I'm looking at how all of these kids look so different. I'm sure she couldn't tell you who fathered any of them."

"Well, just make sure you get a paternity test for yours. Don't be a fool."

"Too late. I'm already a damn fool. I gave the baby my last name before getting the paternity results. Then I come in here to find photos of her with her damn doctor that delivered the baby, as well as a damn near naked picture of the asshole from where we live. These pictures are recent...since she's been supposedly carrying my child," he said, choking up.

"Wow! Well, I guess the ho didn't fall too far from the tree."

"Tell me about it. Do you know how messed up I'm feeling about all of this shit. I have fucked a woman and her child, Eddie. That's crazy! What are the fucking odds of that happening?"

"Let's just hope we don't find out you did the mother of that other crazy girl you've been doing," Edward laughed.

"That shit ain't funny. That girl is really crazy. And now she's telling everyone she's having my baby, but she didn't tell me."

Edward tried to stop laughing. "I'm sorry. I don't mean to laugh. I couldn't believe it when you told me earlier. Sounds like you might need a restraining order or something. I kind of figured she was a fatal attraction type."

"I think so."

Charles' phone beeped. He looked at his caller ID and saw his home number. He debated whether or not to answer it.

"Eddie, let me go. That's Charlotte calling me, and she doesn't be up this time of night."

"Alright, get back with me and let me know if everything is okay."

"Will do," Charles said before clicking over. "Hello?"

"Mr. Charles Webb?" a strange man's voice said.

Charles could hear a lot of noise in the background. "Yes," he hesitantly answered, confused and afraid.

"This is Detective Paige of the Hollywood Hills PD. There's been an incident concerning your wife, Charlotte Webb. We're going to need you to return home as soon as you can."

Charles almost dropped the phone. He immediately assumed Charlotte to be dead.

"Is she okay?" he asked, already knowing she was not if they were calling.

"She's fine, but we're going to need you to return home from your trip. She said you had just left for Sedona. How soon do you think you can make it back?"

"She's fine? Then what's the problem?" Charles asked, both confused and annoyed.

He had enough mess to address where he was, and he certainly didn't want to leave his newborn daughter, if it was his daughter.

"Detective, my daughter was just born earlier this evening, and I really can't get away right now if my wife is alright."

"Baby?" the detective asked, just as confused. "I'm sorry, but we will need you to return within the next twelve to eighteen hours. This is a very critical matter that can't be discussed on the phone."

All of the day's events were beginning to overwhelm Charles. He felt as if he was ready to have a nervous breakdown.

"Fine! I'll be there. Where am I supposed to go?"

"My card is on the foyer table waiting for you."

"I'll call you when I return then."

"Thanks!" Detective Paige said before hanging up.

Charles was exhausted and wanted some rest before getting back on the road. Instead, he took a quick shower to wake himself up and headed back to the hospital with all of the photos in hand.

Since Tapioca was resting peacefully when he arrived, he went to the nursery to see his daughter. The more he looked at her, the more he was convinced that she was indeed his daughter. Immediately at that moment, he opened up to love that little girl unconditionally with his whole heart. He hated to leave her, especially after she seemed to smile in her sleep as he held her. He went back to wake Tapioca.

"I have to leave. There's been an emergency, and I have to get back home."

"What's the emergency? Madison's pussy is calling you? You dirty asshole! How are you just going to leave your own daughter for a piece of ass? And take that bitch to a fucking hotel next time, not my house."

Charles looked at Tapioca as if she were stupid. He then dug into his back pocket, pulled out the envelope he had placed the pictures in, and threw them on her bed. "A piece of ass, huh?"

Tapioca opened the envelope, looking at the pictures. Her anger quickly dissipated to embarrassment. "I can explain…"

"Please save it," he disgustedly snapped. "I'll be back to see my daughter as soon as I clear up whatever the matter is at home. As for you and I, we're definitely done, and so is that fucking Jonathan," he said, picking up the pictures of Jonathan out of the stack.

"What is that supposed to mean?" she asked, concerned.

"You'll find out soon enough, as will he."

Tapioca noticed the picture of her with her mother and sisters in the stack. "What is this about? Why do you have my mom's picture with me and my sisters? Do you think I'm fucking them, too?"

"That *is* your mother?"

"Yes, why?"

Charles shook his head as he walked to the door to leave.

"Trust me, you don't want to know," he replied and left.

23

Charles arrived home three o'clock that next afternoon to find Charlotte gone and the home ransacked. He was careful to avoid passing Tapioca's house because he didn't want Madison to see him.

"Detective Paige, please," he said when he called after finding the detective's card.

"This is Detective Paige."

"Charles Webb here. I'm home. Do I need to come to the precinct or not?"

"It might be best that you do," the detective told him.

"Fine, I'm on my way. Do I need to call a lawyer since I don't know what this is all about?"

"That won't be necessary."

"Do you know where my wife is? Her car is here, but she's not," Charles asked.

"We'll talk about it when you get here."

*****

"Thank you for coming in," Detective Paige said to Charles after they were both seated in an interrogation room.

"Didn't sound like I had much of a choice. I'd like to know where my wife is at now."

"Your wife is being arraigned tonight for a now double homicide charge. When we first spoke, we only knew of one, but now, it's officially two. The second one may or may not hold up, but your wife certainly won't be seeing the light of day again."

Charles sat with a blank look on his face. "Murder? Charlotte?"

"Yes. One Madison Williams and an unborn child. Apparently, Mrs. Webb shot Ms. Williams with a .22 caliber handgun and attempted to perform an abortion with a coat hanger on Ms. Williams while she was still alive. Mrs. Webb then attempted to go home and clean herself as if nothing happened, also attempting to dispose of the gun found in a trash bag along with her bloodied clothes outside in the trash container."

Charles was too stunned to speak. This was all his fault. In one mind, he thought about his feelings he had for Madison and all the wonderful times spent with her. He thought about another of his offspring, which had been so brutally destroyed. In another mind, he thought of all the hell his selfish lifestyle had subjected his wife to, who wanted nothing more than to save their marriage.

The detective continued, "What I need to know from you is, what was your involvement with Ms. Williams? A neighbor informed us that she told them that you two were expecting a baby. We saw there was a nursery set up in the house, although it was severely destroyed, assumingly by your wife."

Charles was delayed in his response. The information was too difficult to process. He was also embarrassed to have to answer the detective's question.

"I… I…We…We were briefly involved romantically."

"Briefly involved? Why were you planning for this baby? We heard the furniture was delivered about a month ago. The embryo was aged at about six weeks. It makes no sense that furniture was purchased before conception for a *brief* involvement. I take it your marriage was seriously on the rocks, particularly since you said you just had a new child born yesterday in Arizona."

Charles covered his forehead with his hand. "I knew nothing about the baby," he answered after a deep sigh. "She was the house sitter for my current daughter's mother. The nursery was set up for my daughter. By the time I arrived to Sedona yesterday afternoon, I learned that Ms. Williams was contacting my wife and my daughter's mother saying that she was pregnant with my child. The information caused my daughter's mother to go into labor while she was fussing at me."

"So do you think your wife committed this heinous act to help protect you?" the detective asked as if Charles was the suspect.

"How would I know what she was thinking? My wife and I have been having a great deal of difficulty in our marriage for the past year. I can't imagine her wanting to help me with anything. She's been aware of my involvement with Ms. Williams. I could only guess that the whole conversation of a baby may have pushed my wife over the edge. My wife hasn't been able to conceive, so it must have been difficult for her to hear."

"Didn't she know about your daughter?"

"Actually, no. Not yet. I was waiting to see the direction my marriage was headed before I told her."

Detective Paige flipped through a chart in front of him. "You said you were trying to conceive?"

"That's correct."

The detective looked at Charles strangely. "How were you trying to conceive with your wife having had a tubal ligation almost three years ago? The only surgical history listed is an appendectomy and a tubal ligation."

"A tubal-a-who?!"

"Her tubes tied… To prevent a pregnancy."

Charles looked up into Detective Paige's blue eyes to see if he was just trying to probe for a reaction. Charles could see the genuine confusion.

"Charlotte? Her tubes tied? There must be some mistake."

"I take it you didn't know then?"

"Detective, I think if I would have known that. I would have strangled her myself. That lowdown bitch! After the hell she has put me through, and I hung on in there hoping and waiting for one fucking child during our marriage. Now I hear this nonsense?"

"Wow! I apologize for being the bearer of bad news."

Charles shook his head in disbelief. "To think, just the other night she wanted to talk about fixing our marriage. At what point was she planning on letting me, her husband, know she voluntarily gave up her right to bear our child? How long did she plan to keep up this charade? Eleven years together and you think you'd know someone. And where the hell did she get a gun from?" he asked as an afterthought. "Was it legal?"

"Actually, it was not. Ballistics show the gun was used in another crime eighteen months ago. Ironically, the previous tenants from the same house had a domestic violence situation where the wife shot the husband for having an affair with a woman in the neighborhood. The husband survived, but the gun was never located until now. We assume your wife must have found the gun hidden somewhere in the house."

"But why wouldn't she tell me that she found the gun?" Charles asked as if the detective really had the answer.

Detective Paige raised an eyebrow and stopped himself from sharing Charlotte's confession of her intentions of killing Charles, too.

Charles began laughing hysterically as if someone had told a joke.

"The bitch was planning on killing me," he stated as though he read Detective Paige's mind. "Wow, I had no children, and it took me to have an affair to finally get a child, but then I was about to have another. I think if Charlotte didn't kill Madison, Tapioca certainly would have. She just went ballistic on me yesterday as soon as I arrived, telling me that Madison told her we were together and about to have a baby. She was so angry, her water broke while she was fussing at me."

"I have to ask, why didn't you just get a divorce if you two were so unhappy? Why all of the affairs?"

"Detective, I loved my wife, but she wasn't the nicest person. When I'd get to my breaking point, she'd start with the tears, and I foolishly kept trying to find ways to make her not be so mean and bitter. That house we're in, she picked it and I had no say, although I have to pay the mortgage. Our marriage was just about sexless, and Tapioca happened to come on the scene at the right time." Charles stopped to deliriously laugh again. "You would not believe what I just learned yesterday."

"What's that?"

"I met Tapioca's mother over twenty-six years ago at my best friend's bachelor party. I couldn't believe it when I saw the picture yesterday. She had one of those glares you'd never forget."

"Is Tapioca your daughter? Isn't she about twenty-five years of age?"

"Oh gosh no! That would be a tragedy. Her mother was a hooker. There's no telling who fathered any of her children. Even at the bachelor party, her and the other girls there were very active. No, no! There's no way," he laughed again.

"Just thought I'd ask. I've seen stranger things happen. Nowadays, with so many men having children in different places, I see many sisters and brothers hooking up without ever knowing it."

"I bet. I guess I had no business getting involved with a girl young enough to be my daughter. No more young girls for me. Too much trouble. Too many changes to go through."

"How so?"

"I probably would have left my wife for Tapioca and lost half of everything in a divorce, but the number of men that girl was taking up with is incredible. It's too much to handle emotionally. Maybe I'll just let her do her thing so I can win custody of my daughter. For that, I'll always be thankful."

"Are you sure it's your daughter then?" Detective Paige boldly asked. "I've heard a few unpleasant reports while we were interviewing last night, and from what we heard about Tapioca, she was the whore of the century. People thought Madison was the new tenant and was glad Tapioca moved away.

"I'm sure. Besides, I took a paternity test yesterday. It should be back in a few days, I guess. I think she looks like she would be my child. Once I knew for certain, I was planning on letting Charlotte know."

"Speaking of Charlotte, do you want to see her quickly before she goes up for arraignment? I'm pretty certain she'll be held without bail. I think they're supposed to get a Psych evaluation on her, as well. You know she's going to need an attorney, don't you? You're still her husband."

Charles looked at Detective Paige like he was crazy. "The woman destroys any chance of giving me the one thing she knew meant the world to me long before we were married and then she kills my child, but I'm supposed to want to help her or see her? Not only that, but she was probably planning on killing me with that gun, too? No thank you. I should see her just to give her a piece of my mind, but no thank you."

"Just thought I'd ask. How about Madison? Do you want to go see her?"

"No," Charles whispered sadly. "I don't think that would be good. I guess I need to get to the house and get it cleaned up for the baby's arrival in a few days."

"Not going to happen. The place is a crime scene. The tape is still on the door. Didn't you see it when you passed by it?"

Charles chuckled while shaking his head. "I was too busy trying to avoid the wrath of Madison. I went around the long way to get in and out of my house. Madison was angry I left her that night after she told me that she loved me."

The detective burst out laughing. "Oh, I can just imagine. Anyhow, I'm not going to hold you up much longer. I know you have a newborn to get back to, and congratulations for that."

"Thank you," Charles said, proud of his daughter.

"I will need for you to stay available, though, because I'm sure we'll have plenty more questions before this is all done. It looks really simple since Charlotte already admitted to the killings, but with these things, you just never know. As for bringing the baby from Sedona, she may have to live with you for a while. The other house will be unavailable indefinitely. I doubt your wife will get bail, so I think you should be okay with the baby in your home for a while."

Charles shrugged his shoulders. He wanted his daughter there, but not Tapioca. "We'll see."

24

Charles had so many mixed emotions on his ride home. He felt guilty for not seeing either Charlotte or Madison. He felt grief for the child he lost that he hadn't known existed. He felt grief over the loss of his sex life with Madison and Tapioca. He felt grief about bringing such madness into Charlotte's life, but then he felt anger about her betrayal. Then he felt joy for his freedom from Charlotte and his marriage. However, as he was pulling into his community and saw Karen James at her mailbox collecting her mail, he felt revenge take over every emotion within him.

"Hey, Charles. Sorry to hear about Charlotte," she lied.

Karen had a crush on Charles for the longest, but he would barely look in her direction. She was thrilled he stopped to speak to her then. The few times she'd seen him with Charlotte, Charlotte acted like a guard dog if Karen so much as looked in his direction. The only other times she'd get to see him was while she was with her own husband, who she had so desperately been wanting to payback since she heard he had slept with Tapioca.

"Yeah, thanks." He dug into his glove compartment and pulled out the photos of Jonathan. "Here, I felt you needed to see this since all the dirt seems to be coming out lately."

"What's this?" she asked, taking the photos from Charles' hand and then immediately recognizing her naked husband barely covered with a sheet over his genitals. "What the…" she said, throwing the pictures to the ground as if they burnt her fingers.

"And please let Jonathan know I said the next time when I say keep away, I mean just that," Charles said, then pulled off towards his home.

That time, he decided to drive by Tapioca's house and saw the crime scene set up. He wanted to see inside, but there was a police car guarding the scene.

He wanted to know how Charlotte got inside the house to do what she did to Madison. He thought of Madison's last words as he was leaving-*"I love you"*-and how he didn't have the decency to tell her the words back. At that moment, he realized had he not ran away from Madison's love, she'd probably still be alive. She wouldn't have been so scorned to the point where she told Charlotte and Tapioca about the baby.

He recalled moments with Madison where the loving was so good that he questioned himself as though he may have actually had love for her. He often compared her to Tapioca and felt she was at least trustworthy. His problem with her was she was a lot clingier than Tapioca, which scared him. She'd often talk as though they were an exclusive couple when there had been no discussions regarding their arrangement. The more she talked about it, the more he thought she was crazy. Still, her loving was irresistible. He rated sex with Madison above sex with Tapioca, and he certainly loved sex with Tapioca. He just became bored quicker with Tapioca than he did with Madison. Madison made lovemaking an art, and each time together was like painting on a brand-new canvas.

As quickly as Charles was pulling into his garage, the doorbell was ringing. He figured it was Jonathan coming to confront him, so he went to the door to greet the confrontation. However, it was Karen. She pushed her way inside and pushed the door shut.

"So I take it you showed me the pictures so it will be you and me, right?" she asked while unbuttoning her blouse.

Charles was shocked and captivated all at once. "Huh?"

"You didn't have to show me those pictures, Charles. All you had to do is say the word."

Her blouse dropped to the floor, exposing her half-cut lace bra that barely contained her bulging 36 double-D's. She unzipped her skirt and let it fall to the floor right in the foyer. Charles was mesmerized by the beautiful body she had. She unsnapped her bra.

"Is this what you want, Charles? You want these, don't you?" she asked with a mixture of seduction and fire in her voice and eyes, pushing her breasts together.

Charles finally found his voice after taking in an eyeful. "Karen, you need to put your clothes back on and go. I am not going to be a part of your revenge. This is childish."

"But you tried to make me part of yours, huh?" she responded, stepping into his space.

Charles could feel the throbbing in his groin as he swallowed hard.

"My husband fucked your wife, so the way I see it, fair is fair. Why should we deprive ourselves?" she said, standing close enough to let her lips touch his lips as she unbuttoned his shirt.

Charles grabbed her hands. "What?! Your husband did what?!

"Please, Charles, that's old news. If you didn't know that already, you're about the only one who didn't know."

Charles stared into Karen's eyes to see if she was lying. She looked so convincing. He couldn't tell if she was lying to him. He let her restrained hands go as his anger about Charlotte's deception grew. He decided he would put a hurting on Karen and send her back to her husband too sore to fuck him, and then he would be done with them all.

"I knew there was a biggie behind door number two," she said as she pulled his hardened dick from his pants and took it into her mouth.

The woman had skills. She sucked him so well, Charles really began to envy Jonathan for having a woman like Karen for a wife. He stopped her long enough to lead her to his brand-new den sofa he wanted to christen. He decided he would let Karen do whatever, send her home with a passion mark on her breast, but he absolutely was not going to taste her. He didn't want to taste "Jonathan's wife". She kept trying to make it happen, but Charles was much more adamant than Karen. He didn't care if she got mad. She would get what she deserved for trying to use sex for her revenge.

After pounding her for over an hour, he was still unable to cum. He told her to suck him some more. At first, she refused because he refused to go down on her, but when he told her that she needed to leave, she quickly changed her mind. She sucked him until he released. He was instantly turned off when he was able to see his own ejaculation coming out. With Madison and Tapioca, they'd swallow every drop. Karen chose to use her hand to coax the fluids out of his volcano.

She was quickly dismissed. She wanted to hang around longer, but he refused her. He wouldn't even give her anything to clean herself up with.

"That's why I lied about my husband and your wife together," she callously said while stepping back into her skirt.

"And that's why you're going home with that big hickey on your tit, bitch!"

Karen looked down in shock. Charles grinned. He was happy that his blow was lower than her low blow.

"Asshole!"

"That's okay, 'cause I still fucked you, didn't I?" he laughed.

She ran out upset before she buttoned her blouse, forgetting her bra. The first face she ran into was Mrs. Vanderbilt standing outside of her house. She left the door wide open, and Charles went to the door still naked, swinging the bra on his finger before tossing it out the door onto the lawn, and closed his door. He wished he had a camera in his hands to capture the look on Mrs. Vanderbilt's face. That look made it all worthwhile.

25

The next day when Charles found out Charlotte was being held without bail, he went out to purchase baby furniture. He hated the idea of Tapioca living with him, but he would be glad to have his daughter with him. A day later, he took the trip back to Sedona. As he explained everything to Tapioca, she seemed happy. Happy to have a family. She was pissed about not having access to her home, but she was glad about living with Charles instead. She was so happy, she offered Charles a blowjob that he gladly accepted. That blowjob made him realize he'd do whatever needed to get Tapioca back in top shape by the time her six-week sexual waiting period was over.

Two weeks later, Charles received a letter from the hospital in Sedona, but he figured it was his paternity test results he no longer needed. He could see, without a doubt, Diamond was his child. His three longtime buddies could even see the striking resemblance.

Tapioca behaved as if she was vying for the role of the next Mrs. Charles Webb. She'd cook, clean, take care of the baby, and give Charles as many blowjobs as he needed to keep him happy. She didn't bother questioning why it was okay for Charlotte to be a thick woman but he had a problem with her extra weight, despite just giving birth to their child. Instead, she worked hard each day to drop the weight after Charles let her know he couldn't deal with the fat on her.

By week four, Charles felt his dreams coming true. As he was taking his morning run, he saw the 'For Sale" sign on Karen and Jonathan's house. Tapioca was getting closer and closer to her "acceptable for Charles" weight goal. He had been happily ignoring all the calls from Charlotte's attorney asking for his cooperation in assisting with Charlotte's defense costs and possibly getting Charlotte out on a bond with the house as collateral. Tapioca also decided to put a "For Sale" sign on her house because she no longer wanted to go back in the house.

By week six, Charles was taking Tapioca to her brand-new woman gynecologist for her postnatal appointment, where she received the green light to resume her sexual activities. She also got a buyer for her house offering her asking price. Charles took a week off from work to spend having all the sex he needed to make up for in between the baby's naps. The following week, he took Diamond and Tapioca to his office to show off his daughter.

When Susan got him alone, she asked, "So I take it you got that paternity test, huh?"

"Look at her. I really don't need it."

"There is no such thing as too sure. That's all I'm going to say on the matter. So how is Charlotte coping?" Susan asked in one breath, annoyed with Charles' disregard for her advice although there was a great resemblance.

Charles held an envelope in his hand and extended it towards Susan.

"What's this?" she asked, taking the sealed envelope.

"I assume it's the paternity results. I received it a few weeks ago. I didn't find it necessary to open it. If it'll make you feel better, then be my guest. And as for Charlotte, I have decided not to make any inquiries since I learned she went behind my back to be sterilized voluntarily. As if everything else she'd done wasn't bad enough, she pulled that shit. Everything done in darkness always has a way of coming to the light."

"Ain't that the truth! I can't believe she'd do something like that. I actually felt kind of sorry for her with this whole baby thing, but now that you tell me that, I guess it's good you got a child out of the deal…or so I hope," she said as she ripped the envelope open.

"Yeah, I guess. Well, let me get back to mother and child," he chuckled. "I'm sure someone's trying to kidnap her by now."

"Mother and child is right," Susan said, handing the letter back to Charles, but he didn't take it.

"Huh? What are you talking about?" he asked, looking at her perplexed.

"Inconclusive! The test was inconclusive," she replied, then started reading from the paper. "Please contact us as soon as possible regarding your test results. Based on the samples provided from mother, child, and possible father, a conclusive finding could not be obtained at this time. We would like to discuss the matter further with you." Susan put the letter on her desk. "I told you! I told you! I freaking told you! Ain't this some shit? You're in here showing off a child that ain't even yours," she said, getting angrier by the second. "I ought to go in there and give that girl a piece of my mind for taking you through this mess."

Charles was reading the letter as Susan ranted. "It doesn't say she's not my child. This does not say I have been excluded. It says 'inconclusive'. Apparently, they must not have had good samples taken to complete the test."

Susan raised her eyebrow. "If you say so."

"It's not a big deal. I'll just give them a call in the morning to find out what the problem was. I already told you, I know Diamond is my daughter. You can't even deny that."

"If I didn't have doubts before, I sure have them now. I can't go by looks alone. I already told you about my daughter who was so sure three times." Susan picked up the handset to her phone. "It's still early.

You can use my phone today instead of tomorrow."

"Well, I did want to discuss this with Tapioca in private first before we call the hospital together," he reasoned.

"PULEASE! That girl is going to put it on you so good tonight, you ain't gonna want to call. You're already whipped by that little young girl."

Knowing she was right, Charles took the phone from Susan's hand and called the hospital after dismissing Susan from her own office to talk in private. When she returned, she found Charles with his chin in hand and forefinger covering his tightened mouth. His gaze was deep. He hadn't realized she was waving her hand in front of his face.

"Charles, what's wrong?"

He got up from the seat behind Susan's desk. "I have to go. Thanks for everything," he said as he quickly left the office to go and collect Tapioca and Diamond to leave.

*****

"What's the matter with you? You've been acting strange since we left your office," Tapioca asked after they walked in the house.

"We need to have a talk."

"Okay, I'm listening. You were quiet the entire ride home. You didn't even say anything when I told you that my house is going to close in a week. I thought for sure it would be like a month before we closed," she said half excited as he still zoned out on her.

When Diamond started to cry, Tapioca went to see about her since Charles was still ignoring her. Tapioca tried to conceal her own anger after overhearing Susan question Diamond's paternity. When she was about to get Charles to leave, that's when she heard Susan insisting that he check the paternity despite Charles telling her that he was convinced. Everyone in his office was kind and agreed that Diamond looked like her daddy, with the exception of Susan. Tapioca figured she was jealous because she was unable to snag Charles for herself.

"Tappy, I have to go out for a bit. Are you going to be alright?" Charles asked, really wondering if he could trust her long enough while he went to talk with Charlotte's attorney, who planned on calling him to testify on her behalf.

"Yeah, I'll be fine, but are you okay?" she asked since he seemed more tense after the phone call he had just received.

"Charlotte's attorney plans on calling me to testify for her. Trust me, I'm not happy right now."

"What happened to our talk you wanted to have?" she asked, still curious.

"We will later this evening," he said, giving her a quick peck on the lips before leaving.

She looked out of the window when Charles pulled off and saw Mrs. Vanderbilt also pulling off. She laughed to herself when she thought about the time when Mrs. Vanderbilt came home and caught her with Mr. Vanderbilt. When she saw Mr. Vanderbilt appear in his window, she got excited between her legs. She missed him. She did what she had done for the few days prior; she opened her blouse and moved her bra beneath her breast so Mr. Vanderbilt could see her through his binoculars.

That day, she decided to give him a little extra since neither Charles nor Mrs. Vanderbilt was around. She stripped naked and touched herself while standing in the window. Mr. Vanderbilt did the same. She quickly grabbed one of her vibrating toys to assist in bringing her to an orgasm while he watched her. It felt almost as good as if he were inside of her.

Her hormones were raging, and Charles alone wasn't properly handling her needs. However, since he didn't leave her a free moment, she didn't know how she'd be able to sneak away for a little extra action on the side. A part of her wanted Charles to divorce Charlotte so they could get married. Another part of her didn't want to be stuck with

Charles for the rest of her life. She even thought of buying a new house across town just to have some freedom. She had flashbacks to the times she was filming the *Pudding Pop* series and how she'd take three dicks at a time. She wished for that again so many times, but settled for the back to back.

During her pregnancy, she tried hard to control her sexual urges and focus on inner peace. Unfortunately, the husband of the retreat facilitator came to her cabin one night to check on her since she was pregnant and disrupted that peace. Each time he'd put his hand on her back, she'd feel a throbbing between her legs despite him being very unattractive. Her peace went out the window, and her mind stayed focused on how to get him to eat her pussy before she left the retreat.

The next time he came back to check on her, she was more prepared for him. She wore a short robe with nothing underneath. She kept the tie loose and would continually move around or reach, trying to give him a peepshow. When she excused herself to change, she kept the bathroom door open as she stepped inside to peel off the robe and slip on her nightgown. She barely listened as he told his story of how he reached the peaceful place in his life. She came back from the bathroom and went to hug him. He didn't hug her back. Instead, he asked why she hugged him. She told him she was just thanking him for thinking enough of her to share his stories with her. She told him other people at the retreat barely spoke to her, and it hurt her feelings.

He spent the next hour on her sofa telling her one story after another, as Tapioca got closer and closer, brushing up against him every chance she could. Eventually, he was patting her thigh, but he went home without going any further. However, he was back the next day with new stories to share and a lot more touchy-feely. Twenty minutes later, he was having a discussion on how women should be less inhibited when it comes to their bodies because of its natural beauty. He let her know he could tell she was uninhibited and didn't have silly hang-ups. Next, he wanted her to prove it by removing the nightgown she was wearing.

After playing coy, she removed the gown. Minutes later, he had pussy on the breath, and Tapioca was happy for the moment.

She ended up finding a villa nearby to rent that would allow her the opportunity to freely satisfy her urges, which was not allowed at the retreat. After being left unfilled by that guy, her first call was to Jonathan so he could scratch that deep itch inside of her. She hated what he did to her that last night in her home, but she knew there would be no other that would be able to handle her the way her raging hormones need to be handled. The retreat owner's husband hardly packed enough in his pants to tickle her clit.

Jonathan hung around for two days, giving her all the dick she needed, but that was short lived. Her attention soon turned to her gorgeous obstetrician, who hadn't responded to her advances until she was already six months pregnant. After only one night together, he was already talking about leaving his wife and having a future with Tapioca. She would often tell him how much she was still in love with her baby's father to emotionally back him up. The sex was boring to her, but she had to take what she could get at that point.

Diamond's screaming snapped Tapioca back to the present. She thought of ways she could find some variety in her sex life. Nonetheless, she spent the next week making Charles feel so good that he couldn't remember what he wanted to talk about. The sex was so good, they were both talking about marriage in the heat of the moment.

26

Tapioca was happy when Charles offered to keep Diamond while she got her first whiff of freedom from them. She made a hair and nail appointment and then attended her home closing, which she didn't have to nor could Charles understand why she had to be present. She went to it just to have an excuse to get away for the day. Her first instinct was to find someone to take to a hotel, but she was afraid of violating Charles' trust and ruining everything, leaving her without a home.

When she arrived at the attorney's office, she saw the twenty-three-year-old, Anna Nicole Smith lookalike bombshell that was about to move into her house, sitting with her youthful- looking, sixty-seven-year-old, African-American, sugar daddy boyfriend who was at least three inches shorter than her without the five-inch heels she wore. Tapioca was half tempted to pull the deal because she could spot an untrustworthy ho a mile away. She could just imagine the woman trying to test the waters with Charles since she obviously had a thing for black dick. However, Tapioca's ego was boosted when the boyfriend began drooling over Tapioca. It was just what she needed.

While making small talk, she learned the woman's pet name was Bunny, while her old man was Snookums. Tapioca wanted to stick a finger down her throat and throw up because the pair was sickening with the lovey-dovey act.

Glad to get out of there, she decided to hit a mall with her free time.

She wanted to have her ego stroked as well as find some sexy clothes to wear around for Charles so he wouldn't focus his attention out of his window on Bunny. Unlike Charlotte, Tapioca figured she knew what it took to get and keep a man. She knew she could take Snookums away from Bunny, if she wanted to.

*****

Charles was greatly annoyed when Tapioca strolled in at seven-thirty that evening with bunches of bags.

"We thought you might have gotten lost or something. I didn't know if we were going to have to go out looking for you," he said, being sarcastic.

She kissed his lips. "I'm sorry, sweetie. I went by the mall to pick up a few things and lost track of time. I'm so excited and can't wait to show you what I got for your eyes only," she answered while happily heading up the stairs with her bags.

Charles followed, less annoyed. Tapioca started pulling the items from the bags. Charles sat patiently as she put on her private fashion show. She put on music while modeling each outfit. As Charles' anger went out the window, so did Tapioca's attention when she noticed Mr. Vanderbilt was also in the audience, watching from his own window with his binoculars. She was turned on by her audience, but Diamond's crying spoiled the moment as Charles ran off to see about his 'precious child' that Tapioca at times felt she had to compete with for attention from Charles.

The doorbell rang. Tapioca figured it was probably Mrs. Vanderbilt coming to complain about Tapioca's provocative modeling with the curtains open. She decided to answer the door in her extra skimpy shorts and see-through bright floral halter top she was modeling for Charles. She would give Mrs. Vanderbilt an eye full since she hadn't been taunted in a while. Her seeing Tapioca with Mr. Vanderbilt taught her not to mess with Tapioca. *Maybe she's coming for a reminder,* Tapioca thought.

"Hold on!" Tapioca yelled as she made her way down the stairs in her platform sandals to answer the persistent ringing. Tapioca was in shock when she opened the door to find her sister Vanilla. "What the hell are you doing here?"

"Well, maybe I should be asking you the same thing since I just saw you sitting on some guy's lap at the mall," she shot back loudly.

Tapioca quickly turned around to see if Charles was anywhere in listening distance. She looked directly into his shocked face as he held a happy-looking Diamond.

"Charles, I swear to you, she's lying. I was not with anyone."

"So is this the guy you're running around telling people is the father of your child? You sure it's not Trey's baby since you were so busy trying to tell him that my baby wasn't really his?" Vanilla said, pointing to Charles who was still speechless. "Maybe he needs to take a test and find out who really fathered your baby, you slut!"

"What?" Tapioca yelled, surprised by Vanilla's accusations. "Why are you here anyhow, and how did you know I was living here now? I didn't tell any of you."

"Oh, you live here now?" Vanilla looked directly at Charles when she asked Tapioca the question. "I should have known your ass wouldn't be able to keep off."

"What the hell is your problem, Nilla? I haven't done shit to you."

"You don't call fucking my husband doing shit to me? And thanks to you telling him not to trust me and to get a paternity test, I see you're now fucking my daughter's father, also."

Everyone was quiet as they tried to make sense of Vanilla's words.

She looked at Charles again and yelled, "You lowlife rapist! You swore you didn't lay a finger on me. I guess I gave birth to my daughter through immaculate fucking conception, huh? The baby ain't Trey's and I ain't fucked nobody else, which leaves either the so-called wine bottle I fucked myself with or your lying, rapist ass."

Tapioca turned to look at a pale, stunned Charles, who stood with his mouth open and no words to escape.

"What the fuck is she talking about Charles?"

"I… I… I don't know," he stuttered.

"You don't know? You don't know? You don't remember feeding me bottles of wine and then taking advantage of me while I was drunk? When I asked you if something happened, you swore it did not. And I see your stuttering condition is back."

"There must be some mistake here," Charles insisted, knowing full well he was lying.

"The only mistake was my believing your ass. Maybe I should have brought your daughter with me so you could see her since you have ruined my relationship with Trey. I know one damn thing, you're going to call my man and explain how you got me drunk and raped me and got me pregnant without my knowing it. Otherwise, your ass is going to be taking care of me and my two children."

Vanilla's eyes scanned the inside of the large house.

"Hell, we won't mind moving up in here if you don't wanna tell him the truth. At least you'll know my daughter is really yours," she said, giving Tapioca a dirty look up and down. "And what kind of ho gear is that shit you're wearing to open the door in? And don't even think about talking shit to me, Tap, because I will tell all your fucking dirt, including that guy's lap you were grinding on in the mall like two hours ago. The only way I saw it was because people were talking about some nasty slut behaving inappropriately with all those kids around. You were wearing a beige pantsuit and a scarf tied around your neck. Am I wrong?"

Charles looked at the panic in Tapioca's eyes and knew Vanilla was telling the truth. Instead, Tapioca tried to turn the table on him. Her voice cracked as she spoke.

"You raped my sister?"

"You were out there fucking just like I figured. You can't be trusted for one fucking day to handle your damn business. I knew I should have gone with you, but I wanted to trust you. You will never change, will you?"

"My sister, Charles?" Tapioca repeated, ignoring him.

"Oh, now you're concerned about your sister after all the fucking I personally had to watch you doing with her husband, boyfriend, or whatever he is? No wonder the damn hospital told me I needed to repeat that paternity test. They said it was inconclusive. You probably had so much cum clogged up in your ass that my DNA got mixed up with some other nigga's cum."

Tapioca looked like she was ready to kill Charles with her bare hands. Vanilla stood with her arms folded and amused, with the exception of the part about Tapioca sleeping with Trey.

"So now Diamond is not your baby? Is that what you're trying to say to me? I know that damn nosey-ass Susan told you that shit. Even you know Diamond looks just like you. Isn't that why we're living here and I just sold my house today…because you know that is your fucking daughter?"

Tears poured from Tapioca's face, but Charles wasn't impressed. He turned and walked up the stairs and away from the sisters.

"Where the fuck are you going?!" Tapioca called out after him.

"Next time, you'll learn to stay the fuck up out of my business. You had plenty of dicks. I don't know why you had to fuck with my man. I know one thing, somebody better fix the shit in my household. Otherwise, it's gonna be 'three's company' up in this camp. I will be coming to stay here with my babies. You must be stupid if you think I'm going to just let you hold back on that lottery money while you sit here living high on the hog while my baby's daddy takes care of your ass and your baby who belongs to lord only knows."

Tapioca hauled off and hit Vanilla in the face with everything in her. "You stay the fuck away from him, you little bitch!"

At first, Vanilla fell backwards, not anticipating the blow, but then she charged Tapioca. The two fought for the longest and made their way outside of the house where both of the Vanderbilt's watched. Mrs. Vanderbilt was happy to watch someone, anyone beat up Tapioca. Mr. Vanderbilt watched happily from his window with his binoculars as the fight produced two sets of tits for his viewing pleasure. Hair was being ripped from each head as the two went at it.

The sound of a siren finally caused Charles to look out of the window where he saw the women going at it. He thought about running down to break it up, but then decided against such since he heard the sirens getting closer. He particularly didn't want to go since he figured the two women would quickly redirect their attention to him and probably scratch his eyeballs out. Not only that, but he'd have to leave the baby in the house alone to break the pair apart. And from where he was watching, the pair looked like they were competing in a woman's professional wrestling match.

After the fight was broken up by three police officers, Charles took Diamond outside where the topless women were being restrained. At that point, the sirens drew other neighbors up the hill to see what was happening. Charles was greatly embarrassed, and even more so when Vanilla yelled out that Charles got her drunk and raped her.

Since both women yelled that they wanted the other locked up, both were cuffed and arrested. Charles had to go inside to get new tops for each of them, while Tapioca fussed about Vanilla having one of her tops. The police officer closed the patrol car door to shut her noise up. Tapioca really started going berserk when she spotted Bunny walk up to Charles extra close to speak to him and then was holding Diamond. Charles walked in the house with one of the police officers while a stranger to Charles stood outside holding and kissing all over the baby.

Just as the patrol car was pulling off with Tapioca, she noticed Bunny go inside of the house and only the police officer came out, closing the door behind him, leaving Bunny and Charles alone in the house.

*****

"You certainly have a way with babies," Charles told Bunny when she handed the sleeping child to him. "I really appreciate it. There was so much going on."

"Tell me about it. I just closed on the house today, and I see all of this excitement. I guess I came just in time."

"Tapioca Pudding's house?" he asked, surprised.

"Yeah. You knew the slut?" Bunny spat with venom.

"Wow! What happened with you two?"

"More like what she wanted to happen. She sat there flirting with my friend as if I weren't even sitting there. I started to give her a piece of my mind, but I decided to focus on my new home Snookums was buying me."

"Snookums?"

"Well, he's like my husband without the marriage. He takes very good care of me. Very wealthy. I think that Pudding chick figured as much and was trying to take him with me sitting there."

"I hate to disappoint you, but my daughter's mother is Tapioca. That's who the police just rode off with."

"Really?! So does she live here now? Is that why the house was available?"

"Pretty much. She lives here now because of my daughter. I can't say how much longer that's going to be the case. That was her sister she was fighting with, who just came by to tell me about some activities my daughter's mother was engaging in after she left the closing."

"Wow! I would have loved to see that one. I heard they were both topless when the police put them in the cars. I didn't hear the name, but I overheard some women saying she needed her butt kicked. I didn't think that was a nice thing to say, so I moved away from them and came over to where you were standing. But, now that I know who they were talking about, I understand the ladies."

Bunny pressed her large breasts on Charles' back and arm as she reached around him to stroke a sleeping Diamond's face with her finger.

"She is precious. I hope you go after custody of her and save this child from that unfit mother of hers."

Charles was annoyed by Bunny's verbal assault on Tapioca, as well as the fact that Tapioca tried to seduce yet another man. On the other hand, he was enjoying the warm, tingly feeling of her body against his back.

"I better go put this girl down. She's already spoiled."

"She's too precious to be spoiled."

"Excuse me," Charles said, taking Diamond up to her room. He was surprised to find Bunny still there when he returned downstairs. "Oh, I didn't know you were still here. I wouldn't have taken so long," he lied. Actually, he was hoping if he took long, she would have left.

"It's no problem. It's not like I was in any rush."

"I guess I better start heading on over to the police station to get Tapioca and her sister out of jail before they both die in there or kill me. One or the other," he said, still trying to hint around for Bunny to leave.

While they stood near the door, out of nowhere, Bunny threw her arms around his neck and kissed his lips. She held him tightly until Charles stopped resisting and closed the gap between their pelvises. He was horny and Bunny was willing. He figured he had better take advantage of the opportunity since he had no clue when he'd get pussy again.

He pulled away long enough to guide Bunny up the steps and into his bedroom. He had her stripped naked before they made it all the way to the bedroom. He laid her on the bed and tasted in between her legs.

He enjoyed the taste so much that he went all in, taking his tongue as deep inside of her as it would go. Her thighs were voluptuously thick, and he loved how she spread her legs apart in a perfect split as his face went in deeper and deeper. He was glad when she let him insert a finger into her loose rectum. That told him he was going to get in it. He ate her pussy as if he had all the time in the world. When she couldn't take the assault his tongue was giving any longer, she pulled him up so his swollen nine inches was snuggled between her breasts as they massaged him. Charles felt that Bunny gave him the best Swedish massage he had ever experienced. She quickly cleaned Charles' cum that exploded on top of her breasts, and then she took him into her mouth, sucking him until he was fully swelled once again.

Charles wasted no time squeezing himself into her young, tight pussy. He got her from the front, the back, the side, and then the other side before pulling out and going into the door that made him explode on insertion. He continued to stroke her in the ass even after he had already come. It felt so good that he didn't want to pull out. When he did, Bunny went into his bathroom to bring his still twitching body a wet washcloth. As soon as he was squeaky clean, she hopped back on top of him and rode him like a mechanical bull, trying to get him hard again.

"You are a fucking piece of work!"

Charles looked around Bunny's big boobs that he was licking and nibbling on to see both Tapioca and Vanilla standing in the doorway looking like two battered women. Bunny tried to quickly run for cover, cornering herself into the bathroom. Unfortunately, her clothing was scattered outside of the bedroom.

"What the…" Charles said as he also tried to quickly cover himself. "How'd you get out without me coming to get you?"

"Apparently, you weren't thinking about coming to get us, were you?" Vanilla said.

"I knew it! I knew the moment I spotted that bimbo, she was going to go after you," Tapioca yelled. "Get her ass out of here, Charles, or I'm out."

"Bimbo?!" Bunny came out covered with a large towel. "You're the one who tried to get my boyfriend right in my face. What was the purpose of you giving him your phone number to call you if 'he' needed to know anything about the house? You think I'm so stupid, don't you? It's my house. Why not give the number to me? Then, not long after that, he mysteriously had to leave me to go take care of some business. Were you the business he had to take care of? What, did you see he was an older, wealthy man and figured you'd just take him from me?"

Tapioca looked at Charles nervously as Bunny outed her.

"An older black guy wearing a grey fedora?" Vanilla asked Bunny as she eyed her sister in addition to Charles' eyes boring a hole through her.

"Why the hell are you standing here listening to this nonsense? I have a man that I am very happy with," Tapioca insisted.

"You were in the mall with an older black man. That's whose lap you were grinding on," Vanilla answered.

"Leave me alone with all of this bullshit. Charles, you have to believe me. This is bullshit. We have a family."

Bunny went and stood near Charles. "Family my behind. Since you weren't thinking of him while you were trying to get my boyfriend, I won't think of you anytime I want to be with him." Bunny used a free hand that wasn't holding her towel to turn Charles' face to her as she kissed his lips with Tapioca watching. "See you later, baby," she said, then made her way out of the bedroom to collect her clothing and left.

Tapioca mentally sized Bunny up, debating on snatching her by the hair, but figured it would be a lost fight without Vanilla on her side.

"I'm going to get this paternity test done over, and you and I are done. I'm going to take care of my daughter…"

"Daughters," Vanilla interjected. "My daughter is your daughter, Charles. That's what I came here to tell you tonight. Trey had a paternity test done upon Tapioca's request, and he was excluded from being the father. I haven't been with anyone else. Although I figured you lied about that night, I thought no one ever had to know about it. Never did I have a doubt that I was carrying anyone but Trey's child, and I certainly didn't expect to find my sister here. I don't understand why she's been so hung up on telling Trey to leave me because I wasn't trustworthy. I haven't done shit to her," Vanilla said as tears poured from her green eyes.

"I'm sorry," Tapioca said not so convincingly. "I was just angry at you for pressing me about money after I already gave you an equal split of that lottery ticket. You got what I got, but you're always trying to be so mean to me."

"You keep sleeping with my man. I'm supposed to be mad. If you wanted him, you should have never introduced us, and you could have kept him for yourself."

Tapioca looked down in shame and then looked back at Vanilla. "I didn't know I had feelings for him. I was angry because I wanted a baby, and he told me you two were about to have another baby. I didn't know I was pregnant at the time. Yes, I wanted to be with Trey, but I can't just think about what I want. Whether you want to believe it or not, I do love you, and my daughter does belong to Charles. I wasn't with anyone else at the time. I wouldn't have been with anyone else anymore had Charles not so coldly given me the boot so he could take his wife back."

She turned to Charles.

"Charles, I love you and always will because we share a child, and I want my daughter to have both of her parents, unlike me or any of my sisters had. After how you crushed my heart that time when you wrote that letter and left it in my mailbox, I don't know if I could ever trust you to love me again. I sometimes feel like I need to keep my options open to protect myself from another blow. Even today, I knew when I saw that bitch that she would try and fuck you, and not a day later, I come in here and find her grinding on you. Do you know how that makes me feel? Then I hear you did my sister, too? That's just fucked up. It seems like you're saying 'everyone is better than Tapioca, but I'll just keep her old, reliable ass around.' That's what you make me feel like: an afterthought. You were the sun in my universe, and I was your afterthought."

"I was your sun, huh?" Charles laughed. "That's why you were giving some old man a lap dance in the middle of the mall with children around? You have no class. That's why I won't take you serious anymore. You think I never noticed how the curtains keep opening after I keep closing them, and how Mr. Vanderbilt stays fixed to his window with binoculars like a permanent fixture? What is he looking at, Tapioca? I started to go with you today because I feel I can't trust you enough to leave you home alone or for you to go out alone. I don't even hang out with my friends anymore because I have to keep an eye on your sneaky ass. I hate living like this. One damn good thing about Madison was that I never had to worry about if she was fucking anyone else. When she told me she loved me, I could believe her."

Tapioca slapped Charles in the face. "How dare you!" she screamed. "How fucking dare you!"

Charles grabbed her arms to restrain her.

"Tapioca doesn't know shit about love. She's always been a selfish bitch. Knowing her the way I do, she'll probably focus on how to take you away from her own daughter," Vanilla laughed. "Hell, she even stole one of our mother's tricks. She cooked and fed him and had him coming to see her instead of our momma. Portia put her ass out when she learned the trick took Tappy for that botched abortion when she was like fifteen or sixteen. Bitch has been giving up her pudding to all the men on our block since she was eleven. That's why no one liked her and always wanted to fight her. Chocolate stayed in fights to keep bitches from beating Tappy's ass. The only reason she cooked was because when she wasn't out screwing somebody's man, she had to always hideout in the house from the ones that wanted to jump her. I bet she didn't tell you how a gang of bitches cut Chocolate's face up to send a message to Tappy since she wouldn't bring her ass out the door. This bitch is all about self, and then she wants to act like she cares about Chocolate so much that she's holding lottery money for her. That's bullshit! "

Tapioca snatched away from Charles and ran out of the room crying. The truth was hurtful, and she didn't want to hear it. Charles was shocked by what he heard. He felt a combination of anger as well as felt sorry for her tragic life that she'd often portrayed as a happy one. Let Tapioca tell it, they were a tight, close-knit unit of sisters, and the neighborhood women only picked on them because of their skin colors. Suddenly, it made sense how she ended up in porn at the age of sixteen. Tapioca always made it sound as if she went that route to financially provide for her family, but what never made sense was the fact that Portia Pudding was a well-paid hooker who made thousands just from Edward's bachelor party alone.

"Well, mister, that leaves you and I to talk," Vanilla said to Charles. "Look, I don't want anything from you. I love my daughter, I love my family, and I have my own money. I just need for you to tell the truth about what happened that night. Trey is not trying to hear it, and I'm not trying to be stuck with two kids by myself. I don't have a problem with you taking any test to prove it. I brought Sapphire with me to California so you can get a test."

"Sapphire?"

"That's her name."

Charles laughed. "So I'd have a Diamond and a Sapphire? Two precious stones from two flavors of pudding. Who would have thought?" He got serious. "First, I need to apologize, because I really didn't set out to take advantage or lie to you. You just scared me when you woke up screaming rape. I thought what we did was mutual. I've thought about that night many times since and wished I stood firm when you insisted on having some wine."

Vanilla looked embarrassed. "Well, I guess I can't totally blame you for what happened, but the fact remains we produced a child from it. I really don't want to lose my man…"

"You need to realize he was never yours to begin with. He never will be. He's in love with your sister, just like she's stuck on him."

Vanilla put her hands on her hips. "So what are you suggesting? That I just step aside and let them be together so you and I can be together?"

Charles laughed again. "No, not at all. I will do whatever I need to do to help you fix things at home, but I just think you need to really look at what you're entangled with. Are you going to be alright sharing your husband with your sister for the rest of your life? I mean, if you can have some guarantees that the two will never be together again, then that's one thing, but you have no guarantees, do you?"

"She's never going to leave him alone," Vanilla said, frustrated as she plopped down on the side of the bed. "What am I supposed to do?"

Charles sat on the chair. "I don't know. I hardly think I'm one to give advice. Take a look at the mess I have gotten myself in. All I ever wanted was to have a child or two. Now I have two children, months apart, who are sisters and first cousins."

"Damn! I didn't think about that."

"I don't want to think about it, but I do know this, you and Tappy are going to have to find a way to be civil with one another. All of that fighting and you didn't accomplish a thing."

"Do you see what she did to my face? She hit me in my face just because she didn't like what I had to say. That's how she is. She never wants to deal with the hard realities. She'd sooner run away and pretend things will just go away if she doesn't deal with it. Just like she doesn't want to accept the fact that Chocolate will be in prison for the rest of her life. Instead, Tap wants to put a fourth of the lottery money in some savings account just in case Chocolate ever gets out. Now how silly is that? Chocolate told her to split the ticket three ways, not four. I feel like Tap is trying to be slick because her name is attached to the account, which means she can take out money if and when she feels like it. For all we know, she could have spent that money already, and we would never know it."

"How would you feel if your sister were to be released… say in ten years, and then was broke and homeless? Maybe you ladies could use some of the money to try getting her a new trial. She may get less time at the very least. If it could be proven that she acted out of the psychological distress of that man killing your mother, it might help a jury have some sympathy and cut down her sentence."

"You think so?" Vanilla asked, bright eyed.

"It won't hurt to try. She also could get paroled. You never know until you try."

Vanilla was deep in thought. "Thank you so much! I can see what my sister sees in you. You're cool. Just wish you weren't Sapphire's daddy, though," she laughed.

Charles smiled warmly. "Why don't you go find your sister and get to know your only niece?"

Vanilla got up and walked to the door before turning back.

"I have a secret confession to tell."

Charles was about to worry. He didn't know if he could stand to hear any more. "What's that?"

"When we were kids, we planned the names for our first daughters. Mine was Sapphire; Tapioca's was Diamond; Butterscotch's was Onyx; and Chocolate's was Jade."

Charles laughed. "Well, do know this; I am looking forward to meeting Miss Sapphire. I'm sure she's a beauty."

Vanilla smiled from ear to ear. "I could bring her here in the morning, if you'd like. I left her at my friend's house. I didn't want to bring her in the cab."

"I'd love that. I can drive you wherever you need to go to pick her up." He smiled, somewhat excited about having a second daughter.

The circumstances were troubling, but they were his, and that's all that mattered. Once he got all of the paternity issues out of the way, he could figure out how to move forward and eventually figure out how he'd deal with his messy divorce from Charlotte who was demanding him to pay her legal fees for killing Madison and his other unborn child.

27

"I don't understand how the test came back inconclusive again. You got the results for Sapphire in two days."

"I don't know, Tapioca. I guess that's why they asked for us to come in to talk to them," Charles snapped.

He was tired of Tapioca pressing him about the paternity results as if he had the answers. He tried his best to stay collected under the circumstances. He received confirmation that Sapphire was 99.98% his daughter. He knew the moment he met the happy little girl that she belonged to him. He felt the same about Diamond, but just couldn't get a positive test for some reason.

Life had become very awkward for him. He let Vanilla and Sapphire stay for a few days so he could get to know his other daughter, who was only a couple of months older than Diamond. The two women had finally started getting along… that is until Vanilla walked out of the bathroom naked and hadn't closed the bedroom door. Tapioca fussed about it, but Vanilla felt it was no big deal since Charles was her baby's father and they had already slept together. She'd also wear sexy clothes around the house, which drove Tapioca, who did the same, crazy. Charles enjoyed the views. That pushed Tapioca to try seducing Charles back into her bed since he refused to sleep with her anymore.

To make matters worse, Vanilla decided she wasn't going to fight to be with Trey anymore because she felt Charles made a better father. She talked about flying back to Pennsylvania to get her son and put her house up for sale so she could move back to L.A. for Sapphire's sake. The plan didn't sit well with Tapioca because she didn't want her daughter to have to share her father with anyone.

To top it all off, Bunny had not hid her intentions of being with Charles since she felt they had good chemistry. Although he was horny as hell from having two sexy women in his home, Charles refused because he didn't want the added drama.

Tapioca and Charles arrived at the genetics lab where their tests were performed.

"Hi, please come in and have a seat." The genetics doctor directed them into his office.

"I will say this is somewhat alarming that we'd have to come in to see you. I just had another test done the same day and had the results in two days."

"Is something wrong with our daughter? Is that why you wanted to see us?" Tapioca asked.

"That's part of the reason I needed to see you two."

Tapioca started to wail before the doctor could barely finish his sentence. She had been on edge about the paternity test since Charles first asked for it. While she played the 100% sure role, she didn't know if by some freakish chance William Vanderbilt had fathered her baby. There was that one time she managed to sneak over for a quick ten minutes when Charles ran to the store while she was cooking dinner for him. When Charles returned accusing her of smelling like sex, she lied and told him that she had masturbated while waiting for the rice to cook. He bought it and was turned on by the thought. Dinner was delayed that night by sex.

She didn't know what she would do if the doctor told her that Charles was not the father. She hated the idea of him being the father to Vanilla's child, but it would be harder to accept if he was not the father to her own. Diamond had enough tint in her complexion to make one think that her father would be a black man, but with Tapioca being an interracial byproduct herself, there was no telling. She also constantly wondered about the time she had smoked weed and drank Hennessy with Trey while she was pregnant but didn't yet know it, or the impact of the sexual activities between her and Jonathan during her pregnancy.

"Tapioca, let the man finish! He never said anything was wrong," Charles scolded. The doctor had a grim look on his face that made Charles begin doubting, also. "She's fine. Isn't she, doctor?"

"We ran our test extensively, and we were unable to find any defective genes in the baby…"

"See, you were getting yourself all worked up for nothing," Charles said as he relaxed back in his seat.

Tapioca straightened herself up just long enough for the next blow.

"However…" the doctor continued, "we have concluded a problem much more disturbing, which would be the reason your tests here and in Sedona are returning as inconclusive."

Tapioca reached over for Charles' hand and squeezed it as the doctor went on.

"After we were unable to get a conclusive answer, we ran a few more tests and found that the baby is indeed the offspring of Mr. Webb."

Charles was on the edge of his seat as the doctor seemed to drag out his words. When he heard that he was Diamond's father, he fell back in his seat. "Hallelujah!!"

Tapioca jumped from her seat to kiss Charles, but the doctor held his hand up to stop their celebration. Tapioca and Charles looked at the doctor fearfully with a plastered smile still on their faces. Tapioca took her seat.

"It was brought to my attention that another test was conducted on the same day with Mr. Webb involving the biological sister of Ms. Pudding. I used the sample from both the mother and the baby and have come to the conclusion, which was triple checked by three other facilities, to include the assistance of the FBI genetics facility, that Mr. Webb is in fact 99.91% the father of one Tapioca Pudding."

"Her name is Diamond. I'm Tapioca," she corrected, glad for the confirmation. However, Charles appeared to have seen a ghost, as he was able to fully comprehend what the doctor said.

"No, ma'am, Mr. Webb is *your* father. Additionally, he is the father of Baby Girl Diamond."

That time, Charles wailed out, while Tapioca sat still unable to understand what was being said. Charles jumped from his seat and ran from the doctor's office. Tapioca was about to follow him, but remained because she needed to figure out what was going on. She still was unable to process what upset Charles so much.

"I... I don't get it. You said that Charles is the father of my daughter, right?"

The doctor nodded.

"Well, what's the problem? I don't get it. Why is Charles so upset now when he was just so happy a minute ago?"

"Ms. Pudding, Charles is *your* father. He is also the father of your daughter. Your daughter is also your sister, which is termed incest."

Tapioca shook her head back and forth over and over. "No! No! He is not my father! You need to run those tests again. How could you say something so disgusting? I would never sleep with my father. Why would you say that?" she said as the tears began to fall.

The doctor sat empathetically as he got his answer. He was under the impression that their incest was consensual, and he tried to contain his anger during their meeting. However, after seeing their reactions, it was apparent that the couple was unaware.

"I'm sorry. I didn't know you were unaware."

"UNAWARE?! You thought I'd fuck my own father? Is that what your nasty fucking ass thought of me? Charles is not my father! You need to run your tests over and get it right, you bunch of incompetent asses!”

“Ms. Pudding, the tests were repeated by an FBI lab in addition to our lab. These tests are completely accurate. We all have the same conclusion,” the doctor tried to reason.

“You said it yourself that you mixed up the results with my sister's baby.”

“Oh no! I did not say we mixed them up. I said we were able to use the samples from both to establish a conclusion in your case. By using the sample from your sister, it helped us isolate the gene pool of your mother since we could not have your mother available for testing. The FBI was able to get a DNA sample from your mother's file, which concluded 99.9% conclusive. Your sister's baby helped us to isolate the genes from Mr. Webb that were clearly present in yourself. Those genes were not present in your sister. We also ran a test against your sister's baby and yourself, and you share enough genetic markers to be considered siblings…”

“Oh, this is some bullshit!” she said, cutting him off. “I'm out!” She grabbed her purse and ran out.

She found Charles in the car completely distraught. When she tried to hug him, he pushed her away from him, which made her cry more.

“Charles! I know you don't believe that mess. It's lies! Please!” she shouted in between her sobs.

“Just don't… Don't touch me,” he said, putting his hand up to keep her at a distance.

He started the car up, and they rode home in silence as the tears continued to flow.

Charles dropped Tapioca off at the door and quickly pulled off. Not knowing where else to go, he rode to Arty's office.

“What the hell happened to you? You look like shit,” Arty said when they were behind closed doors.

“My life is all messed up,” Charles said, breaking down again.

Arty waited a few minutes for Charles to get it together,

occasionally putting his hand on his back for reassurance that his best buddy was there for him.

"That girl is my daughter. My daughter, Art."

"Well, isn't that good news? That's what you wanted, right?"

"Tapioca! Tapioca is my daughter! Diamond is my daughter! Diamond is my daughter and my granddaughter."

Arty fell back in his seat next to Charles, unsure of what to say. "The bachelor party?" he asked.

Charles nodded his head to confirm.

"But how? I thought that situation didn't go too well?"

Charles shrugged his shoulders, then sat back in his seat and closed his eyes. He was ready to stop crying, but still, he was lost and unsure of what to do next.

He was getting himself back in control until Arty asked, "Isn't that incest?"

Charles jumped up and headed to the door, obviously disturbed by the word. Arty quickly jumped up to stop him.

"Yo, I'm sorry, man. I wasn't thinking. Please. Please come back and sit."

Charles returned to his seat, and the two sat for about thirty minutes in silence. Arty was willing to be enough of a friend to skip an important business meeting in addition to cancelling the plans he had with his wife for the evening. Arty was dying to have someone to talk to about the situation. His stomach turned as he thought of all the times Charles talked about the hot, nasty sex they'd have…with who turned out to be his daughter. Arty thought about the many times he himself found himself fantasizing about being with Tapioca. Knowing she was Charles' daughter instead of his hot, young girlfriend totally violated the fantasy for Arty. He kept a bottle of Jack Daniels in his bottom desk drawer for special, stressful occasions. This was certainly a Jack Daniels occasion.

Charles practically drank the entire bottle himself, but Arty didn't mind. Since Arty had no advice to give his good frined, he let Charles ramble on as he got drunker and drunker. When Charles was almost ready to pass out, Arty got him in the car and drove him home. He was so disgusted by the situation that he didn't want to have to go in to help Charles to the bed, causing him to have to see Tapioca. Instead, he was greeted by Tapioca's sister, Vanilla.

"Where have you been? I've been calling and calling," she fussed at the incoherent Charles.

"He's out of it," Arty told her after dropping Charles on the bed. "Just let him sleep it off. He'll be alright in the morning."

"The morning?! The morning will be too late. Tappy left, and she left Diamond here with me. I've been watching two babies all day by myself. I need help. Tappy wasn't in her right mind when she left, so I don't know what the hell is going on," Vanilla explained.

"I don't know what to tell you. You're going to have to be on your own until the morning or when your sister returns. I guess he'll tell you what's going on then. But, right now, I have an angry wife and need to get going."

"What?!" Vanilla yelled out as Arty made his way to the door, refusing to enlighten her about anything.

In her mind, she already figured the paternity test proved that Charles was not the father of Diamond. That made her glad that he would eventually get Tapioca and her baby out of his house. Then she could have Charles all to herself to spoil her and her children. She no longer cared about the age difference as she had before. The more time she spent with him, the more she desired to be with him, especially watching how excellent he was with the babies.

An hour later, she managed to get the two babies to sleep. Tapioca still hadn't returned home, and she was furious. Then she went to check on Charles and saw he still had on his shoes. First, she pulled off his shoes and socks. Then she decided to pull off his pants and help him get comfortable. After peeling off his pants, she noticed his package hanging out of his boxer shorts. It turned her on. She stared at it for a few moments. Then she walked away as she became disgusted by the thought of her sister having been with the same man.

She went to her room, removed her clothes, and hopped in the shower where she pleasured herself. Her moment was interrupted by the sound of yelling. She quickly found a robe and ran out of the bathroom to see what was going on before the babies were awakened.

Charles was in his room sitting up with his eyes closed, yelling and swinging at the air. Vanilla wanted to get him quiet as quick as possible. She tried getting in front of him, but he was flailing his arms violently as he yelled. She decided to climb up on the bed behind him and try to tackle him from the side. It worked as it stopped him from yelling. She climbed over him to grab hold of his legs that were dangling from the side and threw them on the bed, causing him to lie on his back. He began crying loudly in his sleep while saying, "I'm sorry!" repeatedly. Vanilla climbed to the top of the bed and sat where she could console a weeping Charles in her arms. She became annoyed when she heard him say, "Charlotte, please forgive me."

"Charlotte?" Vanilla quietly repeated.

He nestled his face in her robe until his wet face was snuggled against her bare breast. Vanilla got an immediate throbbing inside her vagina. Her eyes shifted to his semi-erect ding-a-ling peeping from the opening of his boxers. Her nipples hardened. She was getting hornier by the millisecond. She pulled one of her feet, which had been folded behind her, and brought it to the front of her, allowing her toe to make contact with Charles' peeping penis. She repositioned one of her breast so that the hardened nipple touched his lips. She then rubbed her nipple against his lips until he opened up like a baby, taking her into his mouth. She used her foot to stimulate him until he was fully erect. She untied her bathrobe and grabbed one of Charles' hands to touch her moistness. In minutes, Charles turned into an unstoppable savage beast, and Vanilla loved it.

Again and again, the thought of her sleeping with her sister's man would pop into her head, but she'd rationalize the fact that her sister did the same thing. Additionally, she reasoned that since she shared a child with him, there was no harm. She let go and indulged in the moment. She only had bits and pieces of vague memory of their one time together. This time, she'd be fully awake and in her right mind.

Charles sucked her pussy so intensely till she wondered if he were trying to squeeze his face up inside her. The more he tried to get in, the more she tried to open up for him. She used a pillow to bite on to prevent her screaming out and waking up the kids. Then, suddenly, there was no movement from Charles as Vanilla's body continued to convulse from her orgasm. Vanilla looked down between her legs and saw Charles passed out.

"Oh hell no! I need that damn dick," she said as she rushed to flip Charles on his back before his erection was totally lost.

She peeled his boxers off and took his semi erection into her mouth to resuscitate. She sucked for dear life but to no avail. Charles was in a drunken coma, and there was nothing she could do but let him sleep it off. However, she had every intention to be snuggled up with him when his big, hard dick woke first thing in the morning. Waiting to seize the moment, she would quickly get back in bed with Charles after the couple of times she had to get up to attend to both her and Tapioca's babies.

She had slipped into such a deep slumber herself that she hadn't realized Charles was buried in the depths of her cave, working her from behind and tickling her clit from the front. At first, she thought she was dreaming, but when she felt his hot, wet tongue inside of her ear as he grunted like a wild animal, she knew it was the real deal.

She moved her hips to match his rhythm. It was everything she had hoped for. He stopped long enough to turn her on her back. He then grabbed her legs and pushed them up in the air as he pressed back inside of her. He stroked her hard and fast, making it difficult for her to catch her breath. She placed the pillow over her face to muffle her noise. He kept her in that position until he collapsed on top of her. She was on the verge of her explosive orgasm when he stopped. She was getting frustrated. She winded her hips rhythmically to get him to cooperate. Instead, he rolled off of her back onto his pillow and snored himself a lullaby.

"This is some bullshit!" Vanilla said, again left hanging.

She thought of getting up to go get in her own bed, but decided to stay put just in case there was another opportunity. What she didn't count on waking up to was, "Damn, Charlotte, this pussy is so good!"

While she took it as a compliment to be told her pussy was good, she had absolutely no appreciation being called Charlotte and decided to wake him from his sleep. The sunlight was making it difficult for him to open his eyes and focus. He looked at Vanilla strangely as he still laid inside of her. As he started pulling away from her, she pulled his chest back to hers and gyrated her hips to encourage him to continue pleasing her. His hips moved with her for about thirty seconds, and then he quickly pulled away from her.

"Vanilla?!" he called out, confused.

"What are you doing?" she asked while still lying with her legs fully apart for his re-entry. She held her hand out to invite him back into her.

"What the hell is the matter with you?" he shouted, grabbing something to cover himself with as he held his aching head.

"What the hell is the matter with me?" she repeated, unsure of what to say next. She wanted him back inside of her to finish the job. "Charles, why are you acting like this with me? We have a daughter together. I need you. I can't go on like this. I'm staying here putting everything on hold so you can get to know your daughter. I just need you to take care of me. It's not like we've never been together before."

"Where is your sister?" he demanded to know rather than address Vanilla's request.

"How am I supposed to know? She came in for like five minutes yesterday and then left. She left me stuck with two babies all by myself. She hasn't tried to call one time since she left."

"Why didn't you let me know yesterday?"

"I tried to call you like a hundred times. Your friend brought you in here drunk last night."

"So you decided you'd try and take advantage of the opportunity while I was out of my right mind?" he angrily asked.

"What, like how you did me and got me pregnant, then lied about what happened?" she shot back while on her knees in the bed.

Charles tried to keep his focus on her eyes, but her large nipples were calling his attention. She noticed his eyes on her body as he became lost for words.

"Fine. If that's how you want it, I'll just go back to my quarters until you summon me. Hopefully, I won't have a new man by the time you call. Or better yet, maybe I'll just go back to P-A with my son instead of worrying about you being a father to your daughter. Why wait on your ass when I could do like Tappy; go find some alternative dicks to stay out all night and fuck, while leaving you with the kids."

She climbed off of the bed and sashayed near him as she was about to leave. He grabbed her arm, yanking her back, and then pushed her back on the bed. She instantly raised and opened her legs, anticipating Charles inside of her once more. His hands squeezed both her breasts as if he wanted to cause her pain. She enjoyed the pain. Her pussy was wide open as he pushed his way back in her.

"That's right, fuck this good pussy. You love this pussy, don't you? Ooh, baby, fuck this pussy. Make it squirt all over that big, black cock of yours. Oh, I love this big dick. Make me cum, baby," she begged, and Charles was trying his damndest to follow her commands.

He hit it from the front, the back, the side, and even upside down. Vanilla was getting more fucking than she bargained for. She had come three times already and was ready to quit, but Charles would not let up.

"Get the fuck away from my man!"

Both Vanilla and Charles' heads snapped in the direction of the voice.

"You heard me. I said get the fuck up!"

"Please! He's my daughter's father," Vanilla shot back, trying her hardest to cling to a slipping Charles.

"Where have you been?" Charles demanded as he covered up his creamy dick that he removed from Vanilla.

"I needed some time to think about everything, and I've decided that I'm going to do whatever I must to fight for my man. I love you, I'm in love with you, and I don't ever want to be with another man again other than you. I want us to be married."

"That's not going to happen. We're done," Charles replied.

Vanilla laughed. "Guess he told you, didn't he?"

"Why can't we be together? You love me, and you always will. We can go away somewhere and never have to come back here again. Don't you understand? It's fate that brought us together. We are destined to be together. We belong together. We need each other. Charles, please just say yes. Say yes to us. Your divorce is almost done. We could be married."

"I said it won't happen. I can't believe you'd come in here talking such craziness," Charles snapped, completely disturbed by what he was hearing.

"Give it a rest for crying out loud," Vanilla said. "You can see clear as day who he really wants, and he doesn't want you anymore. It's over! Finito! So, vamoose! Get the fuck away!"

Charles was becoming increasingly nervous by the delusional woman who stood before him while he was naked and had to relieve his extra full bladder.

"Charles, will you tell her to shut up? Yes, we have some things trying to stop us from being together, but that's why we have to turn our backs on the world and just be together the way we belong."

"I can't hold this any longer," Charles said as he shot off to the bathroom. While in the bathroom, he suddenly remembered why he got drunk in the first place.

"You leave out of here, stay gone all night long, leave your baby on me, and then want to waltz up in here talking about 'your man'…" Vanilla started before getting cut off.

"Seems you get a kick out of fucking my men, don't you? First, there was Trey and now Charles. This ain't no *Between Sisters* bullshit. I fucked up letting you have Trey, but I will not sit back and let you have Charles, too. Charles and I are going to go away to be together, maybe in the South Pacific or something, but you won't be getting your hands back on him ever again."

"Vanilla, can you give us a moment please?" Charles asked when he came out of the bathroom, having heard everything said.

Vanilla looked disappointed, while Tapioca had a smug look on her face. Tapioca waved her hand dismissively as Vanilla grabbed her bathrobe and exited the room.

"Thank you, baby. And I just want you to know I'm not angry. I know yesterday was very difficult to deal with. It was a big pill to swallow, but I have managed to swallow it, and so can you."

Charles looked at Tapioca as if she were crazy. She had to have gone mad to suggest they continue their relationship despite finding out they were father and daughter.

"I think at this point it would be best for us to get counseling. We both need to figure out how to handle this situation."

"Counseling?! Charles, we don't need any counseling. We can just go away and not have any distractions, and we don't have to be bothered with what other people say. We can just be happy. You, me, and Diamond. Think about our little girl. Don't you want our little girl to have her mommy and daddy together? Isn't that what you always said you wanted from the day I first met you?"

"Tapioca, we can't do what you're asking. We're always going to be Diamond's parents, but we can't be together ever again. We had problems even without the test results, whereas we both knew we could no longer be a couple. You wanted to be with other men, and I didn't want to be tied down in a relationship anymore. Now that I know we are biologically connected…" Charles was getting choked up as he tried to speak firm and convincing. "That's not going to happen. There's nothing else to talk about. You and Vanilla can continue to stay here for as long as needed, but there will be no you and I."

Tapioca looked at Charles as if he may have been serious and then waved her hand, laughing. "You're so crazy. That's what I love so much about you. I almost thought you were serious," she replied, completely disregarding everything he said. "Well, you know where my room is, you naughty boy. I'd prefer you don't sleep with my little sister anymore, but I appreciate your being honest with me and not sneaking behind my back…"

"TAPIOCA! Are you hearing anything I'm saying to you?" Charles yelled as if that would cause her to hear him.

She walked up to him, reached up, and kissed his lips. He jerked away, wiping his mouth.

"I heard you loud and clear." Then she quickly grabbed his crotch. "I'm tired, so I'm going to go get some rest now, but you can join me if you like. I'd prefer us to go away from here, but if you'd prefer us to stay here, then that's fine, too. As long as we're together." She walked out of the bedroom.

Charles was deeply troubled because he didn't know what he was going to do about Tapioca. Not only that, but she still turned him on just by her touch. On top of that, he knew after doing Vanilla, she wasn't going to back off either. Everywhere his mind raced it hit a brick wall. He felt like a trapped animal. He couldn't leave the women without losing his daughters…all three of them. Yet, living together underneath one roof was not an option either. There was no one he could talk to that could help him figure out how to handle his crisis.

*****

The pressing on his doorbell disturbed Charles' shower. He didn't know if the ladies had left out and didn't say anything. By the time Charles made it to the top of the stairs, he heard Tapioca at the door talking to Trey.

"Of course she's ready to go home. She's been staying here because you acted like you didn't want her. Now I can't sleep in the bed with my own man because he doesn't want to hurt her feelings. Take your girl home so me and my man can have our privacy back."

Charles was unable to hear Trey's words, but made out what he was saying by Tapioca's responses.

"Don't call my man old. Trust me, there ain't nothing old about him. My man can handle his business... Please! Vanilla's drunk ass came at him. He was just trying to be nice to her... So what did you come here for?"

Smiling, Tapioca looked up at Charles and then called out for Vanilla.

Charles' heart raced at the thought of Trey coming to collect Vanilla and Sapphire, leaving him alone with delusional Tapioca. Within an hour, Vanilla was packed and heading out the door. Charles tried to escape right behind them. He went to his office to work, only to have to come face to face with Susan.

"And? I know you're not going to leave me hanging?" she asked.

Charles tried not to look at her. "That's my daughter. The test was positive."

"Well, why'd it take so long? Are you just telling me that to get me to back off?" she said, looking at him to see if he were lying.

"Just back off! Damn! I said she's my daughter. Now drop it!" Charles raised his voice, then lowered it. "I'm sorry. I'm just a little troubled right now. I was going to try and get some work done. I'm going to just leave."

He quickly exited before Susan could say another word. He felt like he was suffocating.

Everywhere he went, he saw something that fondly made him remember Tapioca. He went to a park, and all the lovers were out. He rode by the beach, and he recalled all of the moments he shared with Tapioca. He didn't know how he was going to stop loving her. He thought of going to see if he could spend some time with Bunny, but the house would bring back his first time with Tapioca.

He thought about Charlotte and realized it was her fault for insisting on that house and him having the office with a view. The odds were incredible. One had a better chance of getting struck by lightening twice in the same place. But, to have a quickie with a prostitute at a bachelor party, who slept with several other men that same night, and then move into the one house right next door to the offspring twenty-five years later and fall in love with her despite his being married and having never cheated? If it weren't his own life, he wouldn't have believed it if it were told to him. It was his life, and he still couldn't believe it.

When he realized he would no longer be able to keep avoiding the situation, he went home. It was eleven-thirty that night when he arrived, and the house was dark. Tapioca's car was in the garage. It was quiet. He didn't hear Diamond either. He quickly slipped into his room and to bed. He watched television on mute to keep Tapioca from hearing him. He tossed and turned for the longest before falling asleep at 2:15 a.m.

He awoke fully rested at 8:45 a.m. He felt unusually relaxed and at peace. When he stretched, his arm hit Tapioca's head. She laid there in a deep sleep, naked.

"Oh damn!" Charles whispered to himself. As he was about to slide out of bed, he realized he was also naked, and the dried white stuff on his penis confirmed he had committed an ultimate sin with his daughter once again.

"Hey, sexy," Tapioca said when she woke up and saw a naked Charles standing there watching her.

He sat back down on the bed. "Tapioca, we cannot do this. It's wrong. It's a sin. It's unhealthy. You have to accept reality. We cannot be together, and you cannot creep into my bed at night. Otherwise, I will have to make you leave this house."

Tapioca looked at Charles surprised. "Huh?! What are you talking about?" she laughed. "You're the one who came and got me out of my bed last night. About three o'clock this morning to be exact. I even asked if you were sure, and you said yes. You said you love me and don't want to have to give me up. I'm sure I don't have to tell you the rest. No one has to know about us, Charles," she said, frowning.

Charles closed his eyes. He couldn't believe it. He didn't want to believe it, but when he woke up in Tapioca's bed the following morning, despite him locking his bedroom door, he knew he was the culprit. By day, Charles went through life trying to convince himself that he was in control of the situation, but each night, his sleepwalking landed him between her legs.

When Tapioca told him that she'd call and make an appointment for them to get counseling, Charles declined. The truth was, Charles knew why he was sleepwalking. He knew what he wanted. He didn't want to get help, and he didn't want to stop loving Tapioca. He didn't want to stop making love to her.

After two weeks of living in sin and in denial, Charles and Tapioca resumed sharing a bedroom and began functioning as a normal couple once again. He no longer cared that his relationship was socially unacceptable. He had the one woman he loved, and that made him happy. He was not interested in letting her go ever again. They both fully acknowledged their father-daughter relationship, but it didn't matter nor was it going to interfere with their love for one another.

Charles began distancing himself from his friends because they were asking too many questions about why Tapioca was still in his house and where she slept. He didn't like the fact that he couldn't openly love Tapioca in front of them. He hated them offering to set him up with a potential new wife. He stayed away from his office because he felt Susan was able to see through his dark secret.

He put his home and company on the market as soon as the ink dried on his divorce papers and Charlotte was convicted. Then he moved his unsuspecting aging mother and family to a small, unknown town in Utah where they were able to be out in the open with their relationship because no one knew their dark secret.

Their second child, Charles Jr., was born a year later, just after they married. They lived happily, in their own world, ever after.

~~~The End~~~

About
The Queen

The Queen has been writing for many years, ranging in short stories, poetry, plays, professional, and other writings. She is a native of (Queensbridge) Long Island City, New York and currently resides in Nevada with her family. She is also the author of the *Between Sisters* series. Her education includes Business and International Business. When she's not writing, she loves to travel to sunny climates with clear and turquoise waters or near the mountains for inspiration.